I0554306

THE DAYDREAMER DETECTIVE RETURNS A FAVOR

MISO COZY MYSTERIES
BOOK 5

STEPH GENNARO

ONIGIRI PRESS

© 2017, Steph Gennaro (Stephanie J. Pajonas, S. J. Pajonas).

Cover design by S. J. Pajonas

This is a work of fiction. Names, characters, businesses, places, events, and incidents are either the products of the author's imagination or used in a fictitious manner. Any resemblances to actual persons, living or dead, or actual events is purely coincidental.

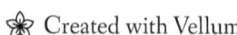 Created with Vellum

THE DAYDREAMER DETECTIVE RETURNS A FAVOR

This book is dedicated to saké.
It was much needed this year.

———

FOREWORD

In Japanese, the most common way of showing respect to another person's social standing is with the use of honorific suffixes that are appended on the end of either first or last names. The most common, -san, means either Mr., Ms., or Mrs.

In earlier versions of this book, and in the whole series, I did use these honorific suffixes. But for 2019 and onward, I have switched to the English way in order to make this series more accessible to English speakers. I hope you enjoy this version!

The town in this novel, Chikata, is completely fictional, though the area I put it in is not. Saitama prefecture is located to the west of Tokyo, and many of the eastern areas are considered to be suburbs of the city. Chikata is located farther out west, nearer to the prefectures of Nagano and Gunma.

CHAPTER
ONE

"Wrap the yarn around the hook and pull it through."

Saya leaned over the table, careful to watch each of the ladies work their crochet hooks through the thick yarn and figure out who needed help. It was her attention to detail that inspired me to hire her for Friday craft nights at Oshabe-cha.

This was now my favorite day of the week. Each week, I offered a crafting class following afternoon tea, free to my VIP members. Last week, we learned about sock mending. This week, crochet. Each of my usual ladies, and one of the usual men, had turned out to take the class, and they were all enjoying it, laughing and talking throughout the lesson. Their smiles warmed my heart. Next week, Saya would return and show them how to crochet plastic bags together to make mats, something we could either use for picnics or donate to the homeless living in Tokyo parks.

"You're doing a wonderful job," I whispered to Murata, my longest-standing client, neighbor, and friend. She smiled up at me as I reached to collect her teacup.

"You flatter me too much, Mei." But she blushed as she continued practicing her stitching.

I maneuvered my small baby belly past her and the woman sitting next to her. At nineteen weeks pregnant, I still wasn't used to the belly I had grown. The new distribution of weight knocked me off balance, and my swollen abdomen caught a lot of errant crumbs even though it wasn't that big yet. I looked strange and lopsided, and my clothes all fit weird. Eventually, I'd have to stop using a hair elastic on my jeans buttons and buy real maternity clothes, but that day hadn't arrived yet. I was happy to be pregnant, but I was also unhappy with how uncomfortable my body was.

My changed figure didn't seem to bother Yasahiro though. He doted on me, waiting on me hand and foot. Some manly instinct must have told him to keep an eye on me whenever he could because he was always around when I was changing my clothes. I smiled and tried not to laugh as I deposited the dirty cups in the back room's sink and made my way back to the front. Oh, Yasahiro. He was so predictable.

Letting the cool air of the air conditioner units waft over me, I took my time ambling through the front room of Oshabe-cha. The late August heat was oppressive, heavy and humid, making me sweat almost the instant I stepped outside. Thank goodness Yasahiro had sold more international property to pay for the heating and cooling upgrade. Oshabe-cha needed to be comfortable for my elderly clients. Many of them didn't have air conditioning, and this was their only respite from the heat.

I gathered the last of the dirty teacups and brought them to the back room. Piling them into the sink, I sighed at the enormity of dishes in front of me this evening. I loved my job, especially with all the good Oshabe-cha did for the surrounding elderly population, but dirty dishes I could live without. Someday, we would renovate this back room and install a real dishwasher, but that day was not today.

For a moment, I drifted off on dreams of loading the dishwasher, pressing a button, and walking out for the evening. Wouldn't that be great?

Resting my hand on my belly, I wondered if the baby was sleeping. He or she was quiet during the day while I was busy and dancing around at night when I was exhausted. Now, the baby's movements were more like extended fluttering and less like kicking and punching, but I still noticed every single instance. And I loved it.

I took a moment while thinking about the baby to rest my eyes on my most recent painting. This one had actual potential, and I was excited to get back to it.

Over the past two months, I had started and given up on several new landscapes. I'd finished the pine forest landscape for Chiyo, and the giant canvas hung in the men's washroom at Kutsuro Matsu. Then I had been waylaid by wedding plans and our honeymoon in Paris.

Since we returned in June, I used every last gram of energy I had to run the tea shop. There was no time for painting things I was unhappy with. But this one inspired me. My rough outline carved a wooded cliff into the foreground, a valley stretching to a craggy mountain in the back. Two suns rose over the alien landscape, and a giant planet hung over the plain on the left.

Growing up, I'd read plenty of science fiction and fantasy manga, but I always left that love in books and movies, never transferring it to my art. Bubbles of excitement stirred in my chest as I closed my eyes and imagined this world, the brisk wind whipping over the trees, the rain falling in the morning, the ghostly light of the planet when the suns were set.

"And we're done for the day," Saya said, ending her lesson in the other room. I snapped out of my daydream and glanced at the clock. 17:50? Where did the day go? I grabbed my rag and returned to the front room.

"Ah! You beat me again," Shigimo said, throwing his arms up.

He was one of my first elderly clients along with Murata, and he came to the tea shop several times per week. The Go board in front of him was a mess of white and black chips, and the young high school boy who sat across from Shigimo tried not to celebrate. Tsutomo had been coming once a week on Friday afternoons to play Go with the older gentlemen who'd show up here. I loved that my tea shop catered to both young and old, women and men. I just needed a cat or dog, and I'd have all the bases covered.

"Tomo, I hope you aren't cheating," I said, winking at the young man.

He cracked a smile and feigned surprise. "I would never do such a thing."

"Such an upstanding young man, you are."

We both laughed as he cleaned up the game and handed the Go set to Shigimo.

"Do you need dinner tonight?" I asked, waving to the leftover bento boxes in the refrigerated case. There were only three left over from lunchtime, and I always marked them down fifty percent at the end of the day.

"No, thank you, Mrs. Suga. I'm meeting my parents at Sawayaka for dinner. They both have the evening off." He smiled as he bowed to me, and my pregnancy hormones spiked, bringing tears to my eyes. Tsutomo was a good kid, but he was lonely. He didn't have a lot of friends at school, and his parents both worked at strange hours. His mother was a nurse, and his father worked in a factory an hour's drive away.

He cringed as his eyes met mine. "I'm sorry?"

I laughed, wiping the tears from my cheeks and waving him away. "It's the pregnancy, not you. I cry at the strangest things now. I saw a little girl feeding birds in the park the other day, and the whole scene made me cry." I laughed again, and Murata joined me, laughing too. "You enjoy your dinner with your parents. I may see you there later."

We bowed to each other, and he left the tea shop, shaking his head. I waved goodbye to everyone else as they filed out the door, and Saya said she was looking forward to coming back the next week. Another successful Craftday complete!

"Would you like me to walk you home, Mrs. Murata?" Heading to the closet to get her shawl, I let my gaze linger over the blank space on the wall, the place I planned to hang my newest painting when it was completed. I was sure the alien landscape would stir conversation, and if I was lucky, maybe it'd even find a buyer.

"No, thank you, dear," Murata responded, following me. "I'm feeling revived after that crochet lesson. I'm going to go home and keep practicing. I will take a bento box though."

"Of course! I'll pack one up for you."

I handed Murata her shawl, packed a bento box into her bag, and saw her to the door. The heat hit us like a wall of jungle air.

"Oof, it's another hot one," I said, walking her to the corner where I could watch her walk the length of the block around to her apartment building.

"Did you hear we're expecting typhoons soon? Maybe within the next two weeks."

"I did. I watched the weather this morning before opening." The weatherman with his long stick and big red dot went on and on about the low-pressure systems to the south of us, but I was sure it would rain like every other storm this summer. Wasn't Japan wet enough? I had the dehumidifiers running twenty-four hours a day back at Mom's house otherwise mold would grow in the shoes in the closets.

"It'll be exciting!" she chimed, and I tried not to roll my eyes. How many typhoons had I lived through since my youth? Dozens, if not hundreds. It would be a nuisance, and that was about it.

"Be careful walking home." I bowed to her and waited the long five minutes for her to walk the length of the block and disappear around the corner.

Back inside Oshabe-cha, all the chatter of the day was gone. Everyone had left for the night, and the space had become mine once again.

I locked the door, grabbed a bento from the case, and sat at the table nearest the register. Sitting at these low tables was becoming difficult, even with my tiny belly. Something about the way the bump sat on my long torso did not help. I either had to lean away from the table or maneuver my belly underneath it, both of which were not exactly comfortable. So instead, I sat turned from the table and rested with my back against the wall eating a leftover rice ball.

I was gathering strength for the thirty minutes of dishwashing in front of me. But at least when I was done, I could catch the bus and have dinner with Yasahiro at Sawayaka. Then I could go to bed early. Ah, I couldn't wait.

Just as I was about to stand up and attend to my dishwashing, movement at the front door caught my eye, and someone rapped on the glass with their knuckles. I couldn't see who it was except to spot the bottom of a wide black skirt and black plastic clogs.

I hefted myself out of my seat and made my way to the door, knowing that whoever was there saw me sitting inside. There was no way I could pretend to be in the back and not hear them, though I wanted to get back to work. But as I came to the door, a smile blossomed on my face.

"Akai! Long time, no see. How are you?" I unlocked the door and pushed it open to my hacker friend, Akai. It was always interesting seeing her in street clothes instead of her usual housecoat. In a skirt and plain red top, she appeared to be a normal human being, capable of interacting with the world outside her computers.

I hadn't seen her in a few weeks, not since bumping into her at a summer festival where we chatted about her neighbors and laughed while Yasahiro and Goro, my police friend, and his wife, Kumi, wandered among the stalls. Kumi had been almost at full-term then. She gave birth only three weeks later to their first son, Taiga.

"Hi, Mei. I hadn't been here to see your place yet, so I thought it was time for me to finally stop in." She entered Oshabe-cha, looking left and right, checking the floors, the tables, even peering up at the ceiling. I tried not to laugh at her need for order. I lived an organic lifestyle of haphazard disorder. Akai bordered on obsessive-compulsive. "It's really cute. I like what you've done with the place. This used to be a..." She snapped her fingers.

"A brush maker's store."

"Riiiiight. I forgot about that man. Bet he's living a cushy life now."

I smiled as she set her bag down next to a table. Hmmm, I guessed she planned on staying?

"So, uh, look, I know you're closed."

"You can stop by anytime. I don't mind." I tried to sound as welcoming as possible even as I pictured the dishes in the back sink teetering over.

"Well, I purposely came when no one else was here. You know I don't like... people." Her lip curled, and she growled. "I'm willing to do all the town festivals because of the food, but that's about it."

I laughed. "The food is the best part."

"It is."

She sighed as she sat down, and I took that as a sign. I would be late to finish up here tonight.

"I guess something is on your mind," I said, picking up the discarded cushions and stacking them against the wall.

"The tables are turned, Mei. I need your help."

Her face fell into a deep frown, and worry pains shot through my chest. The baby stirred, sensing something was up. If Akai was coming to me for help, it must be serious.

"Okay. Let's talk while I wash dishes."

CHAPTER
TWO

"'ll help." Akai threw a dishtowel onto her shoulder. She removed the clean cups and plates from the dish drying rack and placed them on their shelf.

I smiled as I watched her line up the cups into neat rows. I suspected, though I didn't want to pry, that Akai had some sort of obsessive-compulsive disorder. She was constantly washing her hands, using new towels for every little spill, and performing rituals like folding her gum wrappers into six equal parts before throwing them away. I felt honored she was even at Oshabe-cha, that she was willing to step out of her comfort zone to help me wash dishes.

"You don't have to do that," I said, shifting the teacups to the side and turning on the hot water. This was one of my primary jobs and a responsibility I knew I'd have to take on when I dreamed of this shop.

"I can dry dishes, Mei. It's no big deal."

"Okay, fine. But just this once."

She waited with her hands out while I pulled on my dish-washing gloves and got to work.

"So what's on your mind? What do you need my help with?"

I expected her answer to have to do with an elderly parent or aunt or something of that nature. If there was anything I was known for now, it was taking care of the older set, and I was proud of my achievements. I loved my mom, despite our fight earlier in the year, and I loved the family farm, too. I would do anything for her. But I didn't want to be known as a farmer. That wasn't my destiny. This was.

"It's complicated. Did you know I'm only about five years older than you, and that my family goes back in this town for several generations?" She dried a teacup, being careful to wipe the porcelain down thoroughly before setting it on the shelf next to the others.

"No. I didn't know that. Did we go to the same high school?" It was the same high school I had visited last year during the investigation of Akiko's father's death.

"No. I went to high school in Kawagoe, but my best friend at the time went to your high school. Maybe you remember her? Ria Fukuda?"

I fumbled and dropped the teacup I was washing and blew out a relieved breath that it was undamaged. "Do I remember her? I think the whole town remembers her."

Ria Fukuda was Chikata's biggest mystery. Forget the deaths of Akiko's father or Etsuko or Amanda. The disappearance of Ria plagued our town for many years. One day, she had been laughing and playing with her friends at a town festival. The next morning she was gone. No note. No indication that she was unhappy and had run away. Nothing. The search went on for weeks, and her parents pleaded with town residents endlessly for help. They never gave up on her, even when all her friends had moved on to college and their adult lives. Even when their younger sisters and brothers had done the same.

"She was my best friend from birth. We were inseparable until senior high school when we went different ways." Akai's eyes were unfocused and distant, her memories diving back to over a decade ago. "After her mother died, I started visiting two, sometimes three, days a week with her father. You know, helping him with everyday stuff like this." She lifted her dry teacup and placed it on the shelf. "He never recovered from her disappearance, always waiting at the window, looking outside, hopeful she would return. It broke my heart, but there was nothing I could do for him besides making his home life more comfortable."

"That's so sad. I remember her being such a fun girl." I soaped up another dish as I traveled back in time, to the fields behind Akiko's house, where we played with her brother, Tama, and his friends, including Ria. Akiko and I had both looked up to her. Ria was pretty and smart, and she had both male and female friends. Her personality was open and welcoming, which was why so many people were affected by her disappearance. "But I haven't thought about her in years. I always figured she had run away."

"Yeah, everyone suspected the same. But I knew her well enough to believe differently. She loved her parents, and she wanted to make them proud. She was excited to go to college. Wanted to be a teacher." Akai chuckled, shaking her head. "She loved kids."

I smiled as I remembered how Ria had always spent time with us even though the older kids found the little kids annoying.

"Anyway, her father got lung cancer a few years ago. He'd picked up chain-smoking after Ria went missing, and it burned him from the inside out." Akai grimaced, her lip curled in an angry S. "Ria had no brothers or sisters, and her parents had no family left, so her dad left everything to me in his will."

I raised my eyebrows at her as I washed the last teacup.

Akai sighed, her shoulders dropping. "It's not as great as you think. The man was a hoarder, and now I have a fire hazard of a house on my hands, and contracts for network security work are piling up on my desk. I want to get the place cleaned out and on the market before the end of the year, but I don't think I can do it myself." Her voice quavered, and my heart constricted. Akai wasn't one to show emotion, and here she was talking to me about them.

I snapped off my dishwashing gloves and placed a hand on her upper arm. "It sounds really stressful."

My security system beeped, and I tore my attention from Akai to look at the computer monitor. I could only see the top of his head, but I knew Yasahiro anywhere. He had a bag in his hand, and his other was unlocking the front door.

Akai sniffed up and dabbed at her eyes with the wet dish-towel. "It looks like your man is here."

I guffawed a snorting laugh. "Yes, my man." I wiggled my ring finger at her and rolled my eyes. "Is that how we're referring to husbands nowadays?"

She shrugged her shoulders. "Well, maybe not everyone."

"Fuji-ko! I brought dinner!" Yasahiro called from the front room.

"Fuji-ko?" Akai whispered, but I waved her off.

"It's a long story," I whispered back. "We're in the kitchen," I said, raising my voice.

"Oh, hello, Akai," he said, ducking under the curtains over the door and smiling at us both with a bow. "I didn't know anyone was here."

"It's all right." Akai bowed and put away the dish towel. "I was just leaving."

"No. Stay. I brought more than enough food for all of us. And if Mei is still hungry later, I'll be hoofing it to the convenience store for ice cream, anyway." He chuckled while I narrowed my eyes at him.

The flash of annoyance dissolved quickly though. I couldn't be mad at him. The summer had gone well for Yasahiro. Sawayaka, his slow-food, traditional Japanese cuisine restaurant, was booked until the New Year, the tea shop usually sold out of his bento boxes, and now his kitchen could run itself. Of course, he was still there all the time because so many people came to see *him*, not the restaurant. He probably posed for a hundred pictures and selfies a day.

I watched him as he stood in the cool breeze from the air conditioning, remembering that we were married now, still newlyweds in the eyes of everyone around us. His hair had grown longer, and he was wearing his glasses more often. Contacts weren't comfortable in dry, tired eyes, unfortunately. Nights were difficult for me. I had to use the bathroom pretty much every hour and stretch my aching hips, so he wasn't getting a lot of sleep either.

"If you're sure...?" Akai interrupted my train of thought that had left the station and was cruising towards dreamland.

"I'm sure," Yasahiro said. He lifted the bag and jerked his head toward the front room. "I'll go set up for dinner."

Akai and I grabbed clean chopsticks, plates, and glasses of water and joined him at one of the tables.

"Would you mind pulling down the shutters?" I asked Yasahiro before he sat down. "I don't want people to think we're open."

I opened the plastic containers and laid out dinner across the table. Rice, seaweed, pickles, grilled salmon, shredded chicken with spicy cabbage (Yasahiro was into Korean cuisine lately), sweet potato and shrimp tempura... the selection went on and on.

"Wow. You guys do it up when it's just the two of you," Akai said, her eyes widening as more food appeared from the bottom of the bag. "Do you always eat like this?"

Yasahiro handed out bowls and sat across from us. "We try to, but now that Mei is pregnant, she's reverted to some of her old ways. Ramen from the convenience store has usurped my own cooking some days."

He handed a bowl of rice to Akai and invited her to help herself to anything on the table. My mouth watered, thinking of salty, oily ramen noodles. Ever since the nausea of the first trimester had passed, I craved all types of food I hadn't thought about in forever, mostly, to Yasahiro's dismay, total junk food. But whatever. The doctor had said I was in perfect health. For once, I received the good news I felt I had deserved after going through hell right before.

"We all know it's a miracle I like any of this food."

We said the ritual prayer before the meal and dug into Yasahiro's amazing cooking. Akai hummed her agreement after eating a few pickles and rice.

"So what brings you to Oshabe-cha, Akai?" Yasahiro asked, and I jumped as I realized he had no idea what we had been talking about before he showed up.

I quickly filled him in on Akai's situation. "And now she has this house to care for."

"Well, that's not the real problem," Akai said, through a mouthful of salmon. I dipped my tempura in sauce and popped it in my mouth. I'd have to stop eating soon. Once the baby started to grow and overtake my body, my stomach shrank to half its size. I had to eat smaller meals more frequently.

"They never found your friend?" Yasahiro asked, setting his chopsticks down and sipping on water.

"No. She never returned, never showed up dead, nothing." Akai shrugged. "Just perpetually missing."

Yasahiro nodded. "So what's your plan then?"

"Well, I came here hoping to get Mei to help me out." She turned to me, and I could see the favor coming. I owed her for her help with Yasahiro's case. She gave me a steep discount on her services, *and* she delivered the data to me overnight. That was costly, or should've been. "I need someone with keen eyes to oversee the clean-out, and I believe Mei's the right person for the job."

"I think it's a great idea." Yasahiro made eye contact with me, and I knew he was thinking the same thing. We wouldn't have even been there, been together or married, if it hadn't been for Akai's help.

I looked at them both, and Akai elbowed me in the ribs. "You married a smart man."

"Well, of course I did," I said, hiding my apprehension behind sarcasm and a wink. "What exactly do you need?"

Akai set aside her food to explain. "I could hire someone to clean out the house. In fact, I have hired a company, but I don't trust them to throw away possible evidence — evidence that could point to why Ria went missing. What if they dispose of a note or a receipt or something that could tell us what happened to her?"

"Ah. You need someone there you can trust."

"Not just anyone, Mei. It has to be you. You knew her. You knew the people she knew. And you have a background in evidence and a relationship with the police. You'd know what to look for."

I pressed my lips together, considering my situation. I was almost twenty weeks pregnant and running a business by myself. How would I fit this in too?

"I have a great idea," Yasahiro said, spooning more rice into his bowl. "This job won't take longer than two weeks, no?" He glanced across the table at me and raised his eyebrows. I remembered how, a few months ago, I'd wondered when in our relationship we'd know each other well enough to read our thoughts without speaking. That time had come. This was a favor we couldn't refuse, and I didn't want to. I smiled and shrugged my shoulders at him. If he was on board, he'd have a plan.

"Probably less." Akai folded her arms over her chest. "The company I hired is amazing. They clean out houses like this in two to three days. They're willing to go slower for me because of the nature of the situation."

"Perfect." Yasahiro nodded and handed me more food. I sat silently while the two of them negotiated. "I'll take a week off from the restaurant and cover Mei's morning clients and Oshabe-cha. I can look in on Sawayaka in the evenings without having to do much there. Mei would then be available to help you." He reached across the table and grabbed my hand, squeezing it. "We're so grateful for all your help, Akai, during Amanda's murder investigation. Just as long as Mei doesn't overdo it, we'd be happy to help you with this."

Akai turned to me, and I was grateful she looked for my acceptance.

"I'd be happy to help. I would never give up the chance to help with a mystery."

Deep inside, my belly flipped, and the baby gave it a swift kick. I loved my tea shop, and it made me so happy and content to be there every day helping those I cared about. But a good mystery thrilled me to my core. As long as I didn't get involved with apprehending a murderer, all would be well.

I could at least avoid that, right?

CHAPTER
THREE

Monday morning dawned bright and hot, another scorcher in Japan. Earlier in the year, I'd spent my mornings with Murata, but my whole schedule changed once I opened Oshabe-cha. I shifted a lot of my clients who just needed companionship to the tea shop and sandwiched things like trips to the physical therapist, doctors for my clients or even for me, and other errands into Thursday and Friday mornings. The rest of the week was meant for Mom, and I took Sundays off from everything.

I peeled my sweaty body off the bed in Yasahiro's apartment, changed and ate breakfast, and he drove me out to the family house and farm. I found it funny that even after being married to him for two months, I still thought of the apartment as "his" and not "ours." I supposed that mindset took time to shift.

From my passenger's seat, I watched the town go by, everyone slowed in the late summer heat, fanning themselves and hobbling along in the shade of the buildings. The road out to the house was desolate, shimmering in the early morning sun. Akiko's car was gone from the driveway, and Daichi Senahara, the man who helped save me from burning to death in the barn, waved from his front porch as he directed a battery-powered fan at himself. I waved back and made a mental note to bring him something cool later.

Yasahiro pulled into the driveway, parked, and I lingered inside the car, letting the air conditioning keep me cool for an extra few minutes.

"I hope you can handle all of these chores in the coming weeks. If you get too tired or the pregnancy is bothering you, you have to let me know, okay?"

Yasahiro reached over and squeezed my hand, tugging me to him. My chest fluttered with happiness as I looked across the car at my husband. My husband. I still occasionally called him my boyfriend and then laughed.

I leaned over the center divider and let my lips meet his, enjoying this moment of peace. He drew in a sharp breath, bringing a hand to my cheek and sighing through our kiss. I never grew tired of this, how our love strengthened through every difficult situation of the past year. In the beginning, our love was dependent on so many things. I had insecurities to get past and murders to solve. Yasahiro had his own success to foster, and Amanda's constant interference was a drain on his creative energy. I felt it in our kiss that we had conquered the mountains between us, and it was sweet, sweet victory.

I pulled away gently, resting my forehead on his chin. "Don't worry," I said, feeling confident about our situation. "The doctors all say I'm in great health, and I shouldn't change a thing. I love summer, and I love being outside. I'll be careful."

"Be sure to drink lots of water and take plenty of breaks."

I mock saluted him, and he laughed, which was the reaction I wanted. I didn't want him to worry, but I also knew how much I meant to him, how much our baby meant to him. I had to be independent, but I also had to be careful.

"Tell your mom I'll be here tomorrow to take your place."

Not only was he going to help at Oshabe-cha for the next two weeks, but he would also take my shifts at the farm. His eyes sparkled as he gazed out at the produce surrounding mom's house, and I suppressed a giggle. He was looking forward to taking my shifts so he could nab the freshest ingredients for Sawayaka. There was no disguising how much he coveted this rare opportunity.

"I'll see you at lunchtime," I said, grabbing my bag and leaning to him again for a quick kiss. I'd take as many of those as I could.

"Oh, and don't forget to talk to her about our plans for next year. The more we talk about it, the more real this will be."

I sighed as I squeezed the strap on my bag. "You know Mom doesn't want to give up her freedom. It was hard enough when I lived with her."

Yasahiro shook his head. "Who would say no to this? We're offering a lot. Just... Just talk it over with her again."

"Okay."

Yasahiro was hell-bent on our newest plan, to take over the farm, renovate the house and live at home as one big happy family. His apartment was too small for us unless we co-slept with the baby, and we would all be much more comfortable at the family house. I was here almost every day anyway, helping Mom with the farm.

But each time I mentioned the idea to her, she told me to wait. *"It's too soon to be making such decisions, Mei. You'll jinx the pregnancy."* Since when had she been so superstitious about such things?

As I exited Yasahiro's car, the air was a heat and humidity tsunami. Getting to the front door was like swimming in soup, but I wasn't going to complain. Anything was better than freezing temperatures and snow. I left my shoes next to Mom's and found Mimoji stretched out on the cool wood of the dining room table.

"You must be baking in here," I said, scratching him on his head. He meowed and glanced at the fan on the other side of the room. "Got it. One fan on high coming up." I switched on the fan and aimed it straight at him. He lengthened himself into the breeze and promptly fell asleep.

"You spoil him too much, Mei," Mom said, passing by the room with her arms full of dirty potato sacks. "I can't believe you're wasting electricity on keeping him cool."

"Mom, it's only fair! He's wearing a fur coat in thirty-five-degree heat." I left my bag on Mom's desk next to the computer. The security system cameras showed on her monitor, the front door, back door, barn, and both fields. The setup had been running since earlier in the year when we caught that family from Kumamoto camping on our land.

Mom's new employee, Minato Ohno, came into view on the barn camera. He was already on site, gassing up the tractor and attaching the cultivator. With him on staff, Mom spent less time bent over in the fields doing the hard work. It was nice to have the tractor back in operation.

I grabbed my wide-brimmed hat from the hook next to the door and pulled it onto my head before grabbing my elbow-length gloves too. I had to protect my head, shoulders, and arms from the sun exposure. All the extra layers made me feel even hotter, but as long as I wasn't burning in the sun, I didn't care.

"So, Mom, Yasahiro will be here the next couple of mornings instead of me."

"What's going on, Mei?" Mom rushed to me, her eyes wide with fear. "Are you sick? Is everything with the pregnancy okay? Do you need to lie down?"

Her questions were frantic and concerned, and honestly, I was pleased things were almost back to normal between us. I remembered how she kicked me out of the house when I was sick during my first trimester, and her behavior had come a long way since then. I knew she was trying to make up for what happened, and I was glad she was acting like my mom again.

"I'm perfectly fine. Really. Everything with the pregnancy is

great, and no, I don't need to lie down." I finished pulling my
gloves up and tucking them under my sleeve. "I've taken on
another job for the next couple of days, so Yasahiro will cover for
me here and at the tea shop."

Her look of concern did not abate. "Do you two need money?
The harvest has been good this summer, and I can afford to lend
you some if you need it." She grabbed her long gloves from the
hook by the door. "I'm sure that trip to Paris was expensive," she
mumbled.

I tried not to sigh. I really did.

"It wasn't expensive, and we have plenty of money for now," I
grounded out between clenched teeth. My heart rate increased,
and the baby gave me a swift punch in the stomach.

Having conversations with my mom about money always
brought out the worst in us, especially since Yasahiro and I had
started talking about taking the farm over. But the more I thought
about it, the more I realized our problems had a lot to do with our
generation gap. Mom was smart and loving, but she was also old-
fashioned. We wanted to change things, and she wanted them to
stay the same.

"I offered to help out the friend of mine who gave me all the
data on Amanda. Remember Akai?"

"I remember her," she said, plopping her hat on her head.
"She needs your help for something?"

"Yeah. She wants me to help clean out Ria Fukuda's old
house."

Mom paused, and her eyes widened.

"I thought that would get your attention," I said, chuckling.
"Believe it or not, Akai inherited the Fukuda house. Ria's father
died two weeks ago and left his estate to her."

"What a crazy thing to happen," Mom said, opening the door
and ushering me through. "It always bugged me that they never
found that poor girl."

"Me too. I remember playing with Ria when I was a kid."

I turned to look out across the road at Akiko's house and the new greenhouse beyond. The land we used to run and play on as children now belonged to Midori Sankaku, the Tokyo grocery store chain, and they were making great use of it. The greenhouse, started in the spring, was ninety percent complete. They hoped to be up and running by October, almost a year after I moved back home. In the meantime, they were due to break ground on the administrative buildings closer to Akiko's house. Trucks and men in hardhats covered the land. They must've been doing surveys.

"She was such a polite young woman with a promising future ahead." Mom shook her head and clucked her tongue, showing her displeasure over what had happened. "Well, I suppose if Akai needs your help, you should give it to her. Maybe you'll find something that'll point to why Ria disappeared."

"I doubt it. It happened so long ago, and I'm sure the police combed that house when she first disappeared. I'm just going to help out, and I'll be here working with you again in a week. Two tops."

I remembered Yasahiro's insistence from the car.

"Oh, Mom?"

She halted and turned back to me, squinting into the sun.

"Yasahiro was really excited the other day. He found a contractor interested in expanding the house next year. He wants you to meet him soon."

I kept my eyes steady on her, hoping to see acceptance.

No such luck.

"I'm sure it can wait until after the fall harvest in a few months, right?"

I swallowed down my guilt. Was I pushing her too hard? Did she not want to go this step? Almost everyone did this, move in with their parents late in life to make things easier for them. She definitely still cared about me as evidenced by her concern for my well-being. Even though we'd had a rocky few months, I thought our relationship was better after the wedding.

"Of course, Mom. Whenever you're ready."

But maybe I'd done something to give her pause? Maybe she didn't want to live with Yasahiro and me?

I didn't know.

I watched her walk off to the fields and not look back.

CHAPTER
FOUR

I drank a half a bottle of water and got to work picking tomatoes in the field. This was one of the easier jobs that required little to no bending over, so it was always my job now. I had to be careful not to damage the tomatoes, gripping them firmly but not too hard. My mouth salivated looking at each one, red and ripe, and begging to be put in a salad. Yasahiro was going to lose his mind here over the next few days.

Each tomato came loose from the vine and was added to my basket, one after another as I thought about the jobs I had in front of me. Not only did I have a tea shop to care for, but a baby on the way and a mother stuck in isolation mode. Everything was great with Yasahiro, so I was able to shift him to the back of my mind. But I had to deal with a few issues before the baby came.

One, convince Mom we should all be living together in the same house. Originally, I didn't like the idea because I was happy living out of Yasahiro's apartment every day. His place was the height of luxury with a big, beautiful kitchen, spa bathroom, and access to everything downtown. But the more I thought about it, his apartment's location was inconvenient for the rest of my life despite being right over the tea shop. We were going to have a baby. Where would the baby sleep? Where would he or she play? There was no yard at Yasahiro's and no local playgrounds. It would be fine for the first year, but after that, not as much.

Mom's house was better suited for a family since I was there almost every day anyway. All of us could live on the family land together. But how to convince Mom? She loved her house and her freedom, and I doubted she wanted anything to change. I would have to persuade her somehow.

Two, my continuing education. I had a business degree from college that had served me well, once I had a direction in life, but now, I had to make a choice. I loved helping to investigate crimes, but in a small town like Chikata, they were few and far between, and I didn't want to attend a police academy like Goro had. But I could definitely learn more about investments and real estate like Yasahiro had. I saw how lucrative real estate was, and I knew that if we made those decisions together, we could do well for ourselves. How would I fit that in with everything else going on? I was already stretched thin, back and forth to the tea shop, the farm, the restaurant. When the baby came, I'd also have to factor in things like naps and feedings.

Sigh. There was just so much to consider.

When I reached the end of the row and my basket was full, I lugged the tomatoes to the cool shade of the barn.

"Good morning, Mei," Minato said, hauling a bag of white potatoes into the barn. That was my job last year, and boy was I glad I couldn't carry heavy bags this year.

"Morning, Mr. Minato," I said, placing the last of the ripe tomatoes into the plastic bins. They'd be picked up later today, off to someone's table by dinnertime. I clapped my hands together to rid my gloves of the morning's dirt and pulled them off, eager to take a breather from the heat of the day. "How are you?"

He hefted the potato bag and added it to the pile on the other side of the barn. I was really grateful that the new barn looked nothing like the old barn. I feared I would have flashbacks to the barn burning around me, but that wasn't the case at all. I was comfortable in the space and happy my mom was back in business.

"I'm doing well, thank you. It's going to be another hot day today. I think your mom and I will be done by noon." Minato smiled as he crossed the room and opened the barn refrigerator, pulling a bottle of water out and gesturing to me.

"Great idea. Time for a water break."

Minato unstacked two plastic chairs, placed them in front of one of the oscillating fans, and handed me a bottle of water. We took a seat with a view of the rows of green vegetables off into the distance.

We sat in silence for a few minutes, sipping the cold water and staring out at the fields. One thing I really liked about Minato was his ability to ease into any situation. For most of his life, he'd owned a manga store on the other side of town. Then he sold that place and worked at the library. When he became bored of the library, he worked at a local farm stand before coming here to work for Mom. Every place he'd worked, people had loved him. But he grew bored easily of being indoors.

Farming was a good fit for him, despite how interesting he was. Seriously, the man was as handsome as a movie star. He had a perfect goatee, smiling eyes behind his too-hip 1950s style glasses, and muscles on muscles. It was a crime to be that hot in your late forties. His wife was a lucky woman.

"I wanted to let you know that Yasahiro will be here the rest of the week in my place. I'm sure the two of you will have loads to talk about."

"You don't say? Is he itching to get his hands in the dirt?"

"Always." I laughed, spinning the cap back on the bottle of water. "I'm going to be helping a friend the next few days to clean out a house, and Yasahiro will take over my shifts while we get it done."

"That sounds like a lot of work. Aren't you worried about

taking on too much while you're pregnant? When my wife was pregnant, she was in bed all the time. Granted, she had medical troubles, but still."

His son was in high school, so his wife's pregnancy had been a long time ago. I waved off his concern.

"It's fine. It won't be any less tiresome than this, and I think the house has air conditioning even." I fanned myself though it did nothing to help the soup I was sitting in. I'd need another shower before heading to Oshabe-cha.

"Oh, then, that's different." He smiled and winked, and I melted even more. I was a pat of mushy butter threatening to become oil. "Where's this house?"

I thought about his previous occupation, manga store owner. I knew him from those days, my own manga obsession now boxed up and in storage somewhere in the house if Mom hadn't already sold it off. He probably knew Ria from that time.

"It's the Fukuda house on the north side of town. Do you remember Ria?"

His mouth dropped open. "Do I remember her? She was in my store every day for years. Totally hooked on all the romantic manga. Her mom, before she passed away, used to complain about the money she spent on manga." He sat back in his chair and stroked his goatee. "I always wondered what happened to her."

A continuing theme from everyone I spoke to about her.

Minato leaned forward and rested his elbows on his knees, gazing out at the fields. "She was a quiet one. She'd sit in the aisle and read for an hour before buying anything. I liked having her in the store because she was trustworthy, unlike other kids she hung out with."

He drifted off in his thoughts, and I also flashed back to that time, reminiscing about my trips to the store. I didn't remember seeing Ria at the same time I was there, but it could've just been my poor memory of my teenage years. My only clear memories were of my failures in painting and choosing Tama for an inappropriate boyfriend which happened later after she was gone.

I shook my head to clear it. Those days were behind me. I found my love of painting again. I married a fantastic man, and Tama was in jail, where he belonged. I pinched my leg and smiled at the pain. Yep, this was real life.

"Well, her father died recently, and my friend inherited his house and everything he owned. She asked me to help out for the week, so of course, I said yes." I groaned as I got my legs under me and stood up. What I needed was a nap. I wondered if I could get one in. Another hour of work and I could probably pass out in Mom's room until it was time to go. She had air conditioning in her room, and I loved to take advantage of the cool air.

Minato raised his eyebrows at me as he stood too.

"Do you think you'll find anything? About her disappearance?"

"Why she went missing? Doubtful. The police investigated it for years. I'm sure I'll be in and out of there in a couple of days." I grabbed my gloves and pulled them on, eager to return to the work so I could take a nap, something I wanted desperately since the thought entered my mind.

"Mei, I hope you don't mind, but I heard you speaking with your mom the other day about moving into the house sometime next year."

I paused, forgetting that I had indeed spoken with my mom about this a few days ago when Minato had been around. "Yeah, I hope we are. Mom hasn't committed or anything. It's just an idea right now."

I hoped I didn't sound too ambivalent, but I also didn't want to sound confident about the situation, what with all the brushing off I'd experienced.

Minato stroked his goatee while I pulled my gloves back on again. "I think this is a good idea. I've noticed some inconsistencies lately, and I believe you being around more could help smooth things out."

"Like what?" I pulled my hat onto my head, ready to face the sun again.

"Just small things. The tomatoes the other day were labeled wrong, and we had two extra bags of fertilizer that weren't on the invoice. I think your mom has been working extra hard with the summer harvest and missing a few things." He leaned against the open doorway. "It'll be good to have more people around to handle those things."

He waved as he walked off toward the tractor in the next field over.

Well, I'd be happy to help Mom out with these things. She just had to let me.

CHAPTER
FIVE

"Wow. Look at how peaceful he is." I leaned over the portable bassinet and stared at Kumi's baby, Taiga. His chubby, round face was topped with a dark field of hair that Kumi liked to pull straight up into a mohawk. He didn't know it yet, but he was the coolest baby on the block. He stopped grandmas on the street and wowed them with his sweet, pouty lips. I ogled at his long lashes and how they rested along his upper cheeks when he was sleeping like this. I wished my lashes were as long. I was jealous of a baby.

"What's this thing you have him in?" I whispered, being careful not to wake him.

"You'll want one of these. It's a swaddle. You wrap the baby up in it, securing their arms down. It helps him sleep. Kind of like still being in the womb," Kumi said, reaching into the bassinet and tucking a piece of the special blanket under Taiga.

Hmmm, there was so little I knew about babies. There were a lot of decisions to make between breastfeeding or bottles, independent or co-sleeping, rocking, bouncing, carrying... The list was endless, and this was only what I gathered from Kumi who had been a mother for all of three weeks. I had no idea what else to expect in the months ahead. My mom barely remembered raising my brother and me.

"He's such a good baby, hardly ever cries. I spoil him, but he spoils me." Kumi smiled down at him, and I wondered again what my baby would be like. "Aren't you due to find out the gender soon?"

"Late next week. It's the big anatomy scan. I'm a little nervous," I said, closing the door on our bedroom once Kumi had left the room.

Back in the apartment proper, Yasahiro and Goro were setting the table for dinner. Before the baby was born, Kumi, Goro, Yasahiro, and I would often go out on double dates, but that was difficult for them now. We didn't want to lose touch with them, though, especially when they were going through the craziness of being new parents, so we often invited them over for dinner, and sometimes Monday nights worked the best. It felt like a date night for them, and Taiga could sleep while we had adult conversations.

"Don't worry about it. I'm sure everything will be easy. Let's hope the little one doesn't cross his or her legs." Kumi laughed as she sat down at the table.

"How are things going at the bathhouse without you there?" I asked, pouring red wine into everyone's glasses.

"Just a little," Kumi said, pointing to a spot on her wine glass where she wanted me to stop. "Things are good, but I think I'll go back to work next week."

"Why?" I pulled my hand to my heart, shocked to hear this. "Is Chiyo having difficulties covering for you?"

Goro laughed as he set the giant bowl of salad on the table. "Mom keeps telling her to stay home and rest, but Kumi is too bored sitting at home with the baby."

"I'm losing my mind!" She grabbed her hair and rolled her eyes. "I love being a mom, and sure, I'm exhausted most days, but my brain is churning, and I want to be working. Besides, you see him." She waved towards Yasahiro's bedroom where Taiga was snoozing away. "All he wants to do is sleep and eat, and he doesn't even need to sleep on me, which I hear is usually typical of babies. I might as well take advantage of the extra time. Eventually, he'll be awake more or crawling or walking, and my hands will be full. Besides, my mom won't leave me alone," she grumbled. "I'll get more peace at Kutsuro Matsu."

"She can bring him to the bathhouse, and between Kumi and my mom, he'll be doted on night and day." Goro smiled as he raised his glass. "Let's toast. To the good life."

"To the good life," we all chimed before we said, "*Kampai!*"

I sipped and hummed in surprise. This was one of the bottles we brought back from France! The good wine. Of course, I only had about three sips in my glass. I was allowed a taste but not much more. Though the women in France often drank during pregnancy, I was careful about such things. I raised my eyebrows at Yasahiro across the table.

"Don't worry." He smiled as he cut into the flank steak on his plate. "I have a special bottle set aside for after the baby is born."

I imagined us drinking and toasting the birth of our first child, and I tried not to cry, but a tear leaked out, anyway. I dabbed at the corner of my eye, and no one called any attention to it. Everyone was used to my hormones by now. Kumi had been just as bad, if not worse, during her own pregnancy.

"Have you been thinking of names?" Goro asked, spearing salad greens and shoveling them into his mouth. He was always an exuberant eater. "Kumi spent weeks making lists."

Had I been thinking of names? I scoffed in my head. Of course, I had, but everything I settled on didn't feel right after a day or two of thinking about it.

"Mei won't let me name the baby Godzilla, so my choices are out."

Kumi laughed as she took a fork full of mashed potatoes and pointed them at Yasahiro. "It's better than Gundam."

"Barely." Actually, it would be a good idea to go through all my old manga and look at names from there.

Kumi sighed and closed her eyes. "Yasahiro, I love when you make French cuisine." She stared down at her plate, pouting. "I don't get enough of it."

"Kumi's been eating five meals a day! Even I can't keep up." Goro shook his head. "I guess breastfeeding makes you hungry."

"I've heard it does." Yasahiro reached across the table and pushed my dish towards me. I had gotten distracted and stopped eating, not that I could eat a lot anyway at this stage. I got the smallest piece of steak of everyone because I was sure I wouldn't eat it all, but then be hungry in an hour. What I needed was a small, constant stream of food. "And I'm happy to make whatever kind of food you want, Kumi. Just say the word."

"Not that I don't love your food from Sawayaka."

"Of course," he said, stopping to drink. "It's good to have variety though. Speaking of variety, did you hear what Mei is up to the next few days?"

"No! Do tell." Kumi's eyes were wide with the prospect of gossip.

"Akai came to me yesterday —"

"To flirt with you?" Goro asked, leaning forward, eager for news.

"No. Ugh. You are such a pain about this." Everyone else laughed as I blushed. "She's been totally fine, especially since we got married." I cleared my throat as Goro acted like I was just being silly. "Anyway, you'll never guess what Akai inherited."

"A boat," Kumi said.

"A barn full of chickens," Goro guessed.

"Ria Fukuda's old house." I punctuated each word with a stab of my fork into the salad on my plate.

"Ehhhhh!" Goro stopped chewing mid-bite. "Are you serious?"

"I'm serious."

Goro chewed in silence, his eyes focused on the window overlooking the street. The sun was setting, bathing everything outside in shades of peach and strawberry. I suddenly really wanted fruit.

"Wow. I haven't thought of her in a long time." He cut his steak and paused. "Did you know that her disappearance is the reason I became a police officer?"

"No. I didn't know that." I set my knife and fork down, eager to turn all my attention to him.

"I didn't either. Though I remember you mentioning her," Kumi said, finishing her potatoes. She was eating faster than any of us.

"She was in the grade above mine at school, and she used to tutor me in math during study periods. I was always horrible at math. Before an exam, she would quiz me on the walk into town from the bus. That's how I met Akai, on those walks. Sometimes Ria would meet up with Tama, Kohei, and everyone else at the manga shop."

"Wait, wait, wait." I waved my hand in between us, almost knocking over my glass of wine. Yasahiro saved it at the last minute. "Kohei went to our school?"

Kohei Watanabe was that idiot jerk of a policeman who got all up in my business during Amanda's murder investigation. He'd accused me of getting involved with the case because "it turned me on." Gross. There was nothing hot or sexy about murder.

"Yeah. You didn't know that?"

I stopped for a moment, letting this new information sink in. Kayo, Goro's fellow police officer and partner, told me that Kohei's cousin was Haruka Shinaya. I hadn't seen her since Tama went to jail. She had been Tama's old fiancée and my old high school rival. I guessed this was why Kohei had been stationed in Chikata, even though he wanted to serve in Tokyo. Now the assignment made sense.

"Kayo didn't specify why he was here except that he's Haruka's cousin."

Goro shrugged. "Kayo's not from around here. I doubt she would've known. Anyway, Kohei went to our school only for one year. He, Tama, Ria — they all knew each other."

They were all connected, and I had no idea. But I wasn't surprised. Akiko and I were five years younger than Ria, Tama, and Akai. We weren't even in senior high school at the same time as they were. Goro was in his last year of senior high when I entered the junior high school, and Kumi was a year younger than me. There were plenty of years between us all to keep us out of the same social circles.

"So, Akai inherited the Fukuda house? That's interesting." Goro stroked his chin and ran his hand through his hair. "But she did spend a lot of time with Mr. Fukuda after Ria went missing."

"Supposedly, he had no family to give the house to, and Akai has known for a few years she would inherit the house and everything in it."

Goro returned to his meal. "They probably set up a will ahead of time at the prefectural office. I wonder what you'll find in that house."

I returned to my meal as well, glancing across the table at Yasahiro swirling his wine in his glass.

"I made a peach tart for dessert, and there's vanilla ice cream for on top," he said, changing the conversation.

"Sounds delicious. I'll have an extra helping." Kumi's wide grin stretched across her face, the rest of her meal already in her belly. "Sugar. I have a huge weakness for sugar right now."

"You know, Mei," Goro said, helping himself to another serving of salad while Yasahiro got up to prepare dessert. "I'd really like to know if you find anything in the house that pertains to Ria's disappearance. I'd have to look it up, but I think they closed her case years ago. If not, we could look into opening it again, if new evidence was found."

"If I find anything, you'll be the first person I call. But don't worry, I doubt I'll find anything. My days of drama are over." I swiped my hands together like I was ridding myself of extra flour after kneading dough. "I think I've earned it after what happened with Amanda."

"Indeed you have." Kumi reached over to squeeze my hand. "No more drama. No more bad luck."

I laughed, throwing my head back. "Well, I don't think I'll get rid of bad luck that easily."

"Mei and bad luck go together like strawberries and cream," Yasahiro said, cutting into the peach tart. I had helped with the dessert by peeling and chopping the peaches, something I was getting better at the more I practiced. "But don't worry. We always manage to handle it."

"You all need to stop tempting fate," Goro mumbled.

"You're right about that," I replied, raising my wine glass to him.

He raised his as well. "Be careful this week. And remember to call me if you need any help."

CHAPTER
SIX

After three days of wading through junk in the Fukuda house, I could finally see the floors in the front room. No wonder Akai didn't want to spend all of her waking moments sifting through decades of Fukuda's life. He kept every takeout box, every newspaper, every magazine, every receipt, every dried-up pen, every rubber band he'd ever had. His desk was a graveyard of broken and desiccated office supplies.

In one closet alone, he had collected five or six dozen bottles of booze, each with varying levels of liquid left in them. Dumping them down the drain actually gave me a contact high. Several of the workers Akai hired begged me to let them have the bottles. No way. Who knew what was in them? And I didn't want to be responsible if they got brain damage from illegal alcohol.

But his alcohol collection was nothing compared to the soap collection in the bathroom closet. He must've collected them from every hotel he ever stayed in and stole ones from other people too because how else would anyone ever have 378 mini soaps?

The house was like a time capsule. When I thought back to the time in which Ria, Goro, Akai, and I grew up, Fukuda's hoarding tendencies made sense. Our town had been in the dumps, decaying around us as people moved into the city. Jobs became sparse, and many of us scraped by, paycheck to paycheck. This was the leanest time for my family, and I remember several years that brought my own mother to tears. Stockpiling every last resource was what people had done during the Great Depression and the years following, so I wasn't too surprised to find newspapers older than I was. I was surprised to find a dead mouse in a pile though.

"We're going to take the boxes next to the front door, and then we're off for lunch," Abehito, the foreman in charge, said as I pulled a cold bottle of water from the fridge.

"Is it lunchtime already?" I looked at the clock on the wall and cursed myself again for checking a clock that had probably been dead for quite some time. How long had the man gone without changing the batteries?

Abehito laughed. "You should get rid of that clock next. It's a little after noon." He narrowed his eyes at me as I gingerly set myself in a chair at the kitchen table. I'd been on my feet for at least two hours, setting aside the broken junk from the stuff that could be sold at the estate sale. "Are you all right? You look tired."

"I'm fine. I'm always tired. The baby doesn't let me rest." And just then he or she kicked up a storm so much I squealed and jumped forward in my seat.

"Oh my! You have a fighter in there!" Abehito's eyes widened. "You'll have to enroll that one in karate or jujitsu."

"Probably, if I want to get any rest," I said, rubbing my hand over my belly. It wasn't often that anybody else could see the baby move but me. At twenty weeks, I still wasn't big enough for people to even assume I was pregnant. Soon I hoped to have Yasahiro feel the baby move, but it hadn't happened yet.

"Hello!" The front door slammed shut, and Akai's voice echoed through the front of the house.

"We're in the kitchen!" I called out, and Akai, dressed in her

usual out-in-public black t-shirt and black skirt, lumbered past
Abehito. This outfit was preferred over her staying-home flow-
ered housecoat. She nodded at Abehito as she looked around the
room, noting our progress.

"I brought you lunch from your awesome husband," she said,
setting a bag on the table.

I opened the bag and pulled out the containers while Abehito
and Akai spoke about our current state of affairs. Yasahiro sent
me chicken cutlets! Oh, how I loved him. Chicken cutlets, rice,
steamed carrots, and miso soup for lunch. My mouth watered
despite how hot and sweaty I was. He had stayed home this
morning to cook before opening the tea shop for me. I hoped he
didn't have any problems getting things situated. I flipped over
my phone on the table, and there were no new messages. He was
fine, and I was worrying for no reason.

"So, how much is left?" Akai asked.

"The front two rooms have been emptied, and the remaining
boxes are packed up for the estate sale. We now have to finish the
kitchen, the bathroom, and the two back bedrooms. I would say
we have another four days of work left." Abehito consulted with
his phone, scrolling through a list he'd made the day he started.
He was organized and prompt. Akai picked her contractors well.
"Yep, about four days."

She smiled, pleased with the news. "That's perfect. The
people I hired to run the estate sale said they can come sometime
next week and go through all the leftover boxes. You and your
team are doing great work."

They bowed to each other, and Abehito said, "I'm glad you
think so. My company is grateful for the work." He bowed again.
"We're heading out for lunch and should be back around 13:30."
He waved as he left the kitchen, and I was pleased to hear he
didn't let the door slam in the front room.

"I wonder how long that front door has been broken," I said,
sipping more cold water and turning up the air conditioning.

"Probably as long as that clock on the wall's been broken."

"Probably. Are you staying for lunch?" I reached out with my foot and pushed the chair on the other side of the table so Akai could sit down.

"I already ate." She opened the refrigerator and grabbed a bottle of water. "I had to drop off a project to someone across town, so I stopped by your apartment to pick up food for you. But I'll sit."

"Thanks. You didn't have to do that." This was a treat. The bus ride across town would've taken me twenty minutes, so instead, I would've walked to the convenience store and ate substandard food that Yasahiro swore would make the baby come out with two heads.

And he thought I was dramatic?

"It was the least I could do." She watched me as I dipped my chicken cutlet into the sauce and took a bite. I was sure my eyes rolled back into my head. "That good, eh?" She laughed as I immediately took a second bite. "Well, I guess he deserves that Michelin star."

"He'd never admit that he deserves the star, but he does," I said, nabbing a clump of rice with my chopsticks. "You said you finished off a project?"

"Yeah. I had a huge database I had to pull together in a rush job which means you get my help for the rest of the afternoon." Her face was glum and depressed. Being in this house wasn't easy for her, but I had to give her credit for wanting to help.

While I ate, we chatted about the house and what we'd found already, the treasures amongst the trash. Besides the box of unused toothbrushes I unearthed today, there hadn't been any exciting discoveries. A few days ago, Akai had taken home a fairly large collection of black lacquerware and some crystal bowls. She was confident she would make money on the kitchen appliances and the furniture which had all been painstakingly cared for. Otherwise, she was happy to see the random collections carted away. No one needed twenty-year-old rubber bands.

"Well, if you're here to help, we should work on Ria's room," I said, cleaning up my lunch and leading the way to Ria's old room. I paused at the doorway, letting my fingers run over the imperfections in the doorframe. Had something been attached to the door here?

Akai followed slowly, the stride in her step shortening as she neared the room.

"I haven't been in here since she disappeared," she said, hovering in the doorway. I made a path through the empty cardboard boxes we would soon use and parted the curtains on the window to let in more sunlight. "It looks like her father kept the place in good shape."

"Someone must have." I ran my finger along the length of Ria's desk. No dust. "This was the cleanest room in the house."

Akai harrumphed. "Why am I not surprised?" She sighed as she crossed the threshold into Ria's room. "He was always certain she'd come back home and wanted to keep the room just as she left it."

The room was in great shape. Standing bookshelves along the walls were filled with Ria's old manga collection, each shelf buckling under the weight of books shoved into every available space. I came into this room the first day, but not knowing where to start, I concentrated on the other rooms instead. Now that Akai was around, I figured I could get started.

"How about I box up the manga, and you go through her desk?" I grabbed the air conditioning remote control and turned the box on the wall up to high. I was using an excessive amount of air conditioning while here, but I tried not to care. I wasn't getting paid. Might as well be cool and comfortable.

Akai shifted between her feet. "I don't know, Mei. It doesn't feel right."

I groaned as I lowered myself to my knees and into a cross-legged sitting position next to the bookshelf. The least I could do was allow myself to sit.

"I know how you feel. I've had to go through the apartments of two dead people so far, just in the past year. This makes three." I never thought my life would be so morbid, but between the murder investigations and my work with the elderly, I doubted these jobs would ever end. "You get used to it. I always imagine that the person wants me to take care of their stuff after they've gone. That they've given me permission to snoop. It helps. Kind of."

In my daydreams, Ria followed me through the house and told me the history of everything I touched. She told me her father watched too much TV, and that she would spend hours reading in her room. I imagined the pair of red chopsticks with cherry blossoms on them were hers, and that she loved the black sweater in the closet that had been eaten by moths.

Akai pulled out the chair at the desk, and it squeaked as she sat on it. I tried not to watch her too closely as she sifted through the stack of sketchbooks Ria had left behind, but I could tell from the sound of shuffling papers that she was taking her time to look at everything. Good. This kind of work needed the eyes of someone who knew Ria well. I was positive I'd miss something.

I kept myself busy sorting Ria's manga collection, finding missing books in each of the series she owned, and boxing them all together. I would have to ask Minato if he knew anyone who would be interested in buying these. If anyone would know, he would.

While Akai sifted through everything on Ria's desk, I kept my mouth shut. I figured my presence in the room was enough to give her support but not be nosy. Each time I put ten books in a box, I looked up to check on her, making sure she was okay. For the first twenty minutes, she was stony and sniffly. She moved through the pile on Ria's desk like a snail through mud.

But by the time I moved onto my third box, Akai's swift

movements caught my attention. She had switched from hesitant to determined as she picked up each notebook and set it down, opened the desk drawer and searched around inside it, then moved on to the bookshelves farther down the wall.

"Where...?" She huffed out, pulling sketchbooks from the shelves and thumbing through them.

"Where what?"

"I can't find it." She set a sketchbook down and went for another.

"Is something missing?"

"You know, I hadn't thought about Ria in a couple of years," she said, searching the bookshelves and pulling more sketchbooks out to the desk. "It was just too hard. I blamed her disappearance on myself when I was a teen. We'd been going through a rough patch as friends. She liked this guy, and they were dating, but he was a total jerk to me the one time we met. And it bugged me that she would choose him over me. We fought about their relationship two days before she went missing."

Akai turned around and dropped an armful of sketchbooks on the bed. "I remember talking about it with the cops. I was a blubbering mess, blaming everything on me. Of course, everyone thought I was nuts, and thankfully none of the police listened to my blubbering. What girl runs away from home because she has a fight with her best friend?"

I imagined their fight in my head. Akai had never come to hang out with Tama, Akiko's older brother, or I would've known her before recently. This guy Ria had been dating must've been a part of that crowd, and Akai, knowing she wasn't wanted, had stayed away.

"It's missing," Akai said, her hands on her hips, looking at the pile of sketchbooks.

The abrupt change in subject matter threw me sideways. "What's missing?"

Akai grabbed her phone from the desk and turned it on. "Like I said, I hadn't thought about her much lately until her dad died. So I went through some of my old photos from all the crappy cameras I had when we were teenagers. You know me, I keep everything."

She scrolled through her photos for a minute while I waited to find out what this was all about. I didn't think anything missing was my fault. No one had been in the room since we started cleaning.

"Look," Akai said, turning her phone to me.

I took her phone and peered down at the photo of Ria, sitting cross-legged on a bed somewhere, a red sketchbook hugged to her chest. She was exactly how I remembered her, a happy smile, her heart-shaped face with glowing pink cheeks brought warmth to my chest.

"Aw. She was so nice," I whispered, glancing up at Akai.

Akai's frown was frozen and deep. "The sketchbook, Mei." She tapped on the screen, and the phone zoomed in on Ria's arms. "That was her crowning glory. Some manga book she was developing, a romance based on her high school." She turned the phone and looked at the image again, scrolling to something else. "She even sent off copies of a few pages to a famous manga artist who loved them and told her to keep going."

Akai showed me another picture of Ria, sitting at a small table in the garden out behind the house. She was sketching in the red sketchbook again.

"The damned sketchbook never left her side. And it's not here."

"Maybe she took it with her?" My heart beat swiftly, thumping against my rib cage. "Or the cops might have it?"

"I don't know." Akai plopped on the bed next to all the sketchbooks, her pushy behavior puttering to a stop. "It doesn't seem right that it's not here."

I stood up and squeezed her hand, trying to put on a happy

face. "I'll continue looking for it, and I'll check with Goro to see if the police have it. Don't worry. I'll do my best to find it."

She shook her head at me, her eyes dull.

"Maybe it's gone like she is." She sniffed up and headed for the door. "Even if we found the sketchbook, what difference would it make?"

CHAPTER
SEVEN

The late afternoon was still hot and sticky when I locked up the Fukuda house to head home. Akai had left an hour before I did, unable to force herself to spend any more time in Ria's room than she already had. We'd boxed up the manga, stripped Ria's bed down to its parts, and started sorting through the clothes in her closet when Akai had had enough. I stayed on longer than she did so I could put together boxes for work the next day and bag up any trash that would be picked up in the morning.

I clutched the bag strap on my shoulder as I walked the three blocks to the bus stop. Where had Ria's red sketchbook gone? I would search the house again, but I felt certain it wasn't anywhere I had already cleaned out. I was thorough, opening every cupboard, looking on top, behind, and under everything I came across. Granted, I hadn't opened up any of the kitchen cabinets like I had with Etsuko's apartment. Hmmm, I should probably check them.

A slow moving car on the street caught my attention as I shifted my bag to my front. A police car crept up next to me, and my face brightened with a smile. Goro? I crouched down to look inside when I saw Kohei Watanabe instead. Ugh. I snapped back up when he made eye contact with me. I didn't want to talk to him, ever. For a moment, he cruised beside me before he accelerated and turned the corner, heading in the direction of the station. Despite the heat, I shuddered. That man gave me the creeps.

But thinking about Goro, I pulled my phone from my bag and scrolled to his name. Wherever that red sketchbook was, Akai wanted it found.

"Hey, Mei. What's up?"

"Nothing much. I'm on my way home after another day at the Fukuda house."

"Oh yeah. Found anything interesting?" His voice perked up on the other end.

"Does a twenty-year-old rubber band ball sound interesting?"

"It sounds super boring."

"Yeah. I thought so too. Anyway, I was wondering if you had looked into the old case yet."

In the background, I heard typing and voices murmuring. The station seemed to be quiet for the day.

"Nope. But I can if you like. It was a missing persons case, so it's not like we would retain any evidence. There may be photos of evidence and notes, but that would be about it."

I walked for a moment, looking down at my sandaled feet and wondering what the next move here would be. If Mom or Yasahiro went missing, what would I do?

"Hmmm, well, anything you could pull up would be great. If someone goes missing, how long does the police work on the case? I remember it being quite the stir for a few weeks."

Goro sighed into the phone, and I crossed the street, nearing the bus stop. People had lined up in the shade of a giant tree, so I joined the queue.

"Yeah, two or three weeks. People go missing in Japan all the time, and they usually stay missing. It wasn't unusual or anything that Ria was never found. It was just weird she went missing in the first place."

Hmmm. I thought while I kept walking. Ria had been almost seventeen at the time, and that was about thirteen or fourteen years ago. She was underage, which was why there'd been a big investigation. If she had been a few years older, hardly anyone would've budged. She was well-loved, and her life had been scandal free.

"Right. She had a good life. It seemed weird she would want to give it all up to run away."

"Yeah. Anyway, I'll look into the case and see what I find here."

The bus pulled up, and everyone moved forward. I shifted my phone so I could pull out my bus pass.

"The bus is here, so I have to go. Let's switch to text. I have another question to ask."

"Sure." Goro hung up, and I climbed aboard the bus, placing my card at the reader, and took a seat near the front.

"*What can someone do if the police can't help? What's the next step?*" I typed in, waiting for a reply.

"*PI. Many take missing persons cases.*"

Yes, a private detective. Of course.

"*Do you think Ria's father hired one? After the police were done?*"

"*Yeah, I imagine he did. But they're expensive, so I doubt he retained anyone for long.*"

"*How would I find out who he hired?*"

"*You either cold call a bunch of local PI's or ask Akai to go through Ria's father's records.*"

"*Thanks. I'll do that.*" I stored my phone away, believing that was the end of our conversation, but my phone buzzed again.

"*Are you looking for something in particular?*" Goro's instincts must have been pricking up.

"Yeah. A red sketchbook of Ria's that had manga drawings in it. Akai seems to think it's strange we haven't found it yet."

"You looked everywhere in the house?"

I pictured the last few areas of the house we had left to do. "Pretty much. We still have a few places to look, but I wanted to check with you first."

"Okay. I'll get on it. Remember. The house is not the only place she could've left the notebook. Always think of the whole property."

I was thinking of the whole property, and I couldn't discern anywhere else the sketchbook may be. The house stood alone on the lot with no shed or cellar. A large, plastic, locked chest was to the right of the back door and contained Fukuda's gardening supplies. The backyard was a mix of gravel and herb garden, stone and water feature, then a small grassy expanse under a cherry tree.

I'd have to look harder once I was at the house again. I must have missed something.

I climbed off the bus back home, and the tea shop was winding down for the day. Yasahiro was inside, chatting with Murata and several other people, his face animated and alive.

I kept to the shadows so I could watch him for a moment. It didn't matter if it was his restaurant or my tea shop, he was at home any place he was helping other people. Though I gave him such a hard time when we first met, I believed this was what drew us together. He may have more appreciation for food than I did, and I may have more creativity when it came to painting and other physical arts, but we found common ground in helping others.

The spell was broken when Murata looked out the window and caught me snooping. I smiled and waved as I came inside to the air-conditioned space.

"Ahhhh! It's so nice in here. No wonder no one wants to go home." I smiled at them as I placed my bag near the cash register and stood under the cool air from the wall unit. I was a hot and sweaty mess. A shower and bath would do me a lot of good.

Yasahiro leaned in and gave me a quick kiss on the cheek, trying to be discreet while at the same time supportive.

"How was the clean-out today?" he asked, picking up some discarded teacups.

"Busy. But we're making good progress. I should be able to finish a bedroom tomorrow. Can I help with that?" I extended my arm to take the teacups from him, but he maneuvered them out of the way.

"Nope. Sit down and rest."

"Listen to your husband," Murata said, swatting at me to take a seat.

I hesitated but sat across from her, my joints popping on the way down.

"So tell me more about this job you're doing that's taken you away from the tea shop."

I gave her the basics of the situation, and her face widened with each passing minute.

She sighed, shaking her head. "I remember when Ria went missing."

I tried to stifle a laugh. Of course, she did. Everyone in town remembered! There wasn't one long-standing Chikata resident that was unaware of Ria's disappearance.

"I was good friends, am still good friends, with the people who lived next door to the Fukudas. It was a very trying time for them too when she went missing."

This piqued my curiosity, and I sat up taller in my seat. "How so?"

"Oh, you don't know?"

"Know what?" I leaned forward, wishing I had a pot of tea so I could refill her empty cup and keep her talking.

"Well, I don't want to start rumors again..." She trailed off, but I knew that sparkle in her eye. She was ready to gossip. "The boy of the family next door was in love with Ria for a year. They even had a secret relationship for a while, meeting up in their backyards to hold hands or kiss." She fanned herself like she was talking about pornography. Murata was as sweet as they came. "The police asked them questions for days. It really stressed their peaceful family."

"What's this family's name? Do you think you could introduce me?" My heart raced, and the baby fluttered in time with it.

Murata smiled slyly. "I see you're already excited about another mystery." She threw her head back and laughed. "There's no stopping you now. They're the Kato family, and I'd be happy to do the introductions. Perhaps tomorrow?"

"Thank you! I'll discuss it with Yasahiro tonight."

My phone buzzed and chimed in my bag, interrupting our conversation. I pulled it out, expecting to see Goro's name on the screen, or even Mom's, but it wasn't either. It was my brother.

"Hirata? Hi."

I almost never talked to my brother on the phone. We weren't particularly close and had little in common. I liked him, and as far as I knew, he liked me too, but not enough to talk to each other regularly outside of family get-togethers. If anything, I got along with his wife better.

"Hi, Mei. I hope I'm not catching you at a bad time."

I stood up from the table, holding a finger up to Murata and whispering that I'd be right back, and made my way to the back of the tea shop where Yasahiro was washing dishes.

"No, this isn't a bad time. Is something wrong?"

"Nothing's wrong. In fact, everything's great. I was wondering if you had time to come out to the house this evening? Sorry to spring this on you so quickly, but I just got word from the bank, and everything's about to be finalized. We only have a few more steps before this deal is done. So I was hoping we could sit down and hammer out the rest of the details together as a family."

I stopped dead in the middle of the room, staring up at the

ceiling, and trying to make sense of whatever Hirata was saying on the other end of the phone.

"Bank? What are you talking about?"

Hirata was silent for a long moment. "Mom didn't tell you."

"Tell me what?" My voice rose two octaves. Yasahiro turned off the sink and faced me.

Hirata sighed. "I had a feeling I should've talked to you before we got this far, but she assured me you knew what was going on. I'm buying the family farm."

I reached for the nearest chair to sit down before my legs gave out.

"Come out to the house, and I'll explain everything."

"We'll be right there," I said, my jaw clenched tight.

My brain melted down in the onrush of anger and fury building up in my body.

Mom's hesitation and avoidance finally made sense.

I was being usurped.

CHAPTER
EIGHT

The ride out to the house was deathly quiet, both Yasahiro and I keeping our tempers tampered down. I didn't know what was going on, but I was going to get to the bottom of it as quickly as possible.

Along the pine trees that lined the driveway, my two nephews were passing a soccer ball back and forth between them. Their mother, Yuna, watched from under the shade of the front porch, her hand shielding her eyes from the glare of the early evening sun and the other clutching a cold glass of tea. She stood up as we arrived, coming to my side of the car as I climbed out.

"Mei, it's good to see you," she said, bowing before giving me a stiff hug. Her demeanor was off, like milk that had expired. The change was so severe from the last time we spoke that I almost burst into tears. Everyone knew a secret that we did not. How did this happen?

"It's good to see you too, though I had no idea you'd be here today."

She pursed her lips, and I felt a modicum of relief over the fact that she looked guilty.

"Yeah. I heard. Hirata's inside with your mom. You should go see him."

She walked away from us towards the kids, and a giant, heavy cloud of dread fell on me. I turned to Yasahiro as tears welled up in my eyes. I couldn't take any more drama while pregnant. I had avoided tears most of my adult life, even when I was a screw-up, but now? No.

Yasahiro grabbed my hand and squeezed. "Let's go."

Inside, Mimoji came running when I stepped in the door. He circled my feet, raising his tail to tickle my legs, and meowed. I bent down to scratch his head but kept moving to the kitchen where the sound of cooking and the air conditioning blowing couldn't drown out Mom and Hirata's voices.

"Yes, well, that's why I'm going to get a storage locker in town," Hirata was saying as we came around the corner. His eyes flicked over to me, and he set down his glass of beer to smile and bow. "Mei, Yasahiro, thanks for coming out here on such short notice."

His face was sweaty, and his dress shirt was undone at the collar. The suit jacket he was wearing hung over the back of the kitchen desk chair. He looked like he had left the office not too long ago though it was at least a two-hour drive in traffic from Chiba to get here.

"Can I get you a beer?" he asked, raising his glass to Yasahiro.

"It's no trouble. I'll get it myself." Yasahiro crossed the room to Mom, kissed her on the cheek, glanced at the vegetables she was chopping, grabbed a glass from the cupboard, and a beer from the fridge like he lived there — which he practically did since we were there, one or both of us, several times a week.

My brother only came to visit once a month or on holidays.

Yasahiro grabbed a bottle of water for me from the fridge and joined me at my side.

"So, I'm sorry this is being sprung on you like this, but I guess Mom didn't tell you she was looking for a buyer for the farm."

"Nope," I said, glaring daggers at my mom from across the room. "She never said a thing."

Mom cringed and set down her knife. She took a deep breath and lifted her head, but she kept quiet.

"Well, it was right around your wedding when she came to me about the finances surrounding the farm." Hirata cleared his throat and pushed his sleeves up. "Mom's been in major debt since the barn fire, and even though the summer has gone well, she wants to get the business back up to one-hundred percent."

My mind blanked as I tried to make sense of this. "That's not what she told me. She told me everything's been great." My voice took on a note of exasperation, suddenly unable to remain placid about anything.

Yasahiro looked down at his shoes, a small smile breaking through his neutral expression. "She lied. Obviously," he added. "I should've known."

"I'm sorry," Mom said, lifting her chin. "I had to. I couldn't not host your wedding. I couldn't tell you the insurance check we received for the barn barely covered our losses. I asked Hirata for money around the time you got engaged."

Translation: she was failing because of me.

It was all my fault.

"But the new tractor and hiring Mr. Minato?"

Hirata raised his beer glass. "I financed those."

I sighed and closed my eyes. "Mom, we have money." I gestured between Yasahiro and me. Everything he had was ours now. And though I struggled with that idea, he wanted me to own it. "Why didn't you come to us?"

"Why wouldn't I go to my son for help?"

I had no answer except for the petty ones that flew through my head. Why wouldn't she go to her son for help? Because he had no interest in the farm. Because he was never here. Because he had his own successful career. Because I was the one who came every day and never asked for anything from it. Because I wanted to make this place my home.

"We're closing on the deal next week. I'm set to inherit the land and the house, but Mom's business is worth money, which is why I got a loan to cover expenses for the next five years. Mom will continue to live here, and she'll be paid a salary." He cleared his throat. "Yuna and the kids are moving here too. Tomorrow. Yuna will take over your role on the farm, and we're enrolling the boys in school here."

I was so stunned I needed to sit down, but the chair at the kitchen island felt like it was a hundred kilometers away.

"What about your house in Chiba? And why is just Yuna moving here?"

"We're selling the house, and I'm moving to Hong Kong for a year." When my mouth dropped open, he continued hastily. "For work. I've been asked to head up a project there. They have a housing crisis in Hong Kong, and the bank is financing new developments. I'll leave the same day the papers are finalized."

When I didn't acknowledge him, he continued.

"So this will work out great. Yuna will be here to supervise the investments and have help with the kids while I'm gone. Really, it worked out perfect for us. We're very happy."

Anger buzzed in my chest like a hive of unhappy hornets. Very happy? Was he kidding me? He didn't once ask if I was okay with any of this!

I stepped forward to give Hirata a piece of my mind when Yasahiro grabbed my wrist.

"Hirata, please forgive me for saying this, but did it ever occur to you once to talk to Mei and me about this? We had been talking with Mom for months about renovating the house and all living together here as a family."

Hirata paled, and Mom dropped her head.

My rage transferred from him to her.

"No. It hadn't." He turned to Mom. "Mom, is this true? Why didn't you tell me?"

Mom licked her lips and glanced at us all. Her face went from wide-eyed and scared to pinched and angry. "Mei spent her entire life telling me she didn't want to be a farmer."

I closed my eyes against the slap of truth.

"She doesn't really want this farm. She wants a convenient life."

I opened my eyes, and everything was blurry with tears. Mom directed her eyes at me.

"I'm grateful you've been here every day, working to make up for the losses I incurred bailing you out last fall. But nothing can make up for all that's happened in the last year. Between the barn fire, almost starving over the winter, town rumors about our family, and then that horrible murder case, and now me..."

She stopped, clearing her throat.

"What about you?" I asked, aware of the change in her demeanor. Was something wrong with her? I just about hated her at that moment, but she was my mom. I didn't want anything bad to happen to her.

"Nothing. It doesn't matter now." She waved my concern away like it was an annoying gnat. "I do feel bad that I've kept this from you. But if I have to choose between you and Yasahiro or Hirata and Yuna, then I choose Hirata. I'm sorry."

And that was that. My contributions meant nothing. I wasn't even given a seat at the negotiating table.

But I had brought most of this on myself. I'd said in the past how much I hated farming. I'd grown to love the house and the farm over the past year, but with my heart set on the tea shop, I'm not sure I'd ever expressed my love of this place to Mom. I thought I'd been communicating it with my actions. Everything I'd done hadn't been enough.

Yasahiro flattened his lips and shrugged his shoulders. There was nothing we could do.

"We're renting a storage space in town for the furniture in the back room, my old room. We plan to put the boys in there. But we're going to need your old room for Yuna and me."

It was a punch to the gut, and the baby jerked to avoid it.

"I understand. I'll go clean it out now."

"Will you stay for dinner?" Mom asked, reaching for her knife. She missed the handle, knocked it, and it crashed to the ground, just missing her foot. "*Ai!* I'm all out of sorts."

I eyed her as she carefully lifted the knife from the floor and cleaned it in the sink. She didn't look out of sorts to me. She was the same Mom she always was. Why had I thought things had gotten better between us?

"No. We'll grab my stuff and head out," I said, bowing to them both. I was a stranger in my own home. "Right?" I asked Yasahiro, hoping he didn't want to stay.

"Yeah. Let's go, Mei. I'll help you."

CHAPTER
NINE

"I'm so sorry," I wailed out between sobs on the ride home. The trunk contained two bags worth of the last of my belongings from my mother's house, and I had cried through every second of packing them away. "I had no idea. Really, I didn't."

Yasahiro glanced over at me at a red light and handed me his handkerchief. "Try to calm down, Mei. I am one-hundred percent positive this is not your fault."

I mopped up my face and blew my nose. I was a mess. My life was a mess. Nothing would repair this except going back in time and making different decisions.

"Remember two months ago, after we returned from Paris, you offered to sit down and go over the finances with your mom?"

"Yes?"

"And what happened?"

"She..." I sucked in a shaky breath around my quivering bottom lip. "She said she hired someone from Tokyo to take care of it."

"Then she went on vacation with Chiyo." He nodded his

head. "Classic evasion. I suspected things weren't right back then, but it wasn't my place to push her."

"That's when you started calling contractors!" I examined my new husband as he pulled up to our parking spot outside of the apartment. Had he seen this from the beginning? "You knew something was wrong? Why didn't you say anything to me?"

He laughed. "I did, though I attributed it to her reticence over us all moving in together."

Right. He had said that.

"I never expected *that*." He waved back in the general direction of the house, indicating the brotherly overthrow that just happened. "Especially since your brother took no interest in the farm before now." He sighed, and the sound was so deep, he must have brought it up from his toes.

"I'm so sorry."

"Stop apologizing, Mei. There's nothing to be done."

"I feel like it's all my fault." I hung my head. "I never told Mom how much the farm means to me now. I should've said something."

Yasahiro kept the car and the air conditioning running.

"Look. You'd have to be deaf, dumb, and blind to not know how much that farm means to you. You may not have said it in words, but you said it in actions. You practically starved yourself to save your mom's reputation. We held our wedding there. You went there every day to help your mom. Without pay. No one does that without love."

"Then why did she do this?"

He shrugged his shoulders. "Sounds like these plans have been in motion for almost six months. She probably started going to your brother for money in the winter before she got the insurance check. We were only still dating then. Just think of how much has happened this year."

All at once, gratitude washed over me for this man. Yasahiro was full of good sense and practicality. When I let emotions carry me away, like Mt. Fuji on a stormy day, he was the first person to keep me grounded.

"She lied to me. Several times," I whispered, and he reached over to squeeze my hand.

"Pride does stupid things to people. Trust me. I've seen things my own parents have done that boggle the mind. That generation is caught up in the old ways," he stressed, pulling my hand to keep my attention, "she still loves you. She cares. I know she does. Maybe it *is* time for your brother to take over. We could've done the job, and done it well, but he's first in line." His lips twisted into an evil grin. "Let's see what a banker can do with a farm."

I tried not to laugh as I imagined my brother as he was in his teens, sully and unhappy in the fields with Mom. If I talked about hating farming while growing up, he was just as bad. I always thought that was why he went into finance and moved two hours away.

"What about us?" I asked. "We have a baby on the way, and now all of our plans have fallen through." Tears trickled down my face, and he brushed them away with his thumb.

"Whatever. We still have our money and investments. There's loads of open land in this town. We'll find our spot and build a house. And if you need help, more than what I can provide, I'll hire someone." He shrugged his shoulders again. "Try not to worry too much about it. We'll figure it out. We have time."

He leaned over and kissed my salty lips and my forehead. Knowing we would conquer this together made all the difference.

My bad luck had reared its head again, but I was lucky in love, that was for sure.

But two things from our conversation struck me as Yasahiro turned off the car and popped the trunk.

First, there may be trouble on the horizon when Hirata was done with his year in Hong Kong. From Hong Kong, he could just funnel money home and have Yuna take care of things. But if she didn't like her new life, Hirata would never hear the end of it when he returned. Also, when he returned, he would be expected to help on the farm. It's possible the whole situation would fall apart in a year's time.

Second, Mom's words, *"She wants a convenient life,"* struck me hard in the chest. This was certainly true of my life before I moved home last year. I'd been immature and whiny, and I put Mom through tough times after everything that happened with Tama trying to kill me and then Amanda's death. But I thought I had changed.

Hadn't I?

Worry bounced around my chest, a lost bird trying to find its nest.

Had I been ungrateful? Unsupportive?

Had I disgraced or dishonored Mom in some way?

I checked the mirror and watched Yasahiro lifting the bags of my belongings from the trunk. He was oblivious to the anxiety welling up in me like a newly-discovered hot spring.

Whatever I had done wrong, I would fix it.

Somehow.

CHAPTER
TEN

"Why are you so quiet?" Murata asked as we drove up to the Fukuda house. Yasahiro gave me the use of the car today since neither of us had to go to the house to help on the farm. Those days were over, at least for the short term, and now I was able to use the car to commute instead of the bus.

Today, Murata was along so she could make introductions to the next door neighbor before I got on with the continued business of cleaning out the house. Though I longed to take a day off, curl up at home, and be babied by Yasahiro, I had to keep my promise to Akai. Mom thought I wanted a convenient life? Well, I would prove to her my life was anything but.

"No reason. I was just thinking about real estate, actually. Yasahiro and I are considering buying some land in town. Maybe a little farm with a spot to put a new house. I was looking at those new Panasonic homes. They're pretty advanced now. Earthquake and fire proof —"

"I thought you said you were going to move in with your mom?" Murata narrowed her eyes at me as I parked the car.

I paused as I considered how many people I told this to.

Goro, Kumi... I probably mentioned it to most of my clients and a few others too. Ugh. Great job, Mei. Way to put the cart before the horse.

"That option is no longer on the table," I muttered. "It turns out someone else snagged that opportunity before I could."

"Hmph," she huffed while grasping her door handle. "I always thought your mom was a little on the hasty side. Bet she regrets that decision."

Murata shut her door, and I had to jolt myself into action. I wondered how many other people felt the same way.

I hurried from the car to escort her next door. We crossed the pavement between the two houses, past the dead plants in containers that had belonged to Fukuda to the lush greenery of the next door neighbor, his house and front yard impeccably kept. We rang the bell and waited as the sound of the TV inside muted and footsteps approached.

"Why, Mrs. Murata! What a surprise!" An older graying man stood in the doorway, his face joyous with a big smile. Thank goodness, too, because I had been worried about catching this man off guard without calling ahead of time.

"Takashi, it's good to see you. I hope you're well." Murata bowed to him, and he stepped off the front door threshold to usher us inside before we could even finish greetings.

"I'm good. Healthy. Can't complain."

"Takashi Kato, this is my good friend, Mei Yamagawa."

"Actually, it's Suga now, though I'm still not accustomed to it." I laughed because I often introduced myself to other people using my old, unmarried name. I wasn't used to being Mei Suga yet. It seemed like such a short name.

Takashi blinked at me, his head turned to the side. "Where have I met you before?"

"You haven't, I don't think. But I've been helping to clean out the Fukuda house next door, so you've probably seen me around the last few days."

Murata and I both waited as he digested this information, but it didn't appear to vex him in any kind of way.

"That's it!" He snapped his fingers. "I have seen you around here."

"And when Mei told me she was here every day, I insisted she bring me around to visit you." Murata was excellent at bridging gaps in conversations, and if Takashi felt manipulated, he didn't show it.

"Come in, come in! I was just about to make tea, and I have taiyaki from my son's shop in town. You must try some."

Mmmm, taiyaki. My mouth watered as I thought of the sweet treat, and my stomach gurgled right on cue. I could definitely eat one of those this morning.

Inside, the house was cool and relaxing. I looked around, impressed with the modernity of the place and how clean and clutter free the open space was — a marked contrast to the house I had been in all week.

"You have a beautiful home," I said, leaving my shoes at the front door and following them both into a bright living room.

"Thank you. Just built it two years ago. I'd been thinking of selling, since the town had gone through hard times, but my son convinced me to stay instead. We tore down the old house and constructed this smaller, more efficient one in its place."

I helped Murata to sit at the low dining table, close to the air conditioning unit on the wall.

"Is it a model house?"

"It is. This is a Tama Home," he said from the open kitchen. Steam wafted up from a teapot as he poured in hot water from an electric kettle. "I had a hard time choosing which company to go with, but I'm happy with the outcome."

I made a mental note of his choice. Now that Yasahiro and I would no longer renovate the family farm home, I could choose land without a house, or with a run-down house that could be knocked down, and have a new model home constructed.

Though the awful feeling of dread and betrayal hadn't abated since yesterday, this new idea lifted my spirits.

Takashi came to the table and set out tea with a plate of the taiyaki sweets. Taiyaki, sweet, pancake-like breads, shaped like a fish and stuffed with sweet bean paste, were one of my favorite treats. My mouth watered, but I waited for Murata and Takashi to grab theirs first.

"You said your son makes these now? How is Itsuki?" Murata asked, biting into her cake. I took that as a sign I could eat mine. The cake melted in my mouth, and the bean paste was just the right level of sweetness. I tried to keep my composure, but these were super delicious. I hummed and sighed, much to Takashi's delight.

"He's good, thank you for asking. He and his wife run the taiyaki shop over near the station now. Their son is five already."

"How wonderful! You must be so proud."

"I am, thank you."

"And how is business for you?"

"Business is good. I can't complain."

Murata turned to me. "Takashi inherited his father's chiropractor and sports therapy business." She took another bite. "I knew you'd be home this morning. Always took Fridays off," she said, winking at him.

He laughed. "That's right. Just like Dad."

Ah, their connection made sense. Murata had most likely been a patient of Takashi's father back in her younger days. Takashi was maybe around the same age as my mother. I would ask Murata more about him later.

We all ate the taiyaki while Murata and Takashi caught up on town gossip, and I did my best not to be impatient or rush them through the pleasantries. But I watched the clock tick over to close to ten, and I knew we had to hurry this visit along if I would get anything done that day.

I cleared my throat before sipping tea.

"Oh! So, speaking of people moving around in town, Mei here is cleaning out Fukuda's house next door."

Takashi nodded as he finished his cup of tea. "I haven't been here much during the days this week, but I've seen the boxes leaving in the evenings. You must be quite tired. I only ever went into that house once since Ria disappeared, and I never wanted to go back in again. Too much stuff."

"Indeed it was. Now we have the chaos mostly under control."

"That's good to hear. Do you know if the new owner will sell the place?"

I finished my tea. "Yes. Akai plans to sell the place as soon as we have it all cleared out."

He grunted as he leaned over to look out the window. "I don't know why you would bother cleaning it out. I'm sure the next person will just knock down the place and put up something new. Like I did."

"I couldn't blame them! If they saw your house, they would covet it." I smiled at him, keeping the conversation light and easy. "But we wanted to make sure that all the items that were worth money could be sold off to help cover expenses, and Akai was friends with Ria and was hoping we would run into information about why she went missing."

Takashi leaned forward, his shoulders rising. "Have you found anything?"

The air in the room prickled with energy. "Nothing yet. Something is missing from her belongings we're eager to find. But no evidence as to why she would've left."

Takashi took a moment to think before standing up and removing the teacups from the table. I got the feeling he was stalling or trying to gather up the nerve to say something, so I kept quiet. Patience was something I wasn't good at. My lack of patience always got on Mom's nerves, and I was determined to do better.

Except I shouldn't have been thinking about Mom because my emotions flip-flopped from angry to sad while I waited for Takashi to come around. I couldn't cry now.

"Mei, if you don't mind my prying," Takashi began, and I pumped my fist in my imagination, "what's missing that you're hoping to find?"

"Well..." I drew out the word, wondering how detailed I should be. "You know Ria was a gifted artist, no? She was fantastic at drawing manga, and she had a special red sketchbook that she drew in that's missing."

"I do know! I saw the drawings myself." He sat back down at the table with us, and this time his expression was far away. "My son, Itsuki, way back when they were in high school, dated Ria for about a year."

I gasped, and Murata elbowed me. "You don't say. Really?"

He laughed, not put off by my question. "Ria was the girl next door. Bright and beautiful. I often wished they would grow up and marry each other. You know how it is, the dreams of parents. I knew her family, and that they were good people." His face lost its happy glow. "But then my wife and I divorced, and she remarried and moved to Tokyo. The separation was hard on us. Itsuki was angry with me, so he decided to go to senior high school in Tokyo and come here on the weekends. He would see Ria on those weekends, but it was never enough for both of them. She broke up with him about five or six months before she went missing. He was devastated. Stayed away from her and me. We're good now, but those were hard times."

"I'm so sorry. That sounds really stressful."

Murata shook her head in sadness.

"It was extra stressful because I could hear the fights she would have with her mother and father. Old Japanese houses have thin walls, you know? They would scream at each other for hours."

"About what?"

He waved his hand. "Teenage stuff. This and that. Ria staying out too late, hanging out with the wrong crowd. Her father was angry with her for spending all of her time drawing instead of studying. They fought fiercely the night before she went missing. I heard plenty of door slams, and then in the middle of the night, I thought I heard strange noises in the backyard, but when I looked out there the next day, everything was normal."

"Did you tell all of this to the police when they questioned you?"

"I did. They said Ria's father had been up drinking the night before so it could've been him in the yard." He shrugged his shoulders. "Anyway, they questioned both my son and me, but that was it. I never heard from them again after that."

So, now I had two suspects to consider in Ria's disappearance — her father and Takashi's son, Itsuki.

But Takashi said Itsuki and Ria had broken up six months before she went missing, and Akai seemed to think Ria was dating someone, someone she had only met once. This meant there was another boyfriend unaccounted for.

"Ah, look at the time," Murata said, bringing my mind back to the present. "We don't want to keep you. I'm sure you have plenty of things to do today on your day off."

"In fact, I must be off to go visit my son."

We all stood from the table, Takashi helping both of us to our feet. I had to laugh at the way Murata and I were both hindered by our physical conditions. Murata's hips were going, and my baby belly impeded me from standing up or sitting down with grace.

"You said he owns a taiyaki shop near the station?" I asked as we slipped on our shoes near the door.

"He does. It's the only one there, so you can't miss it." Pride caused Takashi's chest to puff up.

I reached into my bag and pulled out one of the tea shop business cards I carried around. I loved handing them out and seeing the smiles on people's faces when they glimpsed the design Kumi had drawn for me.

"Would you mind giving your son my business card? I run the new tea shop in town, and I bet his taiyaki would be a great addition to my menu. I'm jealous they're so good. I've tried to make them myself and failed too many times to count. I'm a horrible chef!" We all laughed at my self-deprecating humor. "I'd like to talk to him about it soon."

He bowed, taking the card with both hands. "Oh yes. I've heard of your tea shop! It comes highly recommended from all of my older patients at my practice. If you have any fliers you'd like to put in my waiting room, I'd be happy to have them."

I bowed in return. "Thank you so much. That's a great idea. I'd love that."

"I'll let my son know you'll call on him soon."

Outside, the sun was baking everything to a crisp, and the hot air was rich with moisture. I missed the air conditioning immediately.

"Drop me off at the nearest bus stop, Mei. I'll make my way back to our neighborhood alone."

"Oh, I couldn't possibly do that. I'll drive you back."

Her eyes widened as she slapped my arm. "Didn't you hear what he said?" She hastened her steps towards the main street.

"What?" I looked around, hoping the clue would come out and bite me in the leg like a rabid dog.

"He heard strange noises in the yard the night Ria went missing, and I doubt it was her father outside drinking." She nodded, definitively. "You must go search the yard and make sure she's not buried there."

I gasped again, struck dumb by this idea. "That's nuts. There's no way she's buried in the yard. If she had been, I'm sure the police would've noticed the yard torn up and would've figured it out right away. It's unlikely they would've missed something so big."

Murata slid her eyes to the side at me, something I only saw sly teenagers doing nowadays. It was hard not to laugh.

"Leave no stone unturned. You have no idea what the police thought that day they arrived on the scene. They could've been preoccupied with other cases, hungover, sick... Anything. And this was a missing persons case for a teenager. Teenagers run away all the time. I doubt they looked into every possible avenue."

We made it to the bus stop just in time to catch an arriving bus. I helped her up the steps, and she waved me away as she scanned her card.

"Go get back to work. You know what you have to do."

CHAPTER
ELEVEN

Akai and I stood in the backyard, a shovel in each of our hands.

"Are you sure about this?" I asked her, looking out from under my big gardening hat. I used to keep my hat and the gloves at Mom's house, but I wasn't going there anymore, and I'd left them in Yasahiro's car on a whim I would need them. Turns out, my instincts were correct.

Akai sighed, her eyes scanning the tiny yard. "What do we have to lose? I feel like my best friend was a total stranger." She turned to look at the Kato house next door. "She talked about Itsuki. Even said she had a crush on him. But she kept their relationship a secret from me, at the very least. I had no idea, and I guess they dated for quite some time."

"Who else do you think she dated?"

She shrugged. "Not sure. Maybe someone from the crew? Tama Kano's friends? I barely knew them."

I sighed as I thought about going down that path again. My experience of almost burning to death in the barn was still fresh in my dreams. I sometimes woke up, panting and sweating, calling for help. Maybe a stronger person could have shrugged it off, but I couldn't. Whatever I decided to do with this case, I'd have to be careful.

"Anyway," Akai said, sighing and waving her hand at the backyard, "I'm selling the place, and they'll probably rip everything up. Might as well check the whole property."

"What if we don't have to check the whole property?" I jerked my chin at the cherry tree. "Didn't you say she would sit outside under the cherry tree and sketch? That seems like the best place to start."

I led the way since Akai was made of stone. She agreed that we needed to dig up the yard after what I had learned from Takashi Kato, but it wasn't as if she liked it. I got the feeling she still blamed herself for Ria's disappearance, and she didn't want to relive those uncertain days again.

I chose a spot in the grass under the shade of the cherry tree, said a quick prayer for both strength and forgiveness for potentially hurting this beautiful tree, and dug in.

Akai, emboldened by my frank determination, dropped to her knees two meters to my left and got to digging.

With every swift thrust of my shovel into the grass and dirt, my mind focused on my current predicament. Back at my mom's, Yuna was doing my job. She was picking the tomatoes I'd planned on picking, weeding the sweet potato fields I'd cultivated and planted myself, and speaking to Minato. Ugh, Minato. I could guarantee Mom gave him some lame excuse for why I wasn't there. I would have to go visit him at home soon and explain. I enjoyed the casual friendship we had, and I didn't want him to think I was blowing him off.

Shovel, scoop, throw. Shovel, scoop, throw. With each repetitive movement, anger simmered in my gut, the baby eerily quiet, like he or she knew I was close to losing my temper. The last few months rolled through my head, over and over, as I tried to figure out where I'd gone wrong. The last time I'd been a total brat was when Mom kicked me out of the house for being pregnant while not married. And really, my attitude had been tame when I took the circumstances into account. Since then, I'd been a model daughter. I'd never missed a day at the farm, even through most of my first-trimester sickness. I hadn't been snarky or discourteous to Mom. Yasahiro and I had covered almost all the expenses for the wedding, leaving Mom with only the hosting duties, hiring staff to help, and renting the tent. Where had I messed up?

"You're awfully quiet," Akai said, and I was struck by how similar she sounded to Murata earlier today. Was I usually a talker?

"I have a lot to think about."

Akai's shovel sliced into the dirt and a loud metallic thud rang through the tiny yard.

We both froze.

Akai shrank back from the hole. "What if it's a water pipe or something? Maybe we should've asked about that before we got started." She hesitated as she leaned back forward and stared down into the hole she'd dug, her face pinched, uncertain of how to continue.

"I doubt it." I glanced around the yard again. "If it were a utility, it would come in from the street. Let's use our hands."

I sank to my knees next to Akai and peered into the hole with her.

"Mei, I feel bad about having a pregnant woman dig in my backyard."

"Shush," I said, pushing the dirt aside to reveal what was underneath. The scratched surface of a metal box was cool under my fingertips. "I don't want special treatment."

"That's ridiculous." Akai knelt beside me. "Don't you want a seat on the bus?"

"Doesn't everyone?"

She had no answer for that. Yes, I wanted a seat on the bus. But I would wait to ask for one when I was as big as the bus that carried me.

After brushing aside the dirt for a few minutes, we found the edges of the box. It was about the size of A4 paper, and each side was sealed with tape. Akai levered her shovel around the side of the box and heaved. The box came loose, and worms in the dirt squirmed underneath where it had laid for years.

I breathed a huge sigh of relief.

"I'm so glad we didn't find a body."

"Me too." Akai left and came back with a pair of gardening shears she used to cut through the tape. The sun beat down on us, but we didn't want to move. We were both transfixed by the box.

What was inside?

"I don't want to open it." Akai shoved the box at me. "What if this is something personal Ria wanted no one to know about? What if she comes back for it someday?"

I was beginning to understand my new friend, and with every day we spent together, I respected her more and more. She had a strong work ethic paired with a fierce sense of right and wrong. Sure, she hacked Amanda's files for me and sold me the data, but she knew it was for a good cause.

I reached over the piles of dirt between us and squeezed her hand.

"You know this is the right thing to do. If you went missing, wouldn't you want people to explore every avenue to bring you back?"

"No way," she said, shaking her head. "I want people to leave me alone."

I rolled my eyes at her. "Give me the box."

She handed it over with a heavy sigh.

I brushed my fingers over the clasp on the front of the box, clearing away any dirt that would hinder the button from functioning. Then I swung the top open.

Akai gasped.

Inside, looking like time hadn't touched it, Ria's red sketch-book sat with a note on top.

Her cute, curly writing could not be mistaken.

I picked up the note and read it aloud, "Just in case."

CHAPTER
TWELVE

"Where are you?" I texted to Goro, my fingers flying over the screen.

Under the cool breeze of the air conditioner in the kitchen, Akai sat ramrod straight, her hand on the red sketchbook on the table.

"Aren't you going to open it and start reading?" I asked, grabbing waters for us from the refrigerator.

She flipped through the pages rapidly, her face turning green. "I really didn't expect to find it. Why would she bury it?"

I licked my lips, wondering how bold I should be with my guesses. I had a million of them now, my daydreams having taken me to the edge and back.

I sat down across from her. "My guess? She knew she was in some kind of trouble, and this would be the first piece of evidence someone would get rid of to cover up their involvement."

"Who? Do you think someone hurt her?"

I nodded slowly. "The moment we found the box this case went from missing persons to murder." I touched my hand to my chest. "For me, at least."

"Yeah," Akai croaked. "Me too." She pushed the sketchbook

across the table. "I think... I think I'm too biased and too emotional to look at this and make any sense of the story. I'm handing it over to you. Just please, don't lose or damage it."

"Of course," I insisted, bowing my head. "I'll take good care of it."

My phone buzzed. A text from Goro read, *"I'm at the station. Why?"*

"I'll be right there," I replied.

"Do you want me to stick around and help you clean up the backyard? We still have the rest of Ria's room to pack up." I slid my phone into my purse and stood, gently picking up the sketchbook.

"No, thank you." Her lips jerked into a wry smile. "Let me guess. You're off to bring that to Goro?"

"Who else?" I smiled and shrugged. "But of course, I'll stay if you need me."

"No. Really. Go find out what happened to Ria. I can take care of the house. I feel" — she paused, glancing around the kitchen — "better now that we've found the sketchbook. I can do the rest myself. Keep me apprised?" She held up her phone.

"Whatever I find, you'll be the first to know."

I jumped in Yasahiro's car, turned the air conditioning to full, and peeled out of the driveway like I was heading to the Auto-bahn. There was no time to waste!

The red sketchbook was a key piece of evidence in this case, something no one else had before. I didn't know what was in it, but I needed Goro to help me through this. Besides, I promised I would contact him if I found anything.

I parked in the lot at the station, and hugging the sketchbook to my chest, I hurried to the front door. Just as I was about to head in, the door swung open, and Kohei Watanabe stepped out, barreling straight into me. The force of our collision was like being taken out by a football player as we both ran for the ball. I dropped the sketchbook and crashed to the ground, landing right on my behind.

"Ow!" Pain shot up my back, and my heart raced as I worried about the baby. But I hadn't fallen on my belly, so I managed to avoid a near brush with calamity.

Kohei sighed and rolled his eyes as he stood over me. "Why don't you watch where you're going?"

"I could ask you the same question." I glared up at him, wondering if he would apologize and help me up.

No such luck.

"What's that?" He pointed at the sketchbook, and his eyes narrowed as he bent over to grab it.

I was closer to the ground, though, so I got to the sketchbook first.

"None of your business." I swiped it up into my arms.

"What are you doing with that?" he asked, towering over me.

"What do you mean?" Did he know what was in the sketch-book or was I imagining his interest? My skin prickled with goosebumps.

He shook his head, stepping away from me. "Nothing. I never really took you for the artistic type."

My eyes widened. "Pretty much everyone in town knows I paint. You'd have to be an idiot to not know that."

"Whatever. Since when have I paid you any real attention?" he asked, shoving his hands in his pockets as the front door opened again, and Kayo, Goro's partner, ran out.

"Mei, are you okay? What happened?" She offered me an arm to help me up and glared at Kohei just like I did.

"I'm sure pregnancy has made her clumsy." Kohei shrugged as he walked away to a patrol car. "Must be hard being both clumsy and stupid," he muttered, but both Kayo and I heard him.

"Must be hard to be so heartless," Kayo threw back at him. He acted like he didn't hear her, got in the car, and took off.

"Heartless and mean. I thought police officers were supposed to be helpful," I said, brushing myself off.

"Well, he's one-of-a-kind." Kayo sighed, reaching back to adjust her small bun. Her hair had grown longer these last few months. She kept claiming she didn't have time to get it cut, but I think she liked her hair this length. When it was shorter, men wouldn't even look at her. Now, she was getting eyed from across the room more often. I was happy for her.

"Are you here to see Goro?"

"Yeah. Buzz me in?"

"Sure. I'm on my way out for lunch. Oh, that reminds me. Are we still getting together for girls' night tomorrow?"

"I think so. Let me double-check, okay? Things are crazy at home with my mom."

"Okay." She glanced at the red sketchbook and my knees. "You coming straight from the farm, Mei?"

I looked down at my jeans, and the knees were covered with grass and dirt stains. I should've done a better job cleaning up afterward.

"It's a long story."

Goro was eating a salad when I arrived at his desk. He never struck me as the salad type, but when I peered into the bento box, long pieces of thinly cut steak were mixed in with the greens. Of course.

"What's so important, Mei?" he asked around a mouthful of food.

I slid the red sketchbook onto his desk and opened it to the back page. Pointing to Ria's name and the title of the manga work, *After School*, I watched his face morph from puzzled to surprised.

"Look what I found buried in the backyard."

"You found this buried in the backyard of the Fukuda house?"

I nodded as he flipped through the book. I tried to keep my

eyes on the drawings and dialogue, but Goro's face was too much fun to watch.

He leaned in and ran his finger over one dialogue exchange between two characters. One girl's cheeks were blushing as a young man, his hair blond and long over his eyes, stood over her.

"This has to be between us, okay? It would break Hiromi's heart to know we're dating... I'm not sure if I can lie to him... Then it's over between us... No. I promise. I'll keep quiet," Goro read, keeping his voice low. The station was mostly empty, but those left at their desks weren't paying attention to us.

He flipped backwards and forwards in the book, his eyes narrowed.

"What do you think?" I asked, leaning forward. I was eager to find out if his instincts were pinging like mine were. "There was a note with the book." I pulled the "Just in case" note from my purse and gave it to him. He inspected both sides before setting it down and pushing away from the desk to lean back in his chair.

"I don't know. It looks like girly manga to me. Why would she bury it with this note?"

"It has to mean something, no?"

He shook his head. "Not really. I can think of a dozen reasons why she would bury it. Maybe she knew it wasn't very good, and she thought one day she could come back and dig it up like a time capsule. That used to be all the rage when our parents were kids, especially since land never left the family." He scooped up a mound of greens and meat with his chopsticks and paused. "Yeah. That's probably the best explanation."

"That doesn't make any sense. Time capsules had things like money or newspapers or stuff from that time so you could see how things had changed. Who would bury their sketchbook?"

"She might have thought she'd be a big hit by now and that would be just as interesting to dig up."

"Why wouldn't she just stick it on a shelf?"

He shrugged. "I don't know."

I took the sketchbook from the desk and flipped through it again, but without sitting and actually reading it, nothing was popping out at me.

"Akai said this was her masterpiece, and the story was partially autobiographical too." I pressed my lips together as I wondered how long it would take me to read through to the end. Two or three days, tops.

"Do you think anything else is in the ground at her house? Should I get a team out there?" Goro raised his eyebrows at me.

"No. I don't. This is it." I sighed. The sketchbook wasn't much, but it was something. "But I do have a few suspects we can look into around the cause of her disappearance."

"Really? Shoot." He lifted his pen over his notebook and scratched away as I told him everything I learned from Takashi Kato that morning.

"With Takashi Kato aware of his son's love affair with Ria, and then him overhearing her father yell at her, I believe we can count on both the son, Itsuki, and Ria's father being suspects."

I was happy with these two options. They were two more options than the zero options I had the day before even though something felt missing. Besides Ria breaking up with Itsuki, he had no real reason I was aware of to hurt her. No one saw them arguing or angry with each other or the information would've made it into the police report. Her father was dead, so it's not like we could question him either.

"Suspected of what? We've never found a body, so, unfortunately, Ria Fukuda is a missing person until we do."

I folded my fingers around the sketchbook. Was this even worth getting involved in? I had plenty of things to do, especially now that Yasahiro and I were being forced out of the family farm by my brother. I needed to run my tea shop and look for a new home for us too.

I didn't need a mystery on top of all that.

"But..." Goro started, humming under his breath. "I don't see any reason why we can't go talk to Itsuki Kato. You said he makes taiyaki?" He licked his lips, and my stomach growled. It was lunchtime for me too.

"Yeah, and they're delicious. I was thinking about asking him to distribute to the tea shop."

"That would be a nice addition to the menu," he replied, his eyes filled with mischievous delight.

My phone rang in my bag, the buzz-buzz-buzzing stopping a full out laugh from my belly. On the screen, Mom's name flashed. I closed my eyes for a brief moment, trying to convince myself that I wasn't mad at her for taking away my place on the family farm. She was only ever looking to protect the family land and our investment. This situation wasn't her fault.

But it was.

"Hello?" I pressed the phone to my ear.

"Mei, I hope I'm not bothering you." Her voice was irritated, and anger flashed in my vision, my face heating up.

"No. Of course not. How is everything?"

"I was worried about you because neither you nor Yasahiro came out to the house this morning. Are you sick?"

"No. I'm as well as to be expected."

"Then why didn't you come?"

I detected a high amount of passive aggressive behavior on Mom's part. She had replaced me but already missed me? I counted to five before answering. "Seems to me that you have everything under control. Yuna and the boys are going to be a big help."

"They're not, not yet. It'll take time to get them acclimated and learning the business."

"I'm sure it will."

I paused, eyeing Goro who was trying, unsuccessfully, not to eavesdrop.

"I don't remember us saying yesterday that you wouldn't be working here anymore."

"Actually, Hirata said Yuna would be taking over all my duties."

Mom scoffed. "Well, yes, but not right away. I still expect you to come every day. This is a *family* business. Just because I brought in your brother doesn't mean I still don't need you."

"Mom..."

I had so much to say at that moment. What about my tea shop? What about *my* growing family with Yasahiro? What about my hopes and dreams? I barely had time to pick up a paintbrush, and my mom expected me to work for free?

Or was I being selfish?

"I need you to come out to the farm now and take over training Yuna. I'm sure you're done with cleaning out the Fukuda house, and if Yasahiro is still handling the tea shop, then you should have the time free. We'll discuss your schedule too."

I inhaled a long breath through my nose to steady myself. And yet, guilt settled on my shoulders like an angry monkey. Against my better judgment, I felt I owed her. After all, it wasn't Yuna's fault she had no experience running a farm. She worked at the bank when she met my brother, and she grew up in the city, not the countryside. I would be surprised if she knew anything about growing vegetables. As far as I knew, she couldn't even keep houseplants alive.

"I'm hungry, Mom. I'm going to have lunch with Yasahiro, and then I'll come out to the farm this afternoon. I need to check in with Akiko, anyway."

She huffed. "I suppose that will work. See you later." She hung up, and I threw my phone back into my bag with a huff.

Goro's eyes slid to me. "What's going on?"

"It's a long story. I promise to fill you in later."

"Sounds like your mom is pretty mad." He leaned back in his chair. "Let me give you a little advice, from one young person to another. Your mom, my mom — they come from an entirely different mindset. We love our families, but nothing is more important than being happy with your role in the universe." He pressed his hands together in prayer position. "I'm grateful my mom and Kumi have worked out a good relationship, but your mother needs... a push in the right direction."

"You're telling me," I said, smirking.

I stood up and readjusted my dirty jeans. Looks like I wasn't changing anytime soon.

"Let Kayo know I'll call her later. And maybe tomorrow morning we can go to Itsuki Kato's taiyaki place?" He nodded, and I grabbed my bag and prepared myself for a hot exit to the summery outside. "For now, I have work to do."

CHAPTER
THIRTEEN

I t was hotter than the fires of hell outside, and I regretted my decision to come to the farm in the afternoon. I should've told Mom I'd be there the next morning when the weather was cooler. But I was hasty, trying to placate her and not make her any angrier.

Yuna and I were suffering because of my poor decisions.

"I'm going to faint out here, Mei," Yuna said, puffing short, labored breaths.

"Try to concentrate on feeling cool. I always picture a crisp autumn day when I'm working in these conditions."

Yuna glanced sideways at me.

"Forget it. Let's make it through these two things, and we'll go inside."

I was showing her how to pick tomatoes and squash was next. We wouldn't harvest a whole row, not then. It *was* too hot for that. Instead, I decided to show her an example of each so she could get started the next day.

"I don't know how you do this while pregnant. When I was pregnant with both boys, I could barely move."

I shrugged. "Maybe I'm lucky."

Who was I kidding? I was the unluckiest person around, current evidence pointing to my continual state of bad luck.

"Maybe you are." Her voice had a bitter tone to it I wasn't expecting. I stopped and squinted at her, trying to figure out what was going on.

"Are you okay?"

She waved me off. "I'm fine. Let's finish up."

Something in the way she changed the subject so fast told me differently, but I was in no mood to press her. I hurried us through the day's lesson, making sure she knew what to do the following morning, and then ushered her inside. Yuna hesitated in front of the kitchen hooks, not knowing where to hang her hat or gloves. She moved slowly, like she had weights on every joint. I looked out the window, wondering if there was anything else I should do before facing the music. Minato was gone for the day, so I had no one I needed to talk to before spending time with Mom.

In the living room, the boys laid about, sprawled in front of the fan, playing video games on their devices, headphones engaged. Mimoji kept his distance, never fully trusting kids and their grabby hands.

Mom was in her knitting chair, the farm ledger in her lap and a pencil in her hand. Her face was pinched and depressed, and I considered making a run for it.

"I'm going to go cool off in the bedroom," Yuna said, heading off before anyone could stop her.

I pulled up a chair opposite Mom and sat my pregnant butt down where it should be. After digging in the morning and my constant state of activity since then, I was weary and needed a break.

"How is she doing?" Mom asked, referring to Yuna.

"She'll be fine, eventually. She's smart, and she'll catch on.

But I don't think she's done much manual labor in the past." I wiggled my head from side to side. "Are you sure you wouldn't rather put her in charge of the books?" I waved to the ledger in her lap. "She used to work at the bank."

"Well, I could, I suppose."

This was my opportunity!

"Then you could hire someone more qualified to come out here and take over some of the harvesting. Just like you did with Mr. Minato."

Mom squinted her eyes at me like I was a kilometer away in a raging storm. Not good.

"Why would I do that? I have enough help between you and me. I was hoping to increase the yield next year with her help too."

"Well..." I said, drawing out the syllable. "I think, since Yasahiro and I are no longer investing our money in the farm, I'll finally be able to run the tea shop full time. Then I can move on to other things like painting and real estate investment, and of course, raising the baby."

I was proud of myself for coming straight out and saying it. I was polite, but I didn't beat around the bush like most people did. I didn't say no. I just stated my case.

"This" — Mom shook her finger at me — "This is why I didn't ask you and Yasahiro to invest. You know I'm happy for you that you opened the tea shop. But I never expected you to run the place. I find it... irresponsible that you are choosing the tea shop over the family business."

Mom rubbed her forehead as I tried to think of the proper response that didn't involve me jumping to my feet and screaming obscenities at her. She helped me open the place! What did she think was going to happen?

"I... I don't understand. You just cut me out of the family business, so I'm not choosing the tea shop over the family business. That was your choice. Besides, I don't want to be doing hard manual labor in my third trimester, so it's not like I'd be working here much longer, anyway." I rubbed my belly, setting a protective hand over it.

Mom huffed. "I worked in the fields until my due date with both you and your brother. Practically gave birth to you in the middle of the squash."

The image that popped into my head was not pleasant. My overactive imagination needed an off switch. She plowed on.

"I didn't cut you out of the family business, Mei. You're very much still a part of it. The plain truth is that I need you here working. There's more work to do than Yuna and I can handle, and we won't be able to afford another employee. So I will call Yasahiro later this evening and advise him it's time you hired someone to run the tea shop so I can have you back here every day."

A blood vessel in my head throbbed. She wasn't cutting me out, and she still needed me here, so she wanted to run my life. She wanted me at her beck and call.

"You'll call Yasahiro? Why...?" I stopped. Why? Because he was my husband and surely he would have better control over me.

Mom's business was in the present, but her sensibilities were still in the past. All that talk last year about me finding something and someone I loved meant nothing now that she needed me on the farm working for free.

I tried to reconcile that Mom of a year ago with the Mom in front of me. What had happened?

A lot. But I was missing something.

"Maybe he can talk some sense into you." She cleared her throat.

"Maybe he'll talk sense into me? Are you joking?"

I could see it now. Yasahiro's mouth would drop open, and he'd say, "Your mother has lost her mind." Then he'd regret ever marrying me and getting involved with my delusional family. Because everyone was delusional at this point. Hirata had no idea what he was really buying. Yuna would never be able to handle this job. Mom was living in a fantasy world. And I was the one suffering the consequences.

"Don't talk back to me," Mom admonished me. "You have no idea what I deal with concerning you on a daily basis."

"Me? What have I done?" All the blood left my head and settled in my abdomen. The baby fluttered, sensing anxious tension flowing through my body.

Mom stared at me for a solid few seconds, and my dread increased.

"People are talking," she said slowly. And then I remembered what Mom had said the previous day, something about "town rumors about our family." There were always town rumors about our family, but this appeared to be new buzz.

I raised my eyebrows at her, and she reached over to squeeze my hand, a gesture I found more troubling than anything.

"I've tried to stop them, but I can't. You know how small towns are."

"Are people gossiping... about me?" My voice conveyed how unbelieving this was. I laughed, though it wasn't funny. "What could they possibly have to say?"

Mom swallowed and licked her lips. "They say you're a witch."

"A witch?" I couldn't have been more confused.

"That you survived the barn fire because you've sold your soul to Izanami."

Izanami? Wow. Izanami was one of the first gods at the birth of creation. Her son, Kagu-tsuchi, was the god of fire, and he killed his mother by burning her to death.

"And now you're a witch reincarnated. That's how you solved the mystery of Etsuko's death and how you saved Yasahiro from going to jail. How you charmed him into marrying you and giving you a child."

My mind was blank. Utterly and completely blank. I was convinced that my mouth hung open, but I was so detached from my body, I couldn't say for sure.

Mom lowered her head. "For the past few months, I've been having tea with the ladies from the kitchen at Midori Sankaku, the ones I worked with over the winter. It took a while for them to come out and tell me about this, but they eventually did. It only started spreading to my wider circles a few weeks ago." She squeezed my hand again. "This is why it's important for you to continue to work at the farm. What if this all blows up and you lose your business? Or Yasahiro's business?"

My skin crawled with gooseflesh as I imagined people huddling in circles and talking about me behind my back. How did this happen? Why? How many people?

"Mom, this is the most ridiculous thing I've ever heard."

She shrugged before letting my hand go. "I've said the same thing about a dozen times. But don't you think you brought some of this on yourself? Always getting involved in things you shouldn't?"

I threw my arms out to the side. "All I've ever wanted to do was help people. Haven't I helped people?" I stood up and looked down at her. "And I don't believe this at all, that you're worried about me losing my business which is why you want me to work here."

Mom's face shifted from concerned to simmering anger.

"You never wanted me to open the tea shop to begin with," I said, my voice barely scratching the surface of my disbelief. Town rumors, a witch, and Mom had been lying about a heck of a lot more than this farm business takeover. "Have you just been waiting for me to fail?"

She didn't answer my question. "I'm going to go lie down. I have a headache." She stood up, setting her ledger to the side.

I was at a loss for words. The stronger version of me was so angry I saw red. The part of me that cherished my family now that I had grown close to it was shattered and ashamed.

"I'll see you here tomorrow," she said as she walked off.

Yes. Tomorrow.

We would see about that.

CHAPTER
FOURTEEN

Akiko doubled over in laughter, and Kirin barked at her. "Why are you laughing at this? This is serious business!" I couldn't hold in a laugh either. Giggles burst forth, and my head lightened so much I had to sit down at Akiko's table. The air conditioning was on, fluttering Akiko's paperwork and rolling her pencil back and forth. I'd caught her home early on her dinner break. She'd been filling out charts for her patients when I rang the doorbell.

Akiko hooted with laughter, her eyes brimming with tears and her face turning red. "A witch!" She clutched at her stomach. "You? This is possibly the funniest thing I've ever heard." She turned and headed for the kitchen. "Should I get you a broom to go with your glass of water?" She gestured to Kirin. "Go lie down in the bedroom." She trotted off.

"Stop," I pleaded, laughing some more and rolling my eyes. "Maybe I should start wearing all black."

"Get a black cat!" She called from the kitchen. "Lots of black eyeshadow and mascara."

The house rumbled and vibrated, scaring me so badly I jumped up from the table, and Kirin started barking again. Something fell over in the kitchen, and Akiko swore and muttered under her breath.

"What was that?" I asked, leaning to the side to catch sight of her.

"Midori Sankaku construction." She sighed as she exited the kitchen and set my glass of water on the table. I gulped it down, still hot from being outside with Yuna. "They're digging up the back fields for the next few days and laying down pipes and stuff for administrative buildings."

"Pipes and stuff?"

She waved her hand. "You know, water, sewage, power. All that. But the ground has some big boulders about a meter down. That's one reason why we never planted much in those fields." She gathered up her paperwork and set it aside. "They have heavy machinery out there digging away."

"Hopefully not at night."

"No. I'm grateful for that. The foreman came by here a few days ago to let me know what was going on and warn me about the noise. He was very apologetic. Said it would be done soon."

The house rattled and shook again, and Akiko's jaw tightened.

"Well, at least you're not a witch," I said, winking at her.

She sighed. "I'm not pleased about this business with your mom. What happened between you two?"

"I didn't think anything was wrong between us until Hirata showed up on the scene." I shook my head, dragging my fingers through the condensation on the side of my water glass. "But it appears she's been holding a grudge."

"I told you during your wedding that something was up with her."

"You did." I tried not to show my irritation.

My wedding day had been complete bliss for me. The weather had been hot and humid, but everyone who was invited showed up. I'd been so starry-eyed and in love that I'd ignored

Akiko's warnings that my mother was unhappy. I don't know what I would've done differently, though. Akiko had pleaded with me not to leave for my honeymoon, and I went anyway. I would still go if I were to do it all over again, knowing what I know now.

"My trip to France was probably the thing that broke us in two. Mom wanted me to stay home for the planting, and I told her no. She wasn't happy about it." She assumed we would wait until winter to go on our honeymoon, but we defied her and went in June when the weather was beautiful.

"Yeah, well, it's in the past," she replied, and I was grateful she didn't rub my nose in it. Nothing could beat those memories of decadent meals in small Paris restaurants, wine vineyards in the countryside, and lying next to Yasahiro in silk sheets in five-star hotels.

My abdomen clenched, and I brought my focus back to the present.

"I need advice. What should I do?"

"You should discuss this with Yasahiro," she said, pertly.

I pressed my lips together. "I will, but I want your opinion since you've known Mom almost as long as I have."

Akiko kept silent.

"Do you think, if Hirata hadn't gotten involved, she would've let me buy into the farm? Let me rebuild or renovate the house?"

"No." She deflated. "No, I don't think she would have."

I dropped my eyes, once again concentrating on the glass in front of me.

"She loves you, of course. But business-wise? Mei, she never did have nice things to say about all your failed jobs before last year."

"Really? She talked about me?"

She waved her hand. "Of course she did. All the ladies of her generation gossip like the wind is running out and they have to fill the void." She shook her head, a grim frown forming. "People in town would ask after you, and she would say you were doing fine and loved living in Tokyo, but that you were having trouble keeping a job."

I tried not to cry, but my hormones wouldn't let me keep it in. I'd cleaned up my reputation around town by helping with the murder investigations, and my tea shop was a hit, but hearing this news now, I wanted to crawl into a hole.

"How did you hear about this?"

"News travels. One person tells another and another. I heard it fourth or fifth hand, someone trying to pump me for more gossip since they knew we were friends." She huffed. "Ridiculous."

"What did you say?" I asked, my voice low.

Her eyes widened. "I told them to mind their own business."

I smiled. "Thanks." The last of the water in my glass went down the hatch, and I sighed. I really missed beer on a hot day. "Well, I have a multitude of problems now. Supposedly, I'm a witch. Mom wants me to work for free on the farm and hire someone to take over the tea shop, but I want to be at the tea shop. And now I need to look for a new house for Yasahiro and me."

It was her turn to sigh. "I can't believe you're moving, and you won't be right across the street again."

"Have to. Hirata, Yuna, and the boys are moving into the farmhouse." I rubbed my forehead. "A lot has changed in the last day."

Akiko stiffened, and I knew her well enough to identify her angry posture. "What else?"

"I've made progress in the Fukuda case." My face relaxed in a smile. "We uncovered Ria's old manga sketchbook."

"No!" She leaned forward, eager for more.

"Yes. And it's filled with a story called *After School*. I don't know if it'll really have any clues as to why she went missing, but

I'm going to read it and find out. That and I have two new possible suspects in the case."

I explained what I found out at Takashi Kato's house earlier in the day, the news about Ria's father and ex-boyfriend.

"I obviously can't do much about the father, though I'll look into it." Chewing on my lip, I reached across the table to grab a package of crackers Akiko had left out. Dinner time was closing in, and I was starving. "But I need to check into this ex-boyfriend."

We both munched on crackers. "I thought Ria had been dating one of Tama's friends," Akiko said, covering her cracker-filled mouth with her hand. "I saw her with this boy — skinny, with long, bleached-blond hair — once, maybe twice. He didn't live around here, so I never saw him otherwise."

My skin always crawled when I heard Tama's name in casual conversation. He'd tried to kill Akiko and me last year, and the incident still haunted my dreams. I was also certain he was the one who pushed me into the campfire as a kid, leaving me with burn scars on my back that hampered my self-confidence and love life for years until I met Yasahiro. Tama was in jail, and I only had to think of him now and then when prosecutors would call to follow up on details of his case.

Something tickled at the back of my brain.

"Hey, I know we don't talk about this, but..." I let my voice trail off, hoping Akiko would stop me.

"What?" she asked, touching my arm.

"Do you ever visit Tama in jail?" She stiffened. "Or write to him?"

"No." Her face had hardened and lost its good cheer. "Never."

"Never?"

"Mei, I never want to see him again. Never. He tried to kill us both." Her eyes widened, shocked I would even ask. "I don't care that he's family. He can rot in jail forever as far as I'm concerned."

I looked away from her, upset I'd brought up this sensitive subject, but her warm hand squeezed mine.

"Nothing is more important than you, our friends, and my career. Everything else can come second."

I smiled at her, and she smiled back.

"Now, how are you going to solve this mystery, huh? What's next on the list?"

Akiko was always good at changing the subject when it needed to shift.

"Do you remember the boy's name? The blond-haired one you saw Ria with?"

She shook her head. "Nope. But then again, I don't remember the names of most of our classmates, people I saw day in and day out. Their names have all been replaced with nursing terms." She waved to her pile of papers on the table. "Which reminds me! I heard from Kumi we have a girls' night out to plan." She rubbed her hands together with a large smile. "I haven't been out in months. Not since your wedding, I think. It's just been my elderly patients or you when you're able to stop by."

She pouted, and I laughed.

"Aw, poor Akiko. Can you do tomorrow night? I know it's soon, but Kayo has the night off, and Chiyo can watch the baby for Kumi."

"Perfect! We'll go out, have some great food, and everyone else will drink the drinks you cannot drink."

I would've complained, but I was happy the pregnancy was going well. I wouldn't jeopardize it for anything.

"Sounds like a plan."

CHAPTER
FIFTEEN

Nothing could beat a Friday night in bed before 22:00. The bedroom was cool, and I sat in bed, the covers pulled up over my pajamas and the fan whirring in the corner. Yasahiro had closed up the tea shop, cooked dinner for me, and gone to Sawayaka to make an appearance for the Friday night crowd.

This left me at home to read Ria's manga until I was ready to pass out, but that wouldn't be anytime soon. One thing was for sure, Ria knew a good, engaging story.

On the page, the character of Shizuka stood alone in a crowded school courtyard. Her quiet and reserved nature kept her separate from almost everyone but a few close friends. Much like the Ria Fukuda I'd known in real life. This character, Shizuka, though, had a secret. She was in love with her boyfriend's best friend, not her boyfriend.

I flipped the pages and followed her on a group date with her friends to a summer festival complete with fireworks. She ditched her boyfriend, Hiromi, and rendezvoused with the boyfriend's best friend, Kuro, kissing each other in an alleyway.

The story was very dramatic and quite catchy. I was drawn in right away, by both the stories and Ria's art. I loved her style, the quick dash of the pencil, the peachy cheeks of Shizuka, the dashing young love interest who hovered over her. I considered the possible implications of Ria publishing this manga. It wasn't too risqué. Cheating, unfortunately, was commonplace in Japan, and secret lovers was a tried-and-true plot device through most of Japanese literature.

I closed the red sketchbook and picked up my phone to text Akai.

"I've been reading Ria's manga. It's enjoyable, but I haven't run across any clues yet, and I'm not sure I will. Have you uncovered anything?"

I set down my phone and waited, rubbing my thumb over the binding of the sketchbook.

"Really? Are you sure? There has to be a reason why she buried it."

"I'm not totally positive. It's only a hunch. I'll read the whole thing and let you know," I texted back.

"I spent all day in the office hunting through my SD cards. I'm looking for old photos from back when Ria was still with us. I've found three, and I'll go over them tonight."

"Do you ever sleep?"

"No. I should go make more coffee."

I laughed as I tossed the phone aside and snuggled down further into the bed to read.

From the summer festival, Shizuka continued to ignore her secret boyfriend at school and while she was with her real boyfriend. The real boyfriend, Hiromi, was of the brooding, confident variety. Charming but indifferent — an alpha type. He had a big group of friends and led the pack everywhere. The secret boyfriend, Kuro, on the other hand, was understanding and calm, more of a beta hero. He tagged along at the back of the pack, and he always had great things to say about art or Shizuka's favorite subject, fashion. It would've been a hard choice for any young woman to make, but I was rooting for Kuro. They seemed to be a better match.

An hour later, the front door slammed, and I heard footsteps coming up the stairs. Yasahiro was home.

From my spot in the bed, I saw him open the door to the apartment silently and poke his head in.

"I'm still up!" I called out. He sighed, slipped off his shoes, and dropped his keys on the table next to the door.

"I thought you'd be asleep."

I yawned. "I should be, but I was up reading instead."

I yawned again. Now that I'd started yawning, I wouldn't stop until I fell asleep. "Besides, it's nice to have energy back after that disastrous first trimester." When I did nothing but puke and sleep. I was glad that was over.

Yasahiro took off his watch and left it on the dresser, crossing the room to sit next to me on the bed. He leaned over and kissed me on the forehead.

"I'm a bit of a sweaty mess," he said, apologizing.

I grabbed his shirt. "I don't care."

I pulled him toward me and angled my face up to meet his lips. He smiled before connecting with me, and his kiss was hungry but sweet. When we parted, he looked into my eyes, and I felt the love that had been there ever since the night of the barn fire.

"Good," I gasped, short of breath. "I don't think I've bewitched you."

He blinked twice. "What?"

I settled into the bed, taking his hand in mine. "You won't believe what my mom told me. She said there's some rumor going around town that I'm a witch. I've put a spell on you, and that's the only reason why we're together."

His face remained blank. "Mei, I am under your spell."

We both burst into laughter at the same time.

He continued to laugh as he stood up and peeled off his

shirt. The best part of my day. "I can't believe how gullible your mom is. I mean, I love her. You know I do. But..." He rolled his eyes. "You and me. We're a good pair. We have a lot of the same ethics and desires for the future, but we're different enough not to be boring." He slipped his pants to the floor too, and I watched, happy to be awake for this. "I don't understand why anyone would even question our relationship." He ran both his hands through his hair. "And, quite frankly, I'm tired of it. Screw them."

I was surprised at his vehemence. "I'm tired of it too, but we have to live here."

"Then we'll live here the way we want to live here. Speaking of which, I have some properties for you to look at."

His eyes sparkled with that desire to find a good deal on land. This compulsion of his was something he was born with. I didn't really understand it, but I'd never owned property of my own before. This was new territory for me. When we married, I'd gained this apartment and all of Yasahiro's land and businesses as well, but it wasn't the same. They weren't my homes. My heart curled up into a ball like a dog does, burying its nose under its paws. My home was Mom's home, and it wasn't mine anymore.

Move on, Mei.

"Really? Anything promising?"

"Several. One with a nice plot of overgrown yard that would make a perfect kitchen garden. Do you think you'll have time to go see them this week? There's bad weather coming — lots of rain — and I need your expert opinion on them."

"I think so." I sounded hesitant, and all because I was hopeful Mom would turn around and surprise me, want me to take over the farm, not Hirata.

I was living in my daydreams again. Not a good idea.

He sat back down next to me on the bed. "Let's be the successful black sheep of the town. You know the old ladies at the tea shop don't care. They spend all day talking about you and wondering when you'll be back. I found it quite insulting, actually." He winked and laughed, and I smiled.

"I guess you're just not as charming as I am."

"I guess not." He picked up the red sketchbook. "How's the story?"

"It's good, but I'm not getting anywhere with the investigation. I'm going to visit the taiyaki shop tomorrow and do some poking around there. You still fine with the tea shop?"

"Absolutely. You've got me through Tuesday."

"And then Girls' Night Out tomorrow?" I cringed, worried I was taking too much time for myself. Mom already thought I was selfish. I didn't want Yasahiro to think that, too.

He angled in and kissed my cheek. "Of course. Though it'll be a miracle if you can stay awake for it."

"Very funny." I smacked him on the arm. He cried out in mock pain, so I pinched him too for good measure.

He laughed as he tugged on my arm. "Come have a bath with me, my wife."

I flushed, not used to the term "wife." "Nah, I'm going to go to sleep."

"Pllleeeeease," he begged.

I *had* put a spell on him, and he was mine. I should take advantage of it.

"Okay. But only because you begged."

I threw my arms around his neck, and he swept me off the bed and into the bathroom, laughing the whole way.

CHAPTER
SIXTEEN

The air in the taiyaki shop hummed with sugar and laughter. Being in a strip of shops close to the train station, the tiny space held a counter, a glass case, and a spot for the taiyaki grill so people could watch their sweet treats being prepared by a professional. I stood over the grill, watching the young woman my age spoon batter into the fish shapes, let them cook, add the sugary red bean paste and more batter, then close up the griddle for the final baking. Ah, my mouth watered in anticipation.

"It smells delicious," I said to her, smiling over the glass divider.

"My husband makes the best I've ever had," she replied.

How does one become a taiyaki shop owner, anyway? I always believed this was something inherited from a parent. But then, before I started my own tea shop, I would've said the same thing about those.

"I'm sure I'll enjoy them," I said, taking the paper bag from her. The opening steamed, and though I knew I'd burn myself on them, I wanted to reach in and stuff one in my face immediately.

But duty called.

I pulled a business card from my bag and presented it to her. "I know it's a little busy here this morning, but I would love to talk to your husband if he has a free moment."

She looked at my card and startled in surprise. "My father-in-law was just talking about you yesterday! Give us a moment. I'll call our assistant out from the back to handle the front register."

I turned around and assessed the young man at the register. Tall and thin, he was half a meter taller than the little old lady paying for her bag of taiyaki. He sported a sparse goatee, something I didn't often see, that covered a small mole on his chin. Otherwise, he was a shop owner in loose, indigo-striped *jinbei*, those plastic clogs everyone seemed to have, and a navy blue handkerchief on his head.

I tipped my head to the side and tried to compare him to the boyfriend Ria drew in her manga, the one Shizuka was cheating on. Was this the man who killed her? Did he go into a jealous rage because she cheated on him with his best friend?

If so, I had a ton more digging to do. I'd have to find his best friend, and their friends, and question everyone. I wasn't even sure I had the time for that.

His wife whispered in his ear, and he raised his head to find me in the room. I lifted my taiyaki in greeting before taking a decent-sized bite. Mmmm, delicious.

He nodded, cool and collected, perhaps a little annoyed. The store wasn't too busy, so what was the problem?

Worry coursed through me. I wished Goro had come along like we originally planned, but he had to cover for another officer who was sick with the stomach flu. I needed his guidance right then. I couldn't put my finger on it, but I suddenly didn't feel welcome here. His wife was sweet enough, but something about Itsuki's demeanor was cold and off-putting. Was it me? Or was it Ria?

Or I was being paranoid for no good reason. Ever since I became pregnant, I saw shadows where there were none. Or I read situations wrong. Just look at what had happened between Mom and me.

I was about to sneak out of the taiyaki shop when Itsuki left the comfort of his post and crossed the room to me.

"Hello. My wife says you'd like to speak with me," he said, bowing. I bowed in return, wondering for a moment if I should get out another business card, but he pulled mine out of his pocket.

"Thank you for taking the time to step away. Your shop is quite successful, and I love the taiyaki." I rubbed my belly to show how pleased I was.

"Thank you," he replied, glancing around the shop. His silence was awkward, and I wondered if I made the wrong decision coming here. My presence appeared to be unwanted.

But if I was going to help out with this case, I couldn't be put off by a hesitant witness. Goro would've never put up with that. Why should I?

Because it was hard being nosy when all my upbringing told me to keep quiet and not bother anyone.

"I met your father yesterday for the first time. My good friend, Yomé Murata, wanted to stop by and reminisce with him, so I brought her over since I've been working next door for the last week. He mentioned you own this taiyaki shop, and I had to come by and test them out for myself."

He narrowed his eyes, but I kept my smile in place. "You're working next door? To my father's house? I thought you owned the new tea shop, Oshabe-cha."

"Oh, you know who I am?"

"Of course I do." And he looked over his shoulder again.

It hit me like being crushed into a train car in rush hour traffic, the slow but inexorable realization that he knew who I was because people had been gossiping about me.

My hearing rang, and I began to sweat. How was I going to reassure him I wasn't bad for his business? Or maybe I was? My mouth dried up, and I swallowed, wishing I'd bought water to go along with the taiyaki.

"I've been helping my friend Akai clean out the old Fukuda house. It's not a permanent job or anything. Just ... helping," I repeated. When I was nervous, I repeated myself.

His eyes widened. "You're cleaning out Ria's old house?"

"I am. Your father mentioned that you and Ria dated for a little while."

Mistake. His face closed up, a light suddenly turned off.

"We did. We dated for about a year. She ran away about six months after we broke up." He half-turned so he could see his wife who was leaning forward, not hiding her attempt at eaves-dropping.

"Are you sure she ran away?" I pressed him. He was on the verge of dismissing me anyway, so I figured I would give it my all.

"No," he said, perking up. "No. I'm not sure she ran away. Why do you ask?"

I shook my head. "Well, it's been a mystery in the town forever, as I'm sure you're well aware of. And since I was asked to help clean out the house, I thought it was a good time to address the rumors about her disappearance. But the police never found a body, so I'm not sure if it's even worth delving into the whole mess."

I figured honesty would get me farther with Itsuki than any accusations would.

He relaxed, his shoulders dropping. "Is that what this is about?"

"This? Oh, me coming here?"

"Yeah. I spoke to my father last night, and he said you were..." He shook his head. "Never mind."

"What?" My face flushed, and I tried to cool it down with the power of my thoughts.

"He said you were jealous of my taiyaki. I thought you were coming to shut me down." He glared down his nose at me, and I flashed back to the joke I made about being an inept cook at my own expense.

"Me?" I squeaked, and the back of my eyes watered with tears. *Not now, Mei!* "How could I shut you down?"

He rubbed his hands together, worry replacing his stern expression.

"You have contacts in the police department, and I'd rather stay away from the town gossip." He said it, but his voice held a disbelieving note.

If the conversation had started off awkward, it was more so now. I took a deep breath and sighed, squaring up my shoulders and lifting my chin.

"I'm not here to shut you down or cast a spell or cause you any trouble." Unless he killed Ria and then all bets were off. "I came to talk to you about selling your taiyaki in my tea shop. I think my customers would love them, and I'm a poor excuse for a chef, so I have to ask others for help in this department."

My eyes brimmed with hormone tears as I remembered all the times my mother was so disappointed in me for not liking her cooking and for being afraid of the kitchen. It was no wonder she chose Hirata and Yuna over me. Yuna couldn't farm, but she could cook.

"And I wanted to know a little more about Ria. I remember her from my teen years, and I wanted to do something about her disappearance. Maybe finally bring some clarity to the case. But I understand if you don't want to have anything to do with me."

I bowed, turned on my heel, and practically ran from the taiyaki shop, not looking back. I just messed up my first interview with a suspect and probably brought more shame on my family in the process.

I rounded the corner and pressed my back against the wall of the alley I was hiding my tears in. Was I being too sensitive? Was I being a spoiled brat to Mom? Was I doing irreparable damage to my tea shop with all the snooping around? I didn't even know how to address these rumors that I was a witch. At this point, I'd rather just go with it, wear black all the time, get a black cat, and walk the streets at midnight.

I laughed at myself, pressing the back of my hand to my lips. The walls swirled around me, and I felt lost for the first time in months. I thought my troubles were over when Yasahiro and I married, and we opened Oshabe-cha. But that wasn't the case at all. My troubles were only beginning.

If I wasn't going to solve the Ria Fukuda case soon, and Akai didn't need me at the house, and Yasahiro could hold down the tea shop, I'd have to work on fixing things with Mom.

I pulled my wallet with my bus pass from my bag, dried my eyes, and walked towards the nearest bus stop.

———

I ONLY GOT TWO BLOCKS FROM THE TAIYAKI SHOP WHEN I passed a Chikata patrol car and Kohei Watanabe stepped out to the sidewalk right in front of me.

"Well, well, if it isn't the newly minted Mrs. Suga. We meet again."

Ugh. I almost turned around and walked in the opposite direction, but my good manners kept me in one spot. I dropped my head for a moment and wiped my eyes. I couldn't let him see me upset.

"What's the matter? Was someone mean to you?" His voice dripped with hatred, and I had to question again why he disliked me so much. What had I done to him to make him treat me this way?

The only thing I could come up with was that I solved mysteries he either wanted to solve himself or never wanted to be solved in the first place. He was related to Tama's old fiancée, Haruka, but even then, it wasn't my fault Tama tried to burn me alive in the barn.

I lifted my chin and rolled my eyes at him. "Hormones. I *am* pregnant, you know?"

"I thought you had just gained weight."

How could anyone be this big of a bully and keep a straight face? Something told me he was not right in the head.

"Well, I'm married to the best chef in town." I cleared my throat and grasped the strap of my shoulder bag. "What do you want? I'm a little busy, and I'm going to miss the bus if you don't come out with it."

He pulled out his notebook, the same kind Goro kept for writing details of a crime he was investigating. I tapped my foot, trying to exaggerate my need for him to make it quick.

"There've been some complaints around town of items gone missing. Several people seem to think they saw you in the locations where those items were before they disappeared."

What was this?

"I'd like to get a statement from you about your whereabouts the last few days."

"This is ridiculous. Why would I steal stuff from other people?"

He plastered a serious expression on his face. "Yes, why would you steal things from other people? That is a very good question. Would you care to explain yourself?"

My thoughts bounced around, trying to make sense of this situation. First, I found out from my mom that I'm a witch. Now, I was some kind of kleptomaniac? What was next?

"There's nothing to explain. I haven't stolen anything. What are these things I have supposedly stolen?"

Kohei licked his thumb and flipped back in his notebook as people passed us on the sidewalk and glanced our way. I tried not to make eye contact with anyone.

"One person says several of his potted herbs from his back garden went missing. Another says her house was robbed of two heavy iron pots yesterday."

Irritation increased under my skin, heating me from my core outward.

"And how does this relate to me?"

"Both said they ran into you in the past week and then saw you in the neighborhood on the same day. Their statements had nothing in common except for you."

I clenched my jaw and waited for the punch line.

His lips curled into an evil smile. "Since it's well-known around town that you're involved in some kind of dark arts, maybe that you keep demons and *yōkai* in your house, they both suggested you might be a likely suspect."

And there it was. Finally, to my face, Kohei brought it back to the rumors about me. And who knows how long people had been thinking I'm some witchy freak or talking about me behind my back.

I took one solid step toward him, and he stood his ground.

"If I have any yōkai at home, I'm going to send them after you, if you're not careful," I whispered, looking him straight in the eyes. "These claims against me are all lies, and until you have actual evidence of me stealing stuff from other people, you had better step off."

He took one step closer. I tried not to flinch. "Two can play at the game of threats, Mei. If I ever see you in Itsuki Kato's taiyaki shop again, I will completely ruin you. Do you understand?"

My heart pumped blood swiftly through my body. "I'll go wherever I want to, and you can't stop me."

One more centimeter and we would've been nose to nose. It was closer than I ever wanted to be to him.

He shrugged his shoulders and stepped back. "It seems to me you should be more careful. Your mother needs permits to sell at the farmers' market this fall. You also need permits to do any renovations at her house. And I know health inspectors too who would be happy to make surprise visits to your little tea shop." He tucked away his notebook and returned to his vehicle.

"Don't screw with me or I'll make your life a living hell," he called over his shoulder as he slid into his car.

He left me slack-jawed as he peeled away from the curb.

I pressed my lips together and looked back in the direction of the taiyaki shop. Seemed to me, not only was I being watched, but there were people in town who had it in for me.

But what could I do about it? Nothing just yet, but I would come up with something. Oh yes, I would.

I took a deep breath and decided to head home and get the car instead of taking the bus. Kohei had wasted too much of my time, and I just wanted to be cool again. Cool and alone.

CHAPTER
SEVENTEEN

The farmhouse was absolute chaos when I arrived. My two nephews, taking advantage of the slightly cooler weather, played with water guns outside while a giant moving van sat open in the driveway.

I took a deep breath, closed my eyes, and pressed my forehead to the steering wheel. I was still shaky from my run-in with Kohei, the big move was already happening, and there was nothing I could do to stop it. I watched movers in white gloves carry bedroom furniture down a ramp and up into the house as my chest constricted and my gut bubbled with jealousy. Mom stood in the doorway, supervising the movers as they maneuvered through the front door and into the living area. Hirata's car was in the driveway, so he was probably here too.

Great.

Mom spotted me in the car and waved, a genuine smile on her face, and I had to remind myself that I'd been doing my best to hide how upset I was. Mom had no clue I was broken up inside over this betrayal.

And it *was* a betrayal. I would feel that way until the day I died.

I waved back, grabbed my bag, and met her on the front porch.

"Looking kind of busy here today," I said, trying to keep things light and easy.

"Not too busy to not get work done. Mr. Minato is in the barn showing Yuna what to do with the tractor. I figured if she can't pick vegetables, she can drive." Mom nodded and directed a mover towards the door. "Hirata is inside handling the movers." She shielded her eyes and squinted at me. "Are you always going to show up this late in the morning?"

"No. I'm sorry. I should have texted you. I had errands to run." I kept it as vague as possible since I didn't want her to know about my failed meeting with Itsuki Kato.

"Well, you can make up for the time tomorrow." Mom ushered me into the house and closed the door, trying to keep the feeble air conditioning inside where it belonged.

"Tomorrow's Sunday, Mom. I never work on Sunday. It's my day to spend with Yasahiro."

Her lips pinched into a tiny pucker. "Mei, you're married now and pregnant. Family comes first."

I wanted to say, "Well, duh," but that would only enrage her. *Patience, Mei.*

"He's my family, too. If I don't spend time with my husband, whom I love, then what's the point of being married?" My blood pressure rose, my blood vessels threatening to burst. How had Mom crawled all over my nerves in the one point two minutes I'd been in the house?

"Marriage is for family and business," she said, her hands on her hips. "Not for love or any of those other things you young people talk about nowadays."

My mouth dropped open. I had married Yasahiro because I loved him and he loved me. We were a modern couple. This was not the Edo Period, 1700s Japan.

I caught sight of Yuna, standing in the kitchen and eavesdropping. She must've sneaked in through the back door from the barn when we were chatting. She averted her eyes and went to the refrigerator to pretend like she hadn't been listening. I could've been mistaken, but Yuna looked miserable. Her face was set in a frown, her hair was pulled into a haphazard ponytail, and her clothes were covered in dirt. This look was a million kilometers away from her usual well-pressed shirts, perfect makeup, and professionally straightened hair.

When I wasn't looking, Mom tripped over a toy truck on the floor and cursed in a very unlike-Mom fashion. "Ugh. Yuna, please tell those boys to clean up after themselves or one of these movers is going to trip and fall and sue me."

Yuna dipped her head. "Yes, Mom." She breezed past us both, picked up the toys, and escaped out the front door.

I inhaled, trying to calm down my reaction, but it was no use. "Mom, I married Yasahiro because I love him, he's a good man, and he loves me. We make a good team. And I'm not going to jeopardize that." I thought of all the marriages in Japan that had turned cold and cruel because the husband or wife became distant after their kids were born. Many marriages had ended or endured through cheating because someone didn't want to have sex or be intimate anymore.

That would not be me. I refused to let it happen.

I figured Mom was going to fight me, but she sighed and lifted her chin. "Fine. I guess that's what all of your generation wants nowadays, anyway. You're a strong woman, Mei. If that's what you want, I'm sure you'll make it happen."

I nodded and followed her into the kitchen, pleased she got the picture quicker than I thought she would. Maybe this was what she needed, me to stand my ground and fight for the things I wanted. It seemed possible that she could change. I had changed this past year, so why couldn't she?

In the kitchen, Mom grabbed her apron and tried to make her

way around the kitchen island, but she knocked her hip against the hard stainless steel top.

"Ow!" She rubbed her hip and blew a frustrated breath through her lips. "This moving is getting to me. I feel turned around and flustered all the time."

I stepped forward, took her hand, and squeezed it. "How can I help right now? I promised Yasahiro I'd return to the tea shop this afternoon, but I have an hour to spend here."

"Thank you, Mei," she said, squeezing my hand back. "Can you check the seed inventory that arrived yesterday?" She grabbed a sheet of paper from her desk and handed it to me. "I need to stay inside and supervise."

"Sure." It was an easy task, something I could finish in an hour. "I'll do this and get going. Then I'll be back on Monday morning."

"Whatever you decide, Mei." Her voice was resigned, and I wondered if I was on her bad side again. But she left the room before I could question her.

Out in the barn, I ran into Minato.

"Hello, Mr. Minato. How are you?" I tried not to blush as he smiled at me. I really did. But no matter how many times I saw him, he was still handsome as ever.

"I'm good, Mei. How are you? It's cooler out today, thankfully." He set down his socket wrench and leaned away from the tractor to test the connection between it and the cultivator.

"I'm doing well, thanks. And yes, I'm glad it's a bit cooler out today. Not as humid either." I crossed the barn to the plastic tubs we kept the seed stores in and attempted to lift one tub from on top of the other so I could access both, but Minato jumped up and ran to me.

"Let me get that for you. You shouldn't be lifting heavy things now."

I stood back as he arranged the two tubs next to each other. "I keep forgetting about that. My doctor told me not to lift heavy boxes, but then I saw a video of some woman on YouTube who was eight months pregnant and doing deadlifts at the gym." I slipped into my daydreams of being fit and fabulous after having the baby and nearly laughed at myself. When had I ever cared about exercising except for running?

Never.

"I'm sure that woman was a trained professional," he said, winking at me. "How's the painting going?"

I was surprised he remembered since it had been a while since we last talked about my painting. He loved to draw, which is why he had previously owned the manga store, so this was a hobby we had in common.

"It's going well enough."

"Well enough? Is something not right with it?"

"Actually, for once, there's absolutely nothing wrong with the painting. I love it to pieces. You'll have to come see it." I huffed a short breath as I looked at the numbers on the sheet Mom had given me. "But I haven't had much time to paint between working here, the tea shop, and helping Akai with the Fukuda house."

"Oh yes! How's that going? Have you found anything?"

I looked twice at the seed stores and realized it would take a while to go through them all. While it was an easy job, it was also time consuming. So I set it aside for the time being, grabbed a bottle of water with Minato, and told him about everything we'd found out so far.

"Now, I'm stuck because I don't know what to do next. I hoped the manga would be the key, but I guess it was too much to ask for Ria to just declare right inside either why she left or if someone had threatened her."

"You only have the two suspects? Itsuki Kato and Ria's father?"

"That's it so far." I shrugged my shoulders and took a sip of water. "And no body, of course. So who knows? She could be alive in America or Europe for all we know, and this is a giant waste of time."

He leaned back in his chair, letting the front legs hover off the concrete slab of the barn. "I don't know, Mei. I don't think looking into her disappearance is a waste of time. She left many people brokenhearted and sick with worry."

He brought his chair back to the ground and leaned over his legs, folding his hands together.

"I didn't know she dated Itsuki which I find funny." He laughed, sadly.

"What's so funny about that?"

"She normally came into the manga shop on her own. She said she liked the quiet time, just her and the stories. But a few times I saw her with a few boys from her school. They all wore the same uniform. They would drop her off outside, or be there when she was done."

This sounded promising. If they had gone to the same school, I could retrieve the class photos to show Minato and ask him if he could identify any of them. Maybe he would recognize someone from the group that hung out with her.

If only Tama, Akiko's older brother, wasn't in jail for killing his father and attempting to kill us, I would ask him more about this. As it was, I didn't want to even think of him, much less talk to him. And besides, I knew him at the time. He hadn't been dating anyone.

"She never mentioned Itsuki, nor any boyfriend. I figured she was a loner, like everyone else in that crew was. I'm sure Akai could tell you more about that than I could."

I looked out over the fields and across the road toward Akiko's house, remembering Tama and his friends kicking a soccer ball around the field in the back. Ria and Haruka, Tama's eventual fiancée, would show up, and they'd all walk into town together. Akiko and I would watch on, jealous of their freedom.

"Do you remember the names of any of the boys who came by with her?"

"No. It was a long time ago, but I'm pretty sure we never spoke about them. Just things like 'My friends are here. I've gotta go.' Or whatever. She was never specific about it."

"She was a quiet girl," I said, agreeing with him. "It wouldn't be like her to gossip or shout out that she was dating someone."

"If she was," Minato corrected me. "I got the feeling that boys were like aliens to her. That's why she spent so much time reading romance manga in the shop and drawing her own."

Yes, it was possible her manga story I was reading wasn't based on her life at all. It could've been the wishful thinking of an awkward girl who had a hard time relating to boys.

"Have you spoken to the private investigator Ria's father hired to find her?" Minato asked, and I straightened up in my seat.

"How did you know he hired a PI?"

He laughed. "Because the woman came and asked me questions the week after Ria went missing. It was the smart thing to do, to hire someone outside of the police force to look for her. Missing persons cases only get so much quality time with detectives before they move onto cases they can actually solve."

"I didn't know he hired someone. Goro suggested Ria's father *may* have hired someone, but he didn't know for sure."

He stood up, dusting off his gloves and jeans. "I have your email address. I'll dig up her name and send it to you. Shouldn't take me long to figure out who she was."

"Thanks. I'd appreciate that."

We bowed to each other as he left, and I returned to dealing with the seed stores, but after several minutes, I was ready to give up. Nothing matched up with Mom's invoice. Her invoice stated we had twenty packets of cucumber seeds, but we only had sixteen. Several other counts were off too, not always in the negative. Why was everything out of sorts?

I'd have asked Minato for help, but he took off as soon as his shift was over. Sweat poured down my forehead as I searched the barn for missing or misplaced seed packs. Moving aside a pile of empty potato sacks, I found a bag of seeds that had been buried underneath. But something told me this wasn't the full extent of the problem, so I continued to search the barn. Eventually, I made my way to the waste and recycling bins where, amongst the discarded plastic, I discovered several more seed packs.

"What is going on here?" I asked aloud as I lifted them up to the light and read the packaging. They were fresh seeds, date stamped to only a month ago.

Hmmm. I rested my hands on my hips as I scanned the barn. Several tools were out of their usual spots and Mom's workbench was not as tidy as it usually was. Was Minato a slob? I didn't think so. His manga store had been well-cared for, and I'd witnessed him cleaning up after himself here on several occasions. Besides, it wasn't like him to touch or use Mom's things if he didn't need them. He had access to the farming equipment and tools, and he made the farm his home when he was here, but he was careful and kind.

I shrugged my shoulders as I returned to my work. Perhaps Mom didn't care as much about these things anymore. I couldn't really blame her. I was haphazard myself, only keeping my space neat and clean because that's what other people wanted. If she was cutting herself some slack, good for her.

Still, the seed stores were a mess, and I spent an extra thirty minutes more than I bargained for working on righting the discrepancies. Even when I was done, several counts were off.

Back inside the house, I called out for Mom, but no one answered until Yuna came around the corner from the living room.

"Shhh. Mom's taking a nap. She was stressed from the move and needed time alone."

Hmmm. That wasn't like her either. She weathered most

situations with abundant energy and only a few hours of sleep. I pulled my forehead into a scrunch of doubt, but Yuna patted my shoulder.

"Thanks for all your help, Mei. I really appreciate you showing me around. I'm terrible at this."

"Don't worry about it," I reassured her. "I'm sure you'll learn in no time."

"We'll see about that," she replied, doubt coating every syllable.

It looked like I wasn't the only one having trouble adjusting to the new situation.

CHAPTER
EIGHTEEN

We raised our beer mugs and toasted, letting them clink against each other as we chanted "Kampai!" My beer mug was filled with grapefruit soda (I craved citrus fruit like no other) and everyone else was drinking alcohol but me. Oh well. It wasn't forever.

The brand new beer garden had opened only three months ago, right in time for summer drinks outside under the stars. The backyard of this restaurant used to be an overgrown traditional garden, but the new owner had been smart enough to tear out the weeds, install plenty of tables, twinkling electric tea lights and a sound system playing the latest in ambient music. Yasahiro swore up and down that his next venture would do just the same because the place was packed almost every single night.

But being the smart women we were, we got in and claimed our table at the early hour of 16:00.

"I'm not used to drinking so early," Kayo said, after taking a deep gulp of her beer. "But then again, I'm not used to not working."

"You all work too much," Kumi said, laughing. "But you

know Goro wouldn't have it any other way. He's working right now. Thank goodness for my mother-in-law."

Jealousy burned inside of me for a short, brilliant second. Chiyo was watching Taiga tonight so Kumi could go out. Her own parents helped out too at least once per week. Yasahiro's parents lived almost an hour away, and I was no longer sure what to expect from my mom. Would she be willing to babysit? Would she help me out when the time came? I wasn't convinced she would. She didn't seem to care about what I had going on.

Really, I had so little choice of what to do. I could wallow in the rejection and not move forward with my life, which was painful when I thought about it too much. Or Yasahiro and I could move on, get our own place and farm, and try to work with what we had. That option afforded us some happiness, at least, but it also felt like we were abandoning Mom.

I didn't like either of these choices.

"Don't look so down, Mei. We're out to have a good time tonight." Akiko patted my hand, and I snapped my face into a smile. I was being stupid again. Whatever was to come, I had brought it on myself somehow, and I would have to learn to live with the consequences when the time came.

"Of course." I lifted my glass again. "I'm looking forward to dinner. I could really use a hamburger and fries right about now."

"Me too," everyone else said. And that was why we were friends. Always on the same page. Akiko and I had had our hard times after the fire last year, but those days were behind us. She helped me in the spring when I was going through hell, and I owed her so much for that.

I let my mind wander through most of the catch-up small talk at the table. The sky was clear, and the shade from the umbrellas kept the space cool. I took the time to go over most of what I was dealing with in my head starting with Ria Fukuda. I was beginning to doubt my original suspicion that she was dead. At this point, I figured she'd had some secret boyfriend, maybe someone she'd met online, and knowing her mother and father would object, she'd run off to be with him. Or her. I mean, who was I to say for sure she was straight? Even after all the digging I had done on her, I barely knew anything.

My list of suspects was deteriorating by the moment, along with my life situation. The only thing that was going my way was my relationship with Yasahiro. At least he believed in me.

I tried to smile as everyone laughed at a joke Kayo told, but my face slipped into a frown as I remembered my conversation with Itsuki earlier in the morning. He thought I'd come to the taiyaki place to cause mischief or give him a bad reputation. He probably didn't mean it, but I was hurt by that, more than I was willing to admit. I prided myself on helping others, not causing them more harm. If everyone in town was going to believe these stupid rumors, I had a lot of work ahead of me.

Sitting at the beer garden as the outdoor space was filling up with patrons, I could've sworn people were eyeing us. Were they looking at me? Or was I paranoid?

The food came, and it gave me the opportunity to be quiet for even longer. My thoughts spiraled out of control, and I daydreamed my "girl time" away. Inside, I was miserable, and I couldn't stop the self-destructive loop of feelings of inadequacy.

Finally, Akiko caught on. "You're awfully quiet, Mei."

Kumi and Kayo looked up from their burgers, their eyes narrowing.

"I've been hearing that a lot lately." I opened my mouth to confess to them, and then I thought better of it. Maybe if I ignored it, the whole situation would go away.

"Spill it," Kayo demanded. "Whenever you have something to say and don't, you get that fish face." She mimed a fish, opening and closing its mouth underwater. Kumi huffed a laugh through her nose.

"Fish face. I'll just add that to the list of names people are calling me."

"This again?" Akiko asked. "I thought we laughed that off the other day."

"That was before I went to visit Itsuki Kato's taiyaki place this morning."

Kumi's attention bounced back and forth between us. "I'm lost. What's going on?"

"Nothing," I replied, but Akiko jumped in unbidden.

"People around town are calling Mei a witch." Her voice was amplified by the alcohol she'd consumed, and I shushed her.

"Keep your voice down," I hissed at her, as both Kumi and Kayo expressed their surprise.

Kayo turned around to scan the crowd, but despite my earlier paranoia, no one was watching us. Inside the bar, a few men erupted in laughter, and Kayo focused on them for a moment.

"Anyway, I don't want to talk about it."

"You will talk about it right now," Kumi demanded. "I haven't heard this at all. Where did you hear this rumor from?"

"My mother," I mumbled.

"Your mother?" Kumi's face was open in shock. "Why would your mother tell you that?"

"Probably because it's true," Kayo said, returning to her burger. "The rumor, that is. Not that Mei is a witch. I prefer 'goddess' in this case, but no one listens to me."

A brief burst of pride rushed through me.

"You never mentioned this, not once," Kumi said to Kayo, taken aback. Their friendship had tightened over the past year since Kayo worked with Goro often.

"Because it's a rumor started by a complete asshole for no reason whatsoever. I wasn't going to spread it or even acknowledge it."

My entire body seized up like being dunked in cold water.

"You knew about this, and you didn't tell me?" My voice was breathy and light. Would I pass out right here? Anything was possible.

"Sorry." She looked genuinely upset, so it wasn't necessary to jump up and scream at her. My emotions were all over the map. "I didn't think the rumor would make it any farther than the station. You said your mom found out?" She cringed. "Sorry. Again."

"Make it any farther than the station?" I ground out between my teeth.

The men inside laughed again, and Kayo's head whipped around to glare at them.

"Yeah, them," she said, jerking her thumb over her shoulder towards the men at the bar. "Kohei and his crew."

My body went from frozen and numb to red hot in the blink of an eye. I should've known it. If anyone were going to spread rumors about me in town, it would be Kohei. I had no idea why he hated me so much besides the fact that I helped to put Tama behind bars and Kohei's cousin, Haruka, was then unable to marry Tama.

I peered into the bar and squinted my eyes past the glare of the setting sun. Yes, Kohei was at the bar, guzzling beer, and boisterously talking with some guys I'd seen in and around the station on occasion. Most of them were volunteer firefighters.

Sucking in a deep breath, I remembered the manga and mythology books I'd read as a kid. If I were going to be a goddess, I would have to make it work for me. I needed to stand up for myself. No more letting people walk all over me.

I pushed away from the table and stood up, swiping the crumbs off of my maternity skirt and finishing off my grapefruit soda. Everyone at the table paled, and Kumi's eyes were wide with fear.

"Wh-what are you doing, Mei?" she asked, her burger paused halfway to her mouth.

"Oh, nothing. Akiko? I'm going to need backup."

Akiko's face broadened into a wide smile. "Yes, Mei." She popped up from her seat and followed me inside.

Kohei noticed me right away, probably because he'd been spying on us since he came into the beer garden. Never one to miss an opportunity to take a dig at me, he tended to seek me out whenever I was near, especially if Yasahiro wasn't around. Something about Yasahiro rubbed Kohei the wrong way. Perhaps his successful stature in the community? I wasn't sure.

I didn't need Yasahiro tonight though.

"Well, if it isn't our local fire sprite," Kohei said, wiping his mouth with the back of his hand. "Out for a night on the town?"

"Absolutely. I can't keep my lust for heat contained all the time, you know. Gotta get out and spread the love as much as possible."

I cut through their little circle, raising my glass to the bartender, and belatedly realizing this was one of Sawayaka's prep assistants, Ichi. I knew he worked a few jobs around town, but I didn't know he tended bar here. Excellent.

"Mei," he said, smiling and waving, "I wondered if that was you outside. Grapefruit soda?"

"Yes, please." I turned my back to the bar and winked at Akiko. "You know, Kohei, I hear around the rumor mill that I'm the new witch in town." I threw my head back and laughed. "Is that why you're keeping these firefighters around you?" I patted the arm of the nearest guy, and he cocked a saucy smile at me, no doubt four or five beers already in his rounded gut. "Afraid I'll set you on fire?"

I jolted forward at him, and at the same moment, Akiko elbowed him from behind. Kohei jumped like a scared cat, sloshing beer out of his mug all over him and the floor. The guys howled with laughter.

"I literally could *not* believe my ears when I heard that one. I laughed so hard, I cried. Didn't I, Akiko?"

"I said we should buy you a black cat."

"Oh yes. I still think that's an excellent idea. Maybe we could even farm out my new talent. I could show up for bonfires or heat people's houses in winter."

One of the guys smirked. "As long as you used your powers for good, not evil."

"Of course!" I cried, clasping my hands together and batting my eyelashes. "But I do have other hidden talents that could be used for evil." I took my new glass of soda from Ichi and turned to him as everyone leaned in to hear me better. "How's business been, Ichi?"

"Good. Lots of people seem to like the place. I think we'll be busy through the end of the summer."

"Did you know I'm the town witch?" I asked him, and thankfully he played along.

"You, Mei?"

"Me. Although these men have it all wrong. They think I can conjure fire out of nowhere, but really, I feel I identify better with a shōjō." Yes, a shōjō! I definitely identified with a sea spirit who loved her alcohol... and had many other powers, too.

Ichi spread his hands out on the bar, leaning forward. "That... that would make a whole lot of sense. Yasahiro's restaurant took off like a rocket after he met you."

"Same with Kutsuro Matsu," Akiko said, butting into the group of now-silent men. Kohei's eyes narrowed at me, and I decided to lay on the dramatics.

"You know, I'm not feeling all that great about this beer garden."

The guys took a half step back.

Akiko saw her window of opportunity. "You're right, Mei. Something about the clientele here rubs me the wrong way."

"Is that it?" I feigned surprise. "I was wondering what it was."

Just then, a party of five farther down the bar paid their bill and left, and suddenly, the bar felt deserted. It was a stroke of luck I didn't deserve, but I so rarely had this kind of luck, I had to take advantage of it.

"See? Looks like my instincts were correct."

Haha! My shōjō powers actually worked! I might not be able to conjure or tame fire (hadn't it hurt me enough in my life?) but I could bring good fortune to businesses. As the story was told, when a shōjō loved a bar, everyone inside prospered. The alcohol flowed, and everyone remained in good health. When she didn't like the place, the alcohol poisoned people and dried up, and the establishment went bankrupt.

It was all preposterous, traditional nonsense to me, but I would take whatever I could get.

Several of the guys looked at each other while their eyes widened.

"We meant you no harm, Mei," one of the other guys said, raising his hands. "It was just a silly rumor."

"I don't know," I persisted. "I have a bad feeling about this place."

Kohei lurched forward with his finger pointed at me. "Don't you dare. This is *my* territory. I come here five times a week. You're not going to run me out of town like you did to Tama Kano."

I blinked at the mention of Tama's name. Is Kohei sticking up for a murderer? The other guys with him backed away.

"Hey," Ichi warned, coming around the bar. "You're being too aggressive, Kohei. I think you should leave." Ichi was at least ten centimeters taller than Kohei and knew how to handle rowdy patrons by towering over them. "Come back some other night."

Kohei glared at Ichi and then me, slammed his almost empty beer glass on the bar, and stormed out. His buddies dolled out cash to Ichi and followed him to the door, but one guy turned around and shouted, "I never thought you were a witch," at me.

Akiko sidled up next to me. "His father owns the cleaners," she said, cracking a smile. "No one will want to cross you now. Nice one. I had forgotten all about shōjōs."

Ten new people entered the bar as soon as the others had left, and I couldn't help but wonder if my divine influence had brought them there. This kind of magic had never worked in Tokyo. Maybe I had to come home to ignite it?

"You never read as much manga as I did," I said, grabbing my soda. "But I'm not sure I did the right thing. Kohei's just going to be angrier with me now."

Ichi returned to his side of the bar and nodded as he picked up his towel. "Yeah, I'd watch out for that one. Honestly, I'd be glad if he never came here again. He has a wild temper and gets into fights all the time. So thanks for granting your magical influence, Mei."

"Come on," Akiko said, hugging my arm and giggling. "I want to go outside and reenact that whole exchange for Kayo. She's going to die."

CHAPTER
NINETEEN

Sunday mornings were my favorite. Oshabe-cha was closed on Sundays and Yasahiro didn't have to be at Sawayaka until noon, so this meant we could sleep in, eat a decadent breakfast, read, or do whatever we wanted. Mom was hopeful I would devote my Sunday mornings to her and the farm, but this was a tradition I refused to give up. Everyone needed a day off from work. I didn't like working long hours at the office when I lived in Tokyo, and I wasn't going to do the same with my life in Chikata.

"Here you go," Yasahiro said, sliding a plate stacked high with fluffy pancakes in front of me. My mouth watered as I watched the steam rise and melt the pat of butter on top. "I have more coming, so eat up."

I could hardly believe that before I got pregnant I survived on toast and coffee for breakfast. Why had I done that when *pancakes* existed?

I brought my small bowl of maple syrup to the side of the plate and picked up my knife and fork, ready to do some damage. These pancakes were doomed. "It'll be a tough task, but I'll endeavor to eat them all."

"That's the spirit," he said, yawning and rubbing his messy head of hair. "You didn't say how the Girls' Night Out went last night."

"That's because I was in bed and asleep before you ever got home." I sliced off two layers of pancake, dipped them in syrup, and shoved them into my mouth like someone who hadn't eaten in ten years. My word, they were delicious.

"Sorry." He yawned again, the spatula in one hand and a coffee cup in the other. "During my mid-afternoon break, I drove by a few places we should look at later today. I think a few of them are promising, especially since the land itself is so cheap." He flipped a pancake, and my stomach went along with it.

My mind latched onto my original dream of renovating the family house and living there. Over the past few months, the plans had dominated my daydreams. I had built and re-built the house many times over in my head, adding stories and decks and bigger bathrooms and on and on. I'd wanted a big bedroom with an attached bath for Mom and another for Yasahiro and me, a big bedroom for our kids. At one point, I'd even imagined a huge play gym in the backyard, one where my nephews and my own kids would play all day without worry.

It was hard to let go of something I'd wanted with all my heart.

"Oh yeah? Did you want to go today during your time off between shifts?"

He must have heard the hesitation in my voice because he paused and stared directly at me.

"Yes, I'd like to go today and get the ball rolling on this. Are you having second thoughts?"

I delayed by eating another slice of pancake. How could I explain this in the most humble way possible?

"I'm having trouble believing my brother has taken over my place at home." My voice broke over the word "home," and I wished it hadn't. "It's not that I'm having second thoughts about you and me. I'm wondering if there's any way to salvage the relationship with Mom."

Yasahiro was silent for a moment, staring at the pancakes on the griddle.

"It's funny you should say 'salvage the relationship.'" He cleared his throat. "She called me yesterday afternoon, and I'm afraid I wasn't very" — he paused, his eyes lifting to the ceiling — "polite about what she had to say."

My hands shook, so I set down the knife and fork. "Really? What happened?" I could barely bring my voice above a whisper.

He turned off the griddle, plated his pancakes, and sat across from me at the table. By the way he deliberately draped his napkin over his lap, I knew things had gone drastically wrong. My throat closed up.

"She started in on me first. Why wasn't I controlling you? Why wasn't I hiring someone for Oshabe-cha? She went on and on about how she supported Sawayaka both socially and financially. How I owed her, not only for that but because she helped me find a wife."

I was speechless, which was a good thing because the obscenities that went through my head were unspeakable.

He cut into his pancakes and stuffed a few in his mouth while I tried to come back to my senses.

"What did you say to her?"

I thought back to the previous day, how Mom was stern with me, tired, and flustered. That had been before she talked with Yasahiro. Yikes. I bet she was in a horrible mood afterward, and I was glad I hadn't been around to witness it.

"I told her that she did not 'find me a wife.' That I would've met you, eventually. That our relationship was fated."

My heart grew by ten sizes.

"And that we were prepared to support her, the house, and the farm into retirement and beyond. Regardless of whatever happened.

But she would not be bossing you or me around, and if we're not to be the primary support... If she's going to give that role to Hirata and his family, then we'll scale back our involvement accordingly."

My pulse was beating so fast, I was sure it wasn't good for me or the baby fluttering in my belly.

"That all sounds polite to me."

He grimaced. "Well, the conversation got heated after that. She was insistent that you work at the farm the same amount of hours. I was insistent that you take it easy. And then I told her that if she wasn't so mean and rude to you, maybe this all would go a lot more smoothly."

My eyes widened, and I covered my mouth with my hand.

"And then she hung up on me." He sighed, reaching for his coffee. "Sorry. I meant to text you or call you, but I knew you were out having fun. Then the shop became busy, and I got distracted. By the way, I love my restaurant, but your tea shop is a whole load of fun."

I blurted out a quick laugh. "Don't change the subject."

"Sorry. But I mean it."

After everything Yasahiro and I'd been through in the last year, this could've torn us apart. Family meant a lot to him. It's why we called his parents all the time and visited them several times per month. His breakup with Amanda had been hard on them, but they'd come around. They were just as supportive of the tea shop as they were of Yasahiro's restaurant, and his mom fawned over me whenever we stopped in. This situation with Mom would've been difficult had Yasahiro sided with her. But he hadn't.

He had chosen me.

Maybe I wasn't lucky in a lot of things, but I *was* lucky to have found him.

"So, what do we do now?" I asked, sinking my fork and knife into the pancakes.

"We do what's best for us. We give your mom some time to cool off, and we start looking at land for our own house."

"Well, maybe things will change when Mom cools off," I said, avoiding Yasahiro's eyes. I was sure Mom would reconsider once she saw what it was like living with Yuna and the boys. She would miss me. Right? At least, I hoped so.

The apartment buzzer rang, and we both eyed it, suspiciously.

"Who would be calling on us at 9:30 on a Sunday?" he asked, getting up to answer the buzzer.

"Let me guess. It's my mom. Or Goro."

"I'm putting my money on Goro," he said, before pressing the buzzer. "Who is it?" he asked into the intercom.

"Um, it's Itsuki Kato. I'm sorry to bother you, but I need to speak to your wife. Is she there?"

Well, that was unexpected.

———

THANK GOODNESS I WAS WEARING MY GOOD PAJAMAS, AND I had pulled my hair back into a ponytail when I woke up. Otherwise, this would've been a disastrous way to start my day.

"Thanks for seeing me. This was the only time I could get away. The shop doesn't open for another hour and a half." Itsuki rubbed his hands together, worrying them back and forth, back and forth. He was clearly uncomfortable, and the creases between his eyes pulled into a tight formation of lines. I didn't have a lot of love for him so far, but a little compassion could go a long way.

"Won't you sit down and join us for some coffee? Yasahiro and I were just finishing breakfast."

"Oh, I don't want to trouble you."

"It's no trouble," Yasahiro said, gesturing to the table. Itsuki sat stiffly in the end chair, his back straight as a board.

I grabbed my coffee cup from my spot at the table and moved to sit across from him.

"I'm sorry to have interrupted your breakfast. I considered calling you since I have your business card, but I was afraid you'd hang up. I wouldn't blame you. I wasn't very helpful yesterday."

I swallowed a mouthful of coffee and decided to lie. "Please don't worry about it. I wasn't offended at all."

His look was skeptical, but I smiled to reassure him. I had been hurt and upset, but he must've had a change of heart, no?

"My wife convinced me to come here. She's the good person. Not me." He sighed and took the cup of coffee from Yasahiro, thanking him. "The real fact of the matter is that I'm indebted to someone, and that makes my situation regarding you very difficult."

I raised my eyebrows at Yasahiro, but Itsuki plowed on.

"But I want to help out with the investigation into Ria's disappearance if I can."

"It's not really an investigation," I reassured him. "I just thought I'd look into it if I could. My friend, Akai, is still broken up about her going missing."

"I remember Akai from those days." He smiled for the first time. "I see her around town now and then, but from what I gather, she works from home."

"She's a bit of a shut-in," I said, kindly. "She inherited the Fukuda house, so she's been going through everything there."

"She inherited the house? How interesting. But I guess she was kind to Ria's father after Ria's mom died. My dad said Akai was there a lot, taking care of him. Has Akai found anything interesting?" He leaned forward, enfolding the coffee cup in his palms.

"Nope. Mr. Fukuda was a hoarder, and besides his used soap collection, there wasn't much there to find." I shrugged my shoulders. "Your father said you and Ria dated for a short time, so I thought maybe you'd have some insight or memories that would help me figure out what happened."

"Hmmm, I honestly don't remember much about my time with her, like nothing specific. We dated whenever I was home from school in Tokyo. She was very bright and sweet, and I would've proposed to her. I thought she was perfect for me and that we were in love. But she broke up with me months before she went missing."

I looked hard into his face for signs of distress or anger, but instead, I detected resignation. He had been passed over, and at some point, he had accepted it.

"I met my wife the next year at school, so although I always wondered where Ria went, my continued interest in her faded quickly enough."

It seemed a likely scenario though I questioned how much he could've loved her if he moved on that fast. I saw the impact Ria had had on Akai, and most people I talked to who had barely known her still remembered and thought about her on occasion. Something didn't seem right about him putting her in his past that easily.

When I didn't respond, he asked, "Is that the kind of information you were looking for?"

Yes and no.

"What about those three or four months in between your relationship and her disappearance? Did she date anyone else? Did she say why she broke up with you?"

He looked down at his coffee cup and shook his head. "She never said why she was breaking up with me, so I assumed she didn't love me anymore. I stopped coming home on the weekends after the break-up, so I have no idea who she was hanging around with."

The back of my brain itched, and I crossed my legs under the table, readjusting my belly. I didn't like the way he wouldn't make eye contact with me. Maybe he was ashamed of being dumped though. I'd have to check with some other people around town to see if it was something he'd hidden or ran away from. Perhaps Minato would know?

"Anyway, I did want to help out." He pulled a piece of paper from his pocket. "I did some searching, and I asked my dad about it, but this is the name of the private investigator that Mr. Fukuda hired after Ria went missing. You should talk to her and see what she remembers. Especially about Ria's dad."

"Her dad?" I perked up. "Why?"

"He was strict with her, and they fought all the time. I'm sure the PI investigated him too in the course of her work." His eyes narrowed. "I never liked him. He put Ria down constantly for reading manga and drawing, two things she loved. She was smart, and she would've gone to school for something practical, but there was no need to be mean to her about her hobbies."

He sighed as he stood up from the table.

"I wish I had more for you, and I'm sorry we can't do business together." He turned and acknowledged Yasahiro for the first time in the conversation. "If you want taiyaki, please come and get them yourself."

Translation: don't let Mei come back to my place of business again. Ugh. And I loved those sweet confections.

"Sure. We understand."

The two men bowed to each other, and Itsuki beat a hasty retreat from the apartment building.

When Yasahiro closed the door and turned to me, I sank back to my chair.

"His taiyaki aren't as good as mine," he said, coming and kissing me on top of the head. He tapped on the piece of paper on the table. "Looks like you have more digging to do, Mei."

CHAPTER
TWENTY

Yasahiro pulled up outside the rundown building in the next town over and parked the car.

"So, you've got five minutes before you need to go inside. What did you think of the properties we saw today?" He reached across the car and into my foot well, pulling a manila folder out and shuffling through the papers inside.

"I think..." He pulled out the words into two long syllables. "These two are our top contenders."

I tried not to sigh as he turned in his seat and laid the two sheets of paper on the console between us.

"This land is smaller, but it's closer to the elementary school and the bus. But then I also think it may be too noisy."

I stared at the information sheet, recalling everything I could about the property. The house on the land had been abandoned for five years. No one lived in the house next door either, and the whole block gave me the creeps when I thought of how many people had uprooted themselves and left.

But Yasahiro saw this as a clean slate. He only cared about location, location, location. As he should.

"And then this place, I feel good about it too. This location has a stronger neighborhood, but it's farther out from everywhere we would need to be, including the school."

I looked at the second choice and tried to imagine us living there. The house here would have to go as well. There was no way the structure could come back from all the rain and water damage it had suffered for the past ten years.

"Hmmm," I said, wanting to be helpful but not feeling it so much.

"Come on, Mei. Think out of the box. We have the money. What do you want to do?"

I stared out the window of the car, and finally, I let go. Tears brimmed in my eyes, and I didn't command them to go away. I'd had it.

"I want to do what we originally planned. Renovate my mom's house and all live together."

His face fell.

"I want to convince her that we're better partners than Hirata and Yuna. I want to make up for all the hardship I've caused my mother."

"Hey now." He grabbed my hand, and I tried to jerk it away. He held on tighter. "You haven't caused your mother hardship."

"Yes, I have. I'm a horrible daughter. It's my fault the barn burned down. It's my fault we went starving over the winter. It's my fault she lost so much money that she had to call Hirata for help. It's my fault that I'm selfish, and I cause so much trouble."

The tears turned into a waterfall, cascading over my cheeks and plopping onto my shirt and the sheets of paper between us.

"And now all of my misdeeds have caused you and me to have problems. I'm such a stupid fool."

Yasahiro unbuckled his seat belt and leaned across the car to hug me. "Is this what you've been thinking about the last couple of days?"

I nodded into his shoulder, and he sighed.

"Now I know why you've been so quiet."

I would've laughed, but I couldn't find the humor in my own problems.

"Whatever your mother said to you, she's dead wrong. I know that she bailed you out last year and that you both lost a lot in the barn fire, but that's not your fault. I feel confident that if that bastard Tama hadn't tried to kill you, you would've found a job and paid your mom back right away. All of this is his fault, not yours. You've just been dealing with the aftermath since then."

He squeezed me once and pulled away.

"I'm going to do that macho thing I never do and tell you that I don't like all the stress this situation has put you under. You're almost twenty weeks pregnant. You have your own life you want to concentrate on. This" — he waved to the private investigator's office we were sitting outside of — "is what you want to be doing."

"Nah..." I waved my hand at him.

"Please," he said, rolling his eyes. "Don't deny it. You love solving mysteries. I wouldn't even be here today if you weren't so good at it." He squeezed my hand.

"I miss Oshabe-cha. I miss painting too."

"And they both miss you." He cleared his throat and pointed to the properties again. "From now on, we're going to concentrate on us. If your mom doesn't want us to be a whole part of her life, we won't worry about it. And we're not going to work for free either," he stressed. "There are other family businesses, but there's always a stake in it for everyone. My friends in Hakone? The ones we visited over New Year's Eve? They'll inherit the business when her mother dies, and they have a place to live. My other friends help out their parents, and they earn profits. No one gets anything for free."

I nodded, glad he put his foot down. Because he was right.

"Don't worry. I'm coming up with a plan to work it out with her. Business is business." He said the last sentence in English, and I knew it so well, the phrase was comforting at this point.

He jiggled the papers, and I pointed to the first one.

"This one. I like that this plot is closer to the school and the bus, but the vacant house next door creeps me out. Can we look into buying that too? We could turn them into a double lot and garden, no?"

His face split into a wide smile. "I like the way you think. The house next door was listed under a different agency, so I'll call them and ask about it." Glancing at the clock on the dashboard, he clicked his tongue. "You better clean yourself up and get inside, or you'll be late."

———

I'D CALLED THE PRIVATE INVESTIGATOR AFTER ITSUKI LEFT the apartment to see if she was working on a Sunday, and her scratchy and worn voice had said, "Honey, I work every day. Come by my office around 15:00."

The faded sign on the door to the second-floor office indicated that Sakiko Yoshida, Private Investigator was in. The carpet in the hallway was stained and smelled of mildew, and the door squeaked and ground open. A rolling cloud of cigarette smoke wafted over me, and I held my breath before calling out, "Excuse me!"

The front section of the office held two chairs, a water cooler, and a coffee table, all under fluorescent lamps. A three-quarters high cubicle wall separated the front from the back, and over the top of the divider, the aforementioned cigarette smoke puffed along the ceiling, stained brown with nicotine.

How lovely.

"Be right with you," Sakiko Yoshida called out. Hers was the same gravelly voice I'd spoken to over the phone. The tap-tap-tap of a keyboard took over the silence, Yoshida pounding away at something.

I wasn't sure what to do. I didn't want to hang out in her office if she was smoking up a storm. I'd avoided second-hand smoke since becoming pregnant, and the smell really bothered me. I was about to head back out when the sound of a chair scraping across the linoleum stopped me, and Yoshida came around the divider, the cigarette dangling out of her mouth.

"Oh! Oh crap, you're pregnant. I'm sorry," she said, immediately putting out the cigarette and turning on an air filtration unit. "Sorry." She fanned the air. "I should've known better. Get plenty of pregnant wives in here checking up on their husbands, but it's Sunday. I tend to give myself a break on the weekends."

I bowed to her. "Please don't worry about it. I'll be fine."

"Still, it's a shame to meet like this." She bowed back. "You're Mei Suga, you said? Come on back and have a seat."

I tried not to hesitate and followed her around the divider. She moved a fine, cut-glass tumbler filled with two-fingers-worth of whiskey to a side table and pulled a stack of papers off of the chair opposite her desk. Cigarette butts and ash overfilled a glass ashtray to the right of her ancient computer. Really? This woman was living twenty years in the past.

"Sorry to bother you on a Sunday, but I thought I'd call and schedule something for the week."

"It's no bother," she said, waving her hand. "Better to meet now. I have two jobs this week tailing cheating husbands, so I won't be around the office all that much."

My curiosity surged. "Um, is that normally what you do? I've never hired a PI before."

She smoothed out her gray hair, its bun loose at the back of her neck. The black suit she wore was two sizes too big on her, and the white blouse underneath was unbuttoned and stained with coffee.

"You married?" she asked me.

"Yes. My husband is outside in the car."

"Is he well off?"

"Uh yes?" I was unsure where this was going.

"Then you may not have hired a PI before, but his family

probably hired one to investigate you and your family. Count on it."

I squirmed in my seat. Would his family do that? Even if they had, we were married, so it obviously didn't stop the wedding.

"That's my other most reliable income. Cheating husbands and engaged couples."

"What about cheating wives?" I asked, suddenly even more curious.

She laughed, and her yellowing teeth flashed in the fluorescent light. "Those too. I get them all."

I laughed as well, thinking it had to be fun to run around and spy on people. This was the exact opposite way I was raised, but then maybe my attitude said a lot about why Mom and I didn't always get along.

I wondered more about this interesting woman in front of me. Had she enjoyed her job? Would she recommend it to others? She wasn't wearing a wedding ring. Perhaps her job wasn't appealing to suitors though I could imagine a hundred different ways she could fall in love with a client.

"So, what's this about the Ria Fukuda case?" I jolted out of a daydream of a young Yoshida spying on the love of her life cheating on her with someone else. For some reason, my daydreams always went to high drama. She leaned back in her chair and grabbed a paper from the printer behind her. Her eyes scanned over the print.

"Ah, yes. Missing persons. I don't do those anymore." She shook her head. "Too many upset parents or spouses, always begging for me to do more. Too heartbreaking."

She was so business-like that I questioned whether she had a heart to break, but I gave her the benefit of the doubt.

"Disappeared about thirteen or fourteen years ago... Hmmm. Yes. I remember this one. She was a nice girl, not too popular, good at school, in all the school clubs. People spoke highly of her.

I suspected the father more than anyone. He was a real piece of work."

The back of my neck began to sweat. "How so?"

She eyed me for a minute. "What did you say your relationship to this case was again?"

"My friend inherited the Fukuda house, and I've been helping her clean it out. I promised her I'd follow up on any leads if I came across them."

Yoshida was quiet as she examined me. "Wait a second. You're Yasahiro Suga's wife, the one that helped clear his name in that murder case earlier this year."

My face heated, and I was sure my cheeks were rosy red. "How... how did you know about that?" All the news organizations focused on the Chikata police force and Yasahiro. No one ever had the chance to interview me because I never gave them the chance. I ran past every reporter, and I hid out at home until the scandal blew over.

"I have connections," she said, not elaborating. She leaned across the desk. "Ever given any thought to becoming a PI?"

"Ummmm." I drew out the word. Of course, I had thought about it, but I was newly married, pregnant, trying to run a business, thinking about getting into real estate, *and* property shopping at the same time. The chaos was enough to haunt my dreams at night.

"I've thought about it, but it's not something I can do right now."

"What about a year from now?"

Why was she pushing me? I was here to find out more about the Fukuda case.

"Um, maybe?"

"Hmmm. I know you. You more than helped out with that murder case, you were also involved in the capture of Fujita Takahara, that Midori Sankaku executive. And I know about Tama Kano, too."

I squirmed in my seat as her smile broadened.

"Never thought you'd walk into my office."

"Well..." I was tempted to grab my bag and hightail it out of there.

She laughed, grabbing her glass of whiskey and taking a sip.

"So you're here to find out more about Ria Fukuda because your friend asked you to. How well did your friend know Ria?"

I relaxed a millimeter, now on more comfortable ground. "Pretty well. They had grown up together and been best friends until high school."

"Then you ask her this. Why did Ria's father lock her inside on the weekends? Is that how much he trusted his daughter?"

I thought about the door of Ria's room and the imperfections on both the door and the frame. Had he put a lock there at some point? I tried to swallow but couldn't.

"He never admitted it, but I saw the evidence, and his wife alluded to their discipline problems. You can't control teens like that," she said, shaking her head. "It's impossible. If it had been me, and my daughter was sneaking out to meet up with boys, I would've driven her there. Not forbidden it." She picked up the paper again and handed it over to me. "Here's everything I gathered on the case. From what I suspected, I figured she ran away to meet up with her boyfriend and give her daddy a scare. I don't know why she didn't come back."

I scanned down the page, and nothing jumped out at me but Itsuki's name.

"Do you know who she was dating at the time?" I looked at the front and back of the page and saw nothing.

"Whatever I knew, it's there in the report. I get fifteen to twenty cases a month, so I don't remember any specifics."

This stopped me short. "A month?"

"Some months are drier than others, but yeah. That equates to" — she typed into her phone — "about 1800 cases in the last ten years. My brain is fraying around the edges, and I don't hold on to any details in my head from previous cases. That's why reports exist."

She sipped her drink again, and I sighed looking at the report. There wasn't much here I didn't already know.

"Well, it appears that the last few months before her disappearance are a complete mystery. She dated someone after Itsuki Kato, but no one remembers who." I thought of that crowd she hung out with, Tama and his friends. There was no way I was going to speak to Tama about this. He was in jail far away. I could pump Akiko for more information, but it was doubtful she knew anything more. Then there was this information that Kohei Watanabe had been a part of their group at some point. I don't remember him around, and I doubt he would be receptive to me if I questioned him.

This had been my only shot.

I stood up and bowed to her. "Thank you for your time. I appreciate you telling me what you know."

She seemed shocked by my kindness. "Please. It's no problem. Mr. Fukuda is dead, right? So, even if he did do something to his daughter, it's not like me telling you this information will hurt anything."

"He died a few weeks ago."

She nodded, a frown pulling creases into the corners of her mouth. "What's done is done."

"Thank you," I said, bowing again and turning to go.

"Wait, Mrs. Suga."

I stopped at the divider.

"If you ever want to pick up private investigation, let me know. It's a good job. Makes plenty of cash." She raised her eyebrows. "I think it's something you'd be good at. I'm going to retire soon, and..."

"And what?" I was surprised at this turn of events. What was she getting at?

"Nothing," she said, waving and pulling a new cigarette from her pack. "Just call me if you're ever thinking about it."

Out in the hallway, I ambled down the stairs to the exit, pulling my phone from my purse and dialing up Akai.

"Hey, Mei. What's up?"

"I just talked with the private investigator who handled Ria's case for her father after she went missing."

"You did? How did that happen?" Akai's voice was hopeful on the other end.

"A stroke of good fortune brought me to her. Anyway, she didn't have many notes on the case." I braced myself. "She did say, though, that she thought Ria's dad was extra strict and angry with Ria for going on dates in high school when she should've been studying."

"Hmmm, yes. And? Most parents don't want their kids dating in high school."

"That was it. She said that if she suspected anyone of wrong-doing in the case, it was the father."

Akai was silent on the other end of the line, then she sighed.

"Mei, he would never have hurt Ria. He searched for her for years after she disappeared. I can't imagine the psychotic break that would have to happen for him to hurt her, murder her, bury her, and then pretend she was still alive for over ten years."

Yeah, that did sound far-fetched.

"You're right," I conceded, though I wished it had been a clue we could continue to investigate. "One more thing. I noticed marks on Ria's door, at the house. Marks that looked like there had once been screws there. Do you think there was ever a lock on her door?"

Akai was silent again, and I wondered how much more of this she could take.

"Hmmm, I don't know. As long as I knew her, her door never had a lock on it."

That was good enough for me. "Okay. I just thought I should

mention it." Maybe Yoshida had those details mixed up with another case.

"Oh, I was wondering if you could stop by tomorrow? I've found a ton of photos on random memory cards and even found a few in Ria's house. I've been downloading them and sticking them on my server for the past two days. I could use help identifying some of these people."

I approached the door to the outside of the building and paused. "Sure. I might be able to come by in the afternoon."

"Great. See you then."

I hung up the phone and threw it into my bag. My husband waited for me in the car, and we had a life to live, property to buy, and a family to raise. But something about Yoshida the Private Investigator fascinated me. She was independent and had made a career for herself from solving these tiny mysteries. I wondered if being a private investigator was something I could do. Something I could be good at.

I sighed as I pushed open the door to the outside. I had enough problems right now. This was something I'd have to think about later.

A lot later.

CHAPTER
TWENTY-ONE

The sky opened, and rain poured down on me as I snagged the last of the tomatoes from the row.

"Yuna, you head inside. I'll put these in the barn!"

Yuna nodded and ran for the house. She was slowly getting the hang of taking care of the fields, but I could tell her heart wasn't in it, much like my heart growing up. Her face wore a frown the majority of the time we spent together, and I wondered if she was on the verge of depression. Our mental health wasn't something we usually discussed, but I didn't want to neglect her. My mom would gloss over any problems Yuna would have, and with Hirata overseas, she'd need someone to confide in. She probably left behind friends in Chiba she wouldn't see all that often anymore, so who was left here for her?

What a mess.

I made it into the barn before I was soaked, and once again, Minato was there, completing an oil change on the tractor.

"We need to stop meeting like this," I joked with him, and he laughed from under the tractor.

"But I've heard clandestine rendezvouses are the best kind." He winked at me as I added the tomatoes to the shallow crates in the corner. "By the way, I've been looking for the name of the private investigator, but I'm not having any luck finding her."

"Does the name Sakiko Yoshida sound familiar?"

He raised one eyebrow. "I think so, why?"

"I got a tip from someone else that she was the one who handled the case. I saw her yesterday."

"You did?" He hauled himself out from under the tractor. "Did you find out anything new?"

"Same information we all know. Ria was sweet, good at school, etcetera. I still can't figure out who she was dating after she broke up with Itsuki Kato."

"Oh, I remember him. He runs the taiyaki shop in town now, right?"

"He does." I looked past Minato to the pouring rain outside. It was coming down hard, in waves of rain, and the puddles were growing.

"Are you sure she dated someone after Itsuki?"

No, I wasn't sure. There was only a small amount of evidence Ria had dated someone else after Itsuki. Akai remembered a young man she only met once, and a big change in Ria after that, one Akai didn't approve of.

"I don't know. Finding people who spent time with her during that time period is hard. Akiko's older brother and his crowd did, but I can't really go talk to him."

"No, you can't." His expression turned dark, and I was thankful for his countenance. He knew the whole story. Mom had told him everything when he was brought into the family business. Only a few people knew all the circumstances surrounding the barn fire and what happened with Tama. We were keeping it quiet until the big trial to be held in the years ahead.

He thought for a few more moments, and we watched the rain come down outside together.

"What about all the clubs she was in at school? It's possible she was dating someone from there. Or maybe someone from the clubs would know more about who she was seeing?"

"Hmmm, yes, her school clubs. Between her manga artwork and looking into Itsuki Kato, I hadn't gotten to those yet, but I suppose I'll have to soon. Akai is still going through all her old photos, and knowing her, she's sitting at home and spiraling through years' worth of memories. I was hoping she'd have something for me first." I imagined Akai, bleary-eyed and staring at the photos on her computer screen, slipping back in time in her memories and forgetting about her work. I would need to check up on her later in the day.

"Well, if she doesn't come up with anything, you could always go to the school and request to see photos from that year. It would give you a good idea of where to start with more questions."

I sighed, realizing I was in for the long haul on this case. A missing persons case could go on for years or even a whole lifetime as I was seeing first hand. Would I be tracking down witnesses or old friends of Ria's for the rest of my life? The more that time slipped away, the fuzzier memories of Ria would be. I could assume that after another ten years, no one would remember anything helpful.

"I'll keep this idea in mind. Maybe later this week, I'll head on over to the school and see what they can tell me. I went there last fall, so I'm sure the people in the office still remember me."

Minato shrugged. "It's worth a shot." He moved to return to work, but I was reminded of my conversation with Sakiko Yoshida.

"Wait a moment. Do you remember much about Ria's father? Did you know him at all?"

He paused and stroked his goatee. "Just from around town. When his wife was alive, he spent most of his time at home with her. But when I saw him out at the grocery store or during festi-

vals, he was always polite and easy to talk to. Otherwise, no. I
didn't know him well at all. Sorry."

"Do you remember Ria ever complaining about the way he
treated her?"

He narrowed his eyes, that protective fatherly quality coming
out in full force. "What do you mean?"

"The PI felt that if anyone had caused Ria's disappearance, it
was her father. That he prevented her from going out with her
friends or meeting up with her boyfriend."

"How so?"

I shrugged and shook my head at the same time. "I'm unsure.
He may have tried to lock her in her bedroom or tried to keep her
in the house some other way, but I'm only guessing."

If there had been a lock on her door, it could've been there for
a million reasons. They may have used the room for something
else before Ria was born. The house had been theirs for
generations.

I wanted to scrape my hands through my hair and tug in frustration, but with the rain coming down in sheets, I tried not to
touch it. My hair was already a frizzy mess as it was.

"I don't know. Her father didn't seem like the controlling
type, but so many people have secret lives at home. The happy
and helpful man on the street could be a drunk at home who
beats his wife. You just don't know."

And that's the way most people wanted it. They tried to keep
their private lives private and put on a mask for the public, quite
literally sometimes with all the surgical masks we wore. I hadn't
worn mine since allergy season was over.

"That's true. It makes solving mysteries difficult though."

"I can imagine."

The sound of a motor and gravel crunching pulled my attention to the driveway and Yasahiro drove up to the house. I'd taken
the bus and walked this morning, leaving the car to him, but I
thought it was a little early to be picking me up for the day. I

glanced at the clock in the barn. Only 10:00 and another hour till he opened the tea shop.

He exited the car with his messenger bag, opened his umbrella, and looked out in our direction. I waved from the barn door, and he ran across the grass to me.

"Hi! What are you doing here so early?" I asked as he stepped into the shelter of the barn and closed his umbrella. He and Minato bowed to each other in greeting.

"You must've left your phone inside because I texted you. I don't need to take Mrs. Yamida to her physical therapy appointment, so I figured it was time to come out to the house and have that talk with your mom." He patted his bag, and I pulled back in surprise.

"Right now? We haven't even discussed your idea." I looked over my shoulder at Minato, but he was quiet and rubbing his hands with a towel after having rinsed them off.

"I'm sure you'll love it, so I thought it would be a surprise."

Oh boy. I didn't know whether to cheer or cringe. Yasahiro was creative and sure of himself, but Mom had become touchy in ways we both weren't used to. Things around the farm hadn't been normal for a while and throwing more gas on the fire probably wasn't the best idea.

But I looked into his face and knew I could trust him. Besides everything that had happened with Amanda, when had he ever been wrong about anything like this? His skill set was worth millions of yen and people from far and wide clamored to get his opinion on business matters.

I summoned up a smile though apprehension clawed at my stomach.

"Great. Mom's inside. Let's go."

CHAPTER
TWENTY-TWO

"It seems that our original ideas of how we would handle the farm have changed," Yasahiro said, pushing his glasses back up the bridge of his nose and laying his hands on the folders in front of him. Mom sat across the table from us, Yuna by her side. Mom's face was a hard slab of stone. "So I'd like to propose a new business idea I have. One that I believe will be advantageous to both of us."

He opened the folder, took out a sheet of paper, and turned it towards Mom.

"*Teikei*, Community Supported Agriculture." Both Mom and Yuna leaned over the paper to stare at Yasahiro's texts and graphs. My heart raced in my chest, uncertain about what would come next. "This is a community farming concept that has been around in Japan since the 1960s, and I've seen it benefit farms both in the US and in France. With volunteer workers, upfront investments, and delivering straight to the consumer, you can improve your farm output and save for retirement or less-fruitful seasons. Since you've started to grow your offerings and Hirata will now invest in the farm, this model will give you the highest margin for profit and sustainability for the coming decade or more."

My scalp prickled as I watched Mom squint down at the paper and then concentrate on Yasahiro. This was unexpected! I figured he would propose some sort of investment in the business in return for my freedom.

"We can set up a system for next year pretty easily. We'll recruit locally and from the surrounding towns, both through word of mouth and advertising. The whole process can start in June with payment, and then we can set up work shifts to last through the summer and harvest time. You won't have to haul produce to the markets anymore, except for a few local farm stands. Mei and I can recruit the volunteers, and we can use Oshabe-cha as a pickup location. Yuna can handle the work shifts and bookkeeping. Mom, you can handle all the plans for what to farm and when. Not only will this cut back on manual labor for everyone, but the system will also cut back on having to hire part-time workers for harvest season. I estimate it'll bring in an extra 500,000 to 800,000 yen per month next year."

Yuna's eyes widened as she looked at a spreadsheet Yasahiro handed to her across the table.

"Really?" she asked, running her finger down the rows of numbers. "I've never heard of this before. This can make that much more money?"

"It's more work to set the whole system up and to find all the volunteers who become investors in the farm. But once that's up and running, the rest of the work is minimal."

Pride caused my chest to swell as Yuna handed each paper across to me. This was awesome and inspiring, and I could see why Yasahiro hadn't told me any of it ahead of time. My imagination was already running away with the possibilities. I saw down the path ahead, and it was glorious. People I knew, friends working in the fields to help pick vegetables that they would eat themselves. The enormous sense of accomplishment we would feel watching bags of produce disappear into warm and happy kitchens.

This was the future, right in front of us.

But Mom sighed and rubbed her eyes, her mouth set in a deep frown.

"I don't know about this, Yasahiro. This whole new paradigm sounds like a lot of work."

"It will be, up front. I won't lie about that. But once the system is in place, each year after will get easier and easier. I'm certain that this is a good step for us. I've been asking questions around town and in the tea shop. People are open to the idea. It's not something that's been done here in Chikata in at least twenty years, and with the new Midori Sankaku open in town, people are looking for ways to support local farms."

"I love this idea," Yuna said, and for once, I saw a glimmer of happiness in her eyes. "I did volunteer organization for my sons' schools back in Chiba. I know of a few websites we could use to handle a lot of the scheduling."

"No," Mom said, placing her hands on the table and standing up. "No, this won't work. I need to keep everything the same as much as possible. The house is already in chaos with Yuna and the boys living here. This... this would be too much."

Yasahiro's eyes dulled, and he met Mom's stare. "I think you should sit down and hear this through to the end, Tsukiko." I cringed at his use of her full name. He had called her Mom for months since we were married. "The plain truth of the matter is that if you want our financial investment and our personal time and efforts, then you will have to go with this plan."

"Or what?"

Yasahiro sighed. "Or we won't be investing our time and money in the family farm. I was clear about that the other day."

The back of my neck began to sweat, and I turned my eyes to the table.

"Already, you're going to have to hire someone to replace Mei here for the rest of the season. Neither of us wants to jeopardize the pregnancy with hard manual labor." Yasahiro's hand closed over mine on the table and squeezed. "And we won't be working here if there's nothing in it for us."

Mom huffed, but Yasahiro plowed on.

"Hirata already came out and said he's going to inherit the farm, something you indicated would not happen six months ago. You told me over the winter you hoped Mei would come around to love the farm because you wanted to hand the land and business down to her."

I looked up at Mom, and she swallowed hard. She was going to hand down the farm to me? I swept my eyes over the dining room, my painting up on the far wall, and remembered all the years I spent in the house and how badly I'd wanted Mom to change her mind. I'd had a chance at it all?

"What happened?" Yasahiro asked, echoing my thoughts.

The room was quiet except for the hum of the fan. Yuna stared out the window, chewing on her bottom lip.

Mom sat back down at the table. She took a deep breath and said, "I have glaucoma."

"What?" I asked, surprised my lips even moved.

Mom turned to me. "During the winter, I noticed my vision along the edges was getting blurry and harder to see out of. I went to the eye doctor about it, thinking it was stress or that I needed real glasses finally. But no. He did tests, and I have glaucoma. And unfortunately, it's already done damage to my vision."

Panic sped up my thoughts, skipping along my memories of the past few months. Mom had been bumping into things, taking more naps, complaining of headaches. All the seed and vegetable sorting issues and the haphazard way she was storing her gardening tools suddenly made sense.

My mom was going blind.

"I've been using drops, but they irritate my eyes fiercely." She sighed, a deep mournful sigh I wasn't used to. Yuna, across from me, was aghast, her mouth dropped open. She was just as clueless as me. "They're slowing the damage, though, so that's good. But I'll probably be blind within a few years."

"What about surgery?" My voice cracked. I couldn't even look at Yasahiro. The guilt of not knowing this weighed a metric ton and sat right on top of me.

"I can get laser surgery that will delay the onset, and I plan to have it done this year." Mom smoothed out her hair, and I imagined her, blind, trying to take care of herself. My heart constricted and tears fell down my cheeks. "But it's expensive, and it won't cure me."

The room fell into silence again as we all processed this news.

Yasahiro cleared his throat. "Why didn't you tell us when you first found out? We're family. We could've helped you."

Mom scoffed, and I jerked, a stab to my chest. "You and Mei weren't married. You were too busy getting her knocked up and involving her in a nationwide scandal to think about me."

Yasahiro lowered his head, and my cheeks burst into flames. If the earth opened and swallowed me whole right then, I would've been so grateful.

"And then your wedding pushed me over the edge. All I wanted was some peace and quiet, but I had to host a hundred people here for the big event. My eyesight was already in trouble then and only got worse after. You should've held it somewhere else."

Anger flashed red hot across my vision, and I stood up, not realizing I was on my feet before I was towering over everyone. "I asked your permission. I even had a backup plan if you were unable to do it!"

I shouldn't have yelled. Yuna was ready to bolt.

Mom huffed. "What did you expect, Mei? That I was going to say no? I had no choice."

"Not true. I gave you a choice." My face heated by twenty degrees. "I specifically asked your permission to have the wedding here. We would've covered every expense, too, but you insisted on paying for a few items as a gift, though you didn't have to. Yasahiro's parents offered to host. You knew that."

"Ladies," Yasahiro said, standing up and holding out his hands to keep us in our corners. "What's done is done. I'm deeply disappointed in you, Tsukiko. Before I became your son-in-law, I thought we were friends. You should've come to me."

Mom had no reply to that, and a part of me died inside right then. She felt bad about not confiding in Yasahiro, but she didn't feel bad about what went between us. I was her daughter, and I was supposed to obey, right? She was angry with me for stepping out of line, and I was angry with myself for being the kind of person my own mother didn't want to go to for help.

But at least I finally knew why everything had happened the way it did. In the winter, she'd been out of money, and her health was failing. Not able to come to Yasahiro for more money because of her pride, she had gone to Hirata. Now, she was adamant about keeping me around because someday she'd be blind, and she'd need me to keep the business in line. But she was still struggling financially. There would be no salary for me if she were paying for surgery on top of everything else. Health care was not expensive in Japan, but even with national health insurance, Mom would still have to pay thirty percent for the surgery and all the prescriptions.

Yasahiro pushed the folder across the table at my mom.

"This plan would still be good for you. It would take a lot of the burdens off of you in the future when your eyesight is gone. But I want to make one thing clear, we will not help you until you can apologize to Mei for treating her poorly."

"No," I whispered, tugging on his arm. "No. She doesn't have to."

"Yes she does," he said, whipping his head around to me. "And she will treat you better from here on out, or we will be strangers." He set his jaw and looked at Mom. "I will not have it. Most of this is your fault for making Mei keep your secrets last winter and then becoming angry with her for wanting to help you, not coming to us about your health, and not being honest with us about the wedding."

Mom flinched as if she was slapped.

"I realize I caused problems during the investigation of Amanda's murder, but I have apologized and made up for that. These other falsehoods have been ongoing and done much more damage than I ever could on my own."

He took my hand and tugged me toward the door.

"We'll await your answer, whenever you're ready." We both bowed, turned to leave, and Yasahiro closed his hand over mine as we reached the door.

"I hate secrets," he said, not dropping his voice.

I was sure Mom heard him.

CHAPTER
TWENTY-THREE

rip, drip, drip.

The last of the storm's raindrops fell off the awning of the tea shop as I finished my lunch across from Murata. The shop was quiet today. Most people decided to stay home instead of braving the sideways rain for a hot cup of tea and some company. I couldn't really blame them. But now that the rain had slowed down, I would expect people to show up for the afternoon.

Murata was reading one of her favorite newspapers and nibbling on a sandwich Yasahiro made for her. Though I had cleaned out years worth of newspapers from her apartment months ago, she hadn't stopped her subscriptions. I still had to tie them up twice a month and put them out for recycling whenever I could.

The morning's drama dominated all of my daydreams. I couldn't imagine a scenario in which Mom would come to me and apologize of her own free will. In the past, she'd apologized to me on many occasions when I'd confronted her about something, but she would always find some excuse for her actions. That was just her way.

But when we got along, we were great pals. We had a lot of the same interests, and I loved sitting down with Mom for a cup of tea and a chat. Growing up, she had helped me with my homework and encouraged me to try new things. When I was dating, I often told her about the men I met, and she had opinions I valued. We had a decent relationship prior to this year.

Everything was different now though. Our relationship had shifted as soon as I moved back home. Getting married to Yasahiro made it even worse. I seemed to have crossed some line I didn't know existed until I was way past it. The funny part was that, in the beginning, Mom had been excited about me dating Yasahiro. She even encouraged us. So what had changed? I wasn't sure, and I would probably never know what had happened to change her mind. Unfortunately, we were beyond easy apologies and forgiving and forgetting.

"How is that manga you're reading?" Murata asked, jerking her chin at Ria's red sketchbook. Her question throttled me out of my head, and I placed my hand on the red sketchbook. I was almost finished with the story, but nothing struck me as important yet. The heroine, Shizuka, was now meeting up with the side boyfriend, Kuro, daily, and once they were almost caught by her real boyfriend, Hiromi.

"It's good. Very compelling. But I'm sure it'll end tragically soon." I drummed my fingers on the red cover and contemplated whether I had time to finish it tonight. With the rain ending, the rest of my day would be busy, and tomorrow, Yasahiro was due to return to days at Sawayaka. My work with the Fukuda house was done, and now my life with Mom was in jeopardy as we waited for her to come around.

I was in a holding pattern.

"Aren't the best stories those filled with love, loss, and tragedy?" Murata asked, her eyes glistening and focused far away.

I almost laughed. "Uh, sometimes. I like funny stories too.

Tragedy is not always my cup of tea." I raised my cup to her, and she smiled.

The doorbell chimed, and I looked up, prepared to see one of my elderly clients come through the door, to find Goro at the entrance.

"Hey, Mei. I was in the neighborhood, so I thought I'd stop by and check in on your progress with the Fukuda case."

He tucked his police hat under his arm, set his umbrella to the side, and bent over to unlace his shoes. Normally, if people entered the front of the shop and just wanted to purchase a bento or tea, I served them without them having to take their shoes off. But farther back in the shop where people sat on the floor at the low tables, everyone went shoeless. It was our way.

I wasn't sure if I was up for talking about the Fukuda case. The fight with my mom, learning she was going blind, and how she lied to me for months had taken its toll on me. What I really needed was a nap, but Yasahiro was upstairs taking his turn in the bed.

"Sit. Can I get you a cup of tea?" I levered myself out of my spot at the table.

"Sure. Do you have any more of the apple green tea? That was really nice."

"I do! Coming right up."

Once he had his cup and a fresh scone too, I sat back down next to him at the table. Murata watched us like we were her favorite TV show. Everyone wanted to learn more about Ria Fukuda.

"Have you finished it yet?" Goro asked, flipping through the manga.

"No. Almost. Maybe tonight. Things around home have been kind of crazy."

"Really? You and Yasahiro?" He looked skeptical, and I was grateful that so much had changed since the winter when no one believed Yasahiro would date someone like me. We were finally a stable couple, one people trusted to last.

I shook my head. "Mom."

"What's going on with her? She and my mom have been so secretive. Always off to Tokyo together for random jaunts around town. Is it true what I heard? That Hirata is taking over the farm?"

News travels fast.

"Yeah. Hirata and his family moved in over the weekend, and Yasahiro and I have been frozen out. Mom still wants me to work there for free, so we proposed a community share business model to her, and she flipped out."

"Why would she flip out about that? That sounds like a cool idea," Goro said around a mouthful of scone. He brushed some errant crumbs off the front of his uniform.

"Well, she told us she has glaucoma and is going to lose her sight."

I regretted saying it out loud, but it was only the three of us in the shop, and I was done with secrets. The whole town would know sooner or later.

"Oh no. That's horrible. She probably doesn't want anything to change because, if she goes blind, —"

"It'll be hard for her to adapt. Yeah, I get it. But shutting Yasahiro and me out was not the best move. We could've helped."

"She thought she'd get more help from Hirata?"

"Who knows?"

Goro finished off his scone. "But, that explains the trips to Tokyo she made with my mom. Your mother was probably seeing a specialist there, and my mom was the driver." He rolled his eyes. "Typical." He sipped his tea and hummed. "This is my favorite. So your mom is losing her sight, and she still wants you working at the farm for free?"

"Mmm," I grunted, trying to communicate that this situation was too new and raw for me to discuss.

Goro ignored all of my social cues. Murata's smile widened.

"That's a tough deal for you, Mei. I thought you were going to move in and renovate the place. Yasahiro's been talking about it for months."

"You don't say?"

Sarcasm was lost on him.

"I do. I'm really surprised by this."

"Me, too, Goro. Can we stop talking about this? It's been a rough few days, and I just need a few hours to forget about what happened. Get some perspective. Okay?"

He shrugged. "Sure. Whatever you want. I came to talk about the Fukuda case, anyway." He cleared his throat and pulled out his trusty notebook. "You wanted me to look into anything I could regarding her time at high school, so I made a call to the principal of our old high school again."

"You did? That's great! I was just talking about this with Mr. Minato a few hours ago."

"We must be on the same wavelength. I figured I might as well check in with the school since I still go out there to do safety classes a few times per year. Ms. Aizawa, the principal, did some digging for me and found all the club photos for the year that Ria went missing. She was too busy to go through them and send me the lists, so I asked her to set aside the photos in a folder for you."

"Fantastic! I can run by and pick them up tomorrow morning."

"Well," he said, standing up from the table, "the reason why I'm in the neighborhood is to speak to all the local businesses about the typhoon on the way."

Both Murata and I blinked up at him. "Typhoon?"

He sighed. "Haven't you been watching the news?"

"No. I've been a little busy."

"This little storm we had is only a prelude of the good times to come," he said, gesturing to the wet streets outside. "Typhoon Number Nine is on its way, and it looks like it's heading straight for us. None of this small tropical storm stuff that dumps rain for a few hours and moves on. They're talking category two, and it may get stronger by the time it hits us."

My blood pressure dropped, and I began to sweat. A state of alarm was not good for the baby nor me.

"If you're going to go to the high school, I suggest you go now. Tomorrow, you'll be battening down the hatches and staying inside." He glanced out the front window. "I think if you put the shutters down, the shop will be okay. Most of the tea shop is up off the street. The real problem will be out on the farms in the low-lying areas."

Mom. Despite being so mad at her I wanted to move to Europe, I didn't want anything to happen to her, Yuna and the boys, and the farm. The farm could easily flood in a heavy rainstorm, so a category two typhoon would do a lot of damage. There was also a small river a half kilometer away that could cause problems too in a large rainstorm. I chewed on my lip, worried about Mom, but going out to the school had to come first.

"I'll go ask Yasahiro to come down and watch the shop."

"Good idea," Goro said, nodding to Murata and me. "I have to be on my way." He slipped his boots back on and tied them up swiftly. "Give my best to Ms. Aizawa when you see her."

CHAPTER
TWENTY-FOUR

"Mrs. Suga, It's good to see you again," Aizawa said, opening her office door and gesturing for me to enter. I'd been sitting in the main office waiting area for only a few minutes, enjoying the sound of classes being held down the hall and the staff answering phones or typing up notes. It wasn't as if I missed school, but like most people, I craved the nostalgia of times gone past.

"Thank you for seeing me at such short notice," I replied, bowing and following her into her office.

"It's no problem, I assure you."

I sat in the same chair I'd sat in last fall when I visited to find out more about Tama's teaching schedule. It was here that I'd caught him in a lie about where he was when his father was killed. He hadn't been teaching because he'd gone home sick. Would I be that lucky today?

"Did Goro Hokichi brief you about why we need these photos?" I asked, eyeing the manila envelope on the desk.

She shook her head. "Only that you were in the middle of an investigation. What's all this about?"

She was a serious woman but very curious — good traits for a school teacher and administrator.

"We're looking into the disappearance of Ria Fukuda."

"No," she said, gasping and leaning back in her chair. I almost smiled at her reaction.

"Yes. Her father passed away recently, and my friend inherited the house. While I was helping her clean it out, we thought we might try to solve the case." I shrugged my shoulders. "It seemed like a good idea at the time, but I admit the whole situation's been nothing but confusing and stressful."

"I'm sure. The police never got very far with the investigation. I wasn't here then, but I was good friends with the former principal. Having a responsible and caring young woman like her go missing on his watch almost got him fired. There was nothing he could've done though. It hadn't happened at school, and there were no prior warning signs. Just here one day and gone the next."

"Did the police come and question anyone in particular?"

She lifted her eyes to the ceiling. "Hmm, not that I remember. I looked at the principal's logs from that time, but he didn't mention anyone specifically. The police questioned anyone who had been in the same classes with her. That's about it."

"Hmmm..." I wasn't getting any extra useful information from this conversation, and I was sure the principal had plenty of other things she should be doing. "Well, then I don't want to keep you from your duties. I'm sure you're a very busy woman. Might I look at the club photos for that year?" I gestured to the envelope on her desk. "I wanted to get a better idea of what Ria Fukuda could've been doing around the time she disappeared."

"Sure." She handed the envelope to me. "Would you mind looking at them here? These are our only copies on site. I think they've been digitized, but I'm fuzzy on the details of where those are stored."

"Of course."

She stood up and left the room while I emptied the envelope onto the clear desk space in front of me and flipped through the old memories. This school was well-known for the variety of after-school clubs on offer. They had everything from traditional kendo to international fencing, arts and crafts, cooking, photography, hiking and survival clubs. Everything.

Including a manga club.

I sifted through the photos until I found the group photo of the manga club, all eight of the students smiling for the camera. And at the center of the photo, Ria Fukuda stood with her red sketchbook clutched to her chest.

A modicum of calm trickled through my chest while looking into her eyes. In the past week, through every thread of evidence and every story, she'd slipped further and further away from me. She almost didn't feel real. And without a body, how could I ever prove she was alive to begin with?

With memories like these, cast in shades of light and dark on a shiny piece of paper, she became real again.

I ran my finger over the list of people in the photo until I came upon, "Watanabe Kohei (Not Pictured)."

Really?

I looked at the photo again, hoping he would appear there. No such luck.

Maybe he was in other photos, in other clubs. I flipped through the other club photos until I found one other mention of him, also not pictured, in the kendo club. What gives? Was he afraid of the camera or something?

I shouldn't have found it suspicious that he wasn't pictured, but I did. *Think, Mei.* Perhaps he was sick the day photos were taken? That was unlikely. Unless you were on the brink of death, you went to school. That's just the way it was here.

Suddenly, I needed to see a photo of Kohei Watanabe from back then so badly my feet itched to start the search. What had he looked like? Had I seen him around when I was a kid and not even realized he was the same person as the jerk of a cop I knew now?

I shuffled through the photos again and came up empty. Well then, what about the individual school photo for the year? They were usually taken on a different day than the club photos.

I glanced out the door, but Aizawa wasn't in the main office. Could I ask someone else in the office for it?

I laid out the photos Aizawa had set aside for me and took pictures of each with my phone so I could show them to Akai and Goro.

"Excuse me," I said, approaching the young man working at the front desk, "I need to find a yearbook for a particular year. I'd ask Ms. Aizawa, but she seems to have stepped out."

He hummed, scratching his cheek, "I'm not sure where they're kept. Is it possible you can come back later?"

"I can't. Sorry. Do you think you'll be closed tomorrow with the typhoon on the way?"

"Probably. The forecast is for damaging winds and rain. Ms. Aizawa is off discussing this right now with the staff."

I nodded and sighed, unsure of what to do next, when the young man perked up.

"We provide copies of the yearbook every year to the prefectural library. You could go there and look at their copy." He pointed in a vague direction out of the school. "The one up on the hill."

"Really? I didn't know that. How long have you been sending them yearbooks?"

"Since the 1960s. They have all the years in the stacks, but you can't check them out."

What a fabulous idea! I dashed out of the high school, checking the location of the prefectural library on my phone before tearing away up the hill to the library parking lot. Exiting the car, I tried to keep my hair in place as the wind whipped around me. Clouds raced by in the sky, indicating the weather was fast, and the typhoon was approaching. By morning, we would see the first bands of rain.

Inside the library, I asked for assistance right away. I didn't know this library at all. When I was in school, I always went to the one in Chikata, and I never came here after school like many of the local students did.

The woman working the front desk directed me to a reference section along the backside of the library. She ran her finger over the spines of my high school's yearbooks. I saw my own year fly past her fingertip and then land on Ria's year.

"Here you go. You can look at it here, but you can't check it out. Please just leave the yearbook on the table when you're done."

I hurried to the table and immediately opened the book, excited to see Kohei Watanabe for myself. But I knew something was wrong the moment the yearbook creaked open.

"Wait!" I called to the librarian, and she halted in her tracks. "There are pages missing."

Cut clean from the inside binding, the page where Kohei Watanabe should've been was absent.

"What?" The librarian took the yearbook from me, and her eyes widened as she examined the interior. "How did this happen?" she demanded.

"I don't know. This is my first time in this library."

"But why did you ask for this particular yearbook?"

Her eyes drilled into me, and I felt like I was being questioned by the police. My scalp prickled.

"I've been looking for old photos of someone I know, a boy, at the time, connected to the disappearance of a young girl from my town over ten years ago. I don't know why the pages are missing."

Was it related or a coincidence?

The librarian looked at me for a long time before coming to some sort of judgment in her head about me. "If so, then there would be pictures of him from the year before... if this was his graduating year." She went straight to the shelf again, but she wouldn't find anything. Goro had said Kohei was only at our school for a year.

"I'm sure all the other yearbooks are fine," I said, as she set a stack of them on the table. "I believe he only went to the high school for one year."

I opened the vandalized yearbook and flipped through, stopping on Ria's photo and looking at her smiling face. *What happened to you, Ria?* I searched forward and backward a few pages hoping to find other familiar faces, but no one jumped out at me. Akai and Tama had gone to different high schools, and I'd have to go back even farther to find Goro, Kumi, or myself.

After flipping through several of the yearbooks, the librarian seemed satisfied that none of the others were damaged.

"Huh," she grunted, her hands on her hips. "I wonder why this was the only one. I'll have to report this to my boss and see what she says to do about it."

"I'm sorry to have caused drama in your day," I said, standing and bowing. "I was hoping to come here, see what I needed to see, and leave without causing any problems."

She gathered up the yearbooks from the table. "It's funny that life never works out that way, right?"

She had no idea.

CHAPTER
TWENTY-FIVE

checked the weather report in the car after the library. Rains from the typhoon would start sometime in the late morning, almost noon, the next day, so if I was going to get anything more done on this case, it had to be today.

I threw Yasahiro's car into gear and headed back to Chikata. I couldn't waste any more time wondering who Ria had dated after Itsuki. In my mind, Ria's father was innocent, shattered to pieces after his daughter went missing. I wasn't sure why people suspected him in her disappearance. He may have been strict, but according to Akai, he loved Ria more than anything. So maybe he was gruff on the surface and that led people to believe the worst. Still, I trusted Akai's assessment of him. He was out of the running.

That left Itsuki and the mysterious interim boyfriend. I wasn't sure Itsuki was innocent, but he didn't strike me as the jealous type. They'd broken up a few months before she went missing, and that fact was backed up by Itsuki's father.

So, who was the interim boyfriend? I suspected Kohei Watanabe, and only for a few vague reasons. He was in the manga club with Ria, and he'd been friends with Tama, Ria, and their crew when he lived here in high school, making him a part of the "scene." If they had dated, I wasn't sure what Ria saw in him. He was mean and a bully, but mostly to me, though Kayo didn't like him either. That kind of attitude could easily become violent. I had a hard time believing someone as sweet as Ria could date someone like him. Maybe she fell for the "bad boy?" Then I could've sworn he recognized Ria's red sketchbook when he knocked me over outside the police station. But he may have wondered if it was mine? There were no outside markings to indicate the sketchbook belonged to Ria.

Deep in my gut, there were two main reasons I suspected him, and neither of them had to do with Ria's past. One, I couldn't find any photos of him from when he attended my old high school, and that was suspicious for no good reason. And two, he was always in the places I was, and I felt like I was being followed. From that one time outside of Ria's old house to the taiyaki shop to the beer garden, he kept turning up where I hadn't seen him before, always too close. Something about it rubbed me the wrong way.

Kayo would argue with me that I didn't like him to begin with, so naturally, I suspected him. She wasn't wrong. I didn't like him, but only because he didn't like me to begin with.

And it all came down to why. Why? Why did he hate me, anyway?

I pulled up to Akai's house about fifteen minutes later. She'd asked me to come by, and this was the perfect time.

"You won't believe where I've been," I said, patting her dog, Buttercup, on the head as I entered her immaculate house. Akai made a space for my shoes right next to hers and ushered me inside.

"Just tell me." She sounded weary and looked like she hadn't slept in a week. "I'm too tired to guess."

I sat in her extra desk chair as she poured herself a fresh cup of coffee in the kitchen. "Coffee?" she asked.

"No thanks. I've been cutting back. I've just been at my old high school, trying to find photos of the clubs Ria was in. I thought, maybe, she dated someone from there, and that could've led us to who she was with when she went missing."

Akai sat opposite me at her desk and slurped her coffee. She was back in her usual housecoat, bright red with flowers and a pair of black socks. She probably hadn't been outside in days.

"Get this. Each time I went to look for her, Kohei Watanabe was mentioned, but he was absent from all the group photos, the manga club and the kendo club too. So I decided to go to the prefectural library to look at the yearbook for that year, and his page was removed from the book!" I threw my hands up in the air. "Poof! Just gone. Cut out."

"Kohei Watanabe... This is the new police officer in town, right?"

"Yes," I stressed, leaning forward. I was excited to tell Akai everything. "He went to high school for one year with Ria, *and* he was friends with Tama, Ria, and all their crew from Chikata. You may never have met him because he wasn't here for very long."

"Huh." Akai squinted and leaned back in her chair to stare at the ceiling. "Kohei... Kohei... I think I may have met him once." Then her chair snapped forward. "In fact, I think I may have seen him in the photos I've been archiving."

She twirled around to her computer and set her coffee mug on the coaster next to her mouse pad. Clicking through multiple websites, a page loaded on her screen filled with small photo thumbnails, all sorted by date.

"I pulled these together over the last few days. From my cards, my archives, and then a card from Ria's house I found yesterday on the floor behind her bed." Her voice was slow as she scrolled through and stopped at a collection of photos dated to the year Ria went missing. The time stamp read, "April." Ria had gone missing in May.

"Look at these. Do these people look familiar?"

It was a *hanami* party, a picnic amongst the newly opened cherry blossoms all along the river of the next town over. Most people I knew traveled there for hanami parties because the town had a festival to mark the occasion every year. In the photo, picnic blankets covered with people and baskets stretched out into the distance, but right in the foreground, I recognized a few faces.

"That's Tama... and Ria... and I don't recognize anyone else by name. I'm sure I met a few of them before though. Their faces seem familiar." I squinted in at the guy sitting next to Ria. His head was turned from the camera, a cigarette in his hand, his shaggy bleached hair obscuring his face.

"I took these pictures," Akai said, quickly clicking through them. "I was at the next blanket over with my high school friends."

Akai paused on another photo. This one wasn't much better though. The guy sitting next to Ria had his hand out, hiding his face from the camera.

"I remember this guy being really camera shy. Back then, everyone was into selfies and posting photos online, and he was having none of that. Said that someday he was sure that anything online would come back and bite him in the butt."

He was right about that. Just look at all the dirt we had dug up on Amanda, everything she had ever put online and most of the stuff she hadn't either.

Akai clicked through more photos, humming along.

"If this guy didn't like getting his photo taken, are we out of luck?" I sighed as I sat back in the desk chair and scratched Buttercup behind the ears when she trotted up to me. "This whole investigation feels like a huge waste of time. I want to know what happened to her, just like everyone else, but I'm not willing to chase leads until the end of time."

I had too many other things going on between my mom, buying a new house and land, and thinking about the future of the tea shop. Plus, what would happen once Mom lost even more of her sight? Would Yuna and Hirata take care of her? I certainly hoped they would.

My thoughts came to a screeching halt as Akai pulled back from her desk and pointed her finger straight at the screen. "A-ha! I knew I'd find one."

Zoomed in on her monitor, the face of the boy sitting next to Ria was crystal clear in the background of a portrait Akai had taken of two friends making peace signs at her. The camera hadn't been directed at him, so he wasn't able to escape the lens like he usually did.

"Kohei Watanabe," I breathed out. His hair was different, and at the time, he'd been skinnier than a rake. Akiko said the guy Ria had been dating was "skinny" and had "long, bleached hair."

I brought my hand to my lips. Had Ria dated Kohei? Was he the "Hiromi" of her manga? If so, did the secret lover, Kuro, even exist? Maybe the manga was what Ria fantasized her life to be like, yet she was stuck with some sadistic animal like Kohei?

Ugh. I had no idea.

But this photo was reassuring. For a while there, I doubted Kohei had lived here all those years ago, but this was definitely him.

Those eyes. They lacked compassion and understanding, and ever since I'd met him in the early spring, I couldn't shake them.

Akai rubbed her face and hit print. The printer warmed up and spit out the evidence.

"Here," she said, handing over the photo. "It's not much, but I'd give it to Goro and see what he thinks. It could just be a coincidence they were in the same social circle."

I stared down at him, the hair on my arms standing on end.

"But, Akai, he could be the boyfriend in Ria's manga." My eyes filled with tears, confusion tearing at my heart and kicking it to the curb. "What if Kohei is the same guy?"

She shrugged. "There are a million what-ifs here, Mei. We don't even know if the manga is true to life. It could've just been her imagination. But I'm going to guess that there's a reason Kohei's back in Chikata, and it has nothing to do with his career in the police force."

CHAPTER
TWENTY-SIX

The blue sky wasn't going to stay that way for long. I watched the clouds zip by overhead, racing for the northwest like some demon was chasing them. And it was.

"We're expecting the first bands of rainfall to hit Tokyo around 11:00, and then the majority of the storm will drench Tokyo and neighboring Saitama prefecture through the late afternoon," the meteorologist said, using his hands to encompass Tokyo and our area of the map. It was so rare to see our town listed alongside the bigger cities in our prefecture. I was sure I was in an alternate reality.

I glanced over at Yasahiro, sitting next to me on the couch in our apartment. He sipped his coffee and raised his eyebrows.

"Looks like I'm not going back to work today." He stood up from the couch and stretched. "I'll go call Ana and text everyone on staff to stay home. We'll close up both Sawayaka and Oshabe-cha."

"Yeah," I said, distracted by the ongoing news conference on NHK. Several weather experts were talking about rainfall amounts over 200 millimeters and wind speeds over 110 kilometers per hour. It wasn't the worst typhoon we'd ever seen, but it had been a long time a storm of this size would hit us head-on. Usually, Chikata only got scraped by the outer edges of a typhoon.

This would be different.

I wrapped my blanket around me as I pulled my phone from the charging cable and dialed up Murata.

"Morning, Mei. Looks like we have quite the storm coming."

I smiled as I thought of her on her own couch about a block away, drinking her morning tea. "It appears that way, yes. I'm going to keep Oshabe-cha closed today, so I wanted to let you know before you left to come by. Do you have enough water and food to last a few days?"

"Mmm, I do. And I'll fill up any empty bottles too this morning, just in case."

"Great idea," I said, thinking about our recycling bins, both here and downstairs in the tea shop. I should do the same. "Will you call a few people to spread the word about being closed today? I could really use the help."

"Of course, Mei. I'll do that right now. Are you going out to the farm today to evacuate your mom?"

"I hadn't thought about it. Do you think it's necessary?" After the way we left Mom on Monday morning, I hadn't spoken to her at all yesterday. She was angry with us, and we were angry with her, and I wasn't sure who was going to break first. It should've been us, but Yasahiro wanted to give her time to think everything over before making a hard and fast decision about the farm and our future.

"Probably. They're saying that low-lying areas will flood."

I knew this situation all too well. Mom's fields flooded when it rained too much, and this usually damaged a lot of crops. We hadn't had a big flood in about five years, and she was more than due.

"And the river on the other side of your mom's property may overflow as well."

That was true. The Kino-Tsukoshi River had swollen this year on several occasions during heavy storms. It was on the other side of the woods, maybe a kilometer away from Mom's main fields, so it wasn't a direct threat to her on a regular basis.

But today would be anything but regular.

My stomach churned, and the baby kicked and twisted, urged on by the small amount of caffeine from my morning half-cup of coffee. I needed to set aside my anger with Mom and get out to the farm to help them as soon as possible. There was no way I could let this situation come between us.

"Thanks for all the news, Mrs. Murata. You stay safe, and I'll check in with you later today."

"Be safe, Mei," she said and hung up.

"Yasahiro!" I called out, heading to the bedroom. I needed to get changed. "We should go!"

———

OUT AT THE FARM, THE WIND PICKED UP, BENDING THE long grass and pushing it to the ground. I craned my neck to see the status of Akiko's house and caught sight of Yuna's boys kicking a soccer ball around in her backfields. At least they were close by and hadn't gone to school today. Come to think of it, I wasn't sure when and where they would be going to school. Maybe in a week, they'd be at my old elementary school on the other side of town. Akiko's car was in her driveway. Good. If I needed her, I'd know where to find her.

Yasahiro followed me into the house as we searched for Mom and Yuna. The papers we'd given to Mom two days ago still sat on the dining room table, and Mimoji was laid out next to them, not a care in the world.

"Mei?" Yuna came out of the back of the house, wiping her hands on a towel. "We weren't expecting you today."

I hefted a huge sigh of relief. "We closed up Sawayaka and Oshabe-cha and came out here to help you prep the house for the typhoon."

"Really?" She raised her eyebrows at me. "What is there to prep?"

I held my temper in check. It wasn't her fault she knew nothing about the farm. She hadn't grown up here, lived through countless typhoons, survived off canned foods for an entire winter because the crop was destroyed when the fields flooded.

"A lot. Anything almost ripe needs to be picked and brought in or it could rot in the wet fields. Mom's fields flood during a typhoon, and we're going to get hit hard with this one."

Her face fell. "I had no idea. Mom is outside now getting out the wooden shutters for the house. Mr. Minato is out in the fields."

I looked at Yasahiro, and we nodded at each other. "Let's divide up," he suggested. "We have an hour before the wind gets too strong, and the rain comes."

Thankful for the cooler weather, I promised to handle the last of the tomatoes, zucchini, and other summer squash. Smaller pumpkins and winter squash peppered the fields, not ready to be picked yet. We'd hope for the best with those. Yasahiro helped Mom cover the windows with the typhoon shutters, bring the potted plants into the barn, and pick up any of the toys the boys had left on the lawn. Minato hauled potatoes into the barn with the tractor, way too heavy for me to lift or care for.

"There's still a lot of produce in the fields, Mei," he said, leaning against the wind ripping through the open barn doors. "You may lose the sweet potatoes, beans, and several other crops."

"I know. Not much can be done about that," I replied, draping the tomato flats with a length of burlap and tying it down to protect them. They were one of our best selling items, and I didn't want them to go to waste.

"I'm going to head home now and help my wife prepare the house if that's okay with you."

"Of course." I squealed as the wind picked up and nearly took my hat away.

He laughed, pulling the rear door closed and latching it tight. Yuna, to my surprise, pushed a wheelbarrow across the grass to the barn with a big smile on her face.

"Mom and I loosened up a few sweet potato fields yesterday, so I knew just where to go."

I was impressed with her gumption and ability to work in an emergency. Though this whole situation with Hirata and Yuna taking over the farm made me angry to the point of tears, at least Yuna was taking things seriously. Hirata wasn't even here to give her support, yet she was determined to learn.

"Fantastic," I said, stepping to the side so she could get in.

I joined Minato at the open barn door, his eyebrows drawn together and eyes staring into the distance. I followed his line of sight out across the road to Akiko's house, both of our eyes trained on the scene in the far fields. The workers for Midori Sankaku had left at some point this morning, if they had arrived at all. The heavy equipment was absent, and the torn up fields sat quiet and desolate... Except for one man climbing out of a hole or some depression, and Yuna's boys running back to Akiko's house.

"What... What is happening there?" asked Minato.

"I don't know."

And then the clouds rolled in, and the rain began.

CHAPTER
TWENTY-SEVEN

It was amazing how the weather went from a few drops of rain here and there to a torrential downpour in a matter of moments. I grabbed my umbrella and skirted the side of the house, hoping Yasahiro and Mom had finished putting up the typhoon shutters.

"We're all done," Yasahiro shouted over the heavy rain. He was already soaked. "Your mom is inside."

"Mei!" Yuna called out, running up to us. "The boys. They're still over at Akiko's." Her forehead was pinched with worry.

"I just saw them running to Akiko's house. I need to go check in with her, so I'll go get them." I was already wet, but not too much to enter Akiko's house. Yasahiro, on the other hand, would drip everywhere.

"Go. I'll dry off, and we'll head back to the apartment when you return." He squeezed my arm as we passed each other, going in opposite directions.

Crossing over to Akiko's house, I almost lost my umbrella twice in the wind. Before long, it would be shredded and unusable. It was a good thing I had three more at home.

"Oh good! I was wondering if I should send them home or

not, but they keep telling me something weird is going on out back in the fields." Akiko held the door open as I ducked into the wind and jumped into her house's entrance area. I didn't want to go any further and get anything wet, especially since Kirin barked from her temporary prison in the bathroom.

Both of the boys' eyes were wide, their faces pale.

"What's going on?" I placed my hand on Korota's shoulder. He was the older of the two and a little more reliable.

He shook his head slowly, his lips pressed together.

"Out with it," I demanded, only able to be stern for a moment as his skin whitened.

"Yushin and I were kicking the ball around out back. I swear we weren't going to snoop or anything."

"Okay..."

"And then we saw a police car drive up to the temporary lot, you know, where all the diggers are and everything. The ones digging for those buildings next to the greenhouse. A police officer got out of the car, grabbed a shovel from the trunk, and walked out past where all the dirt was." He waved his hand in the general direction of Akiko's backfields, where Midori Sankaku's greenhouse was. "Yushin and I thought it looked funny. He went to a specific spot where there was already a big hole and started digging."

I glanced at Akiko, but we were both too curious to stop him.

"We came over the top of the hole and asked him what he was doing, then he yelled at us and told us we were going to be arrested for trespassing if we didn't leave right then." His face hardened. "I swear we didn't know we weren't supposed to be there. Are they going to put us in jail?"

The tips of my fingers cooled as I reached out to pat his shoulder. "No, I'm sure you're fine."

I kicked off my boots and took Korota by the arm through Akiko's house to the back door. "Come here. Do you know where the man was? Can you point to the spot?"

"Ummmm." He bit his lip before pointing. "You see that mound right there? He was right on the other side."

"You sure?"

"I could show you." He straightened up, squaring his shoulders.

"No. Your mom is worried about you. You go to the front and put your shoes back on. Akiko will take you home."

He nodded and left, but Akiko grabbed my arm.

"What's going on?"

I bit my lip as I looked out at the pouring rain. How could I put my fears into words? I couldn't. Akiko was still recovering from the shock of her older brother killing her father and trying to kill us too. What would she say when I told her I thought one of his old friends was a killer too?

And he was a police officer in our own town.

I needed to be ambivalent. "I don't know yet. Let me go find out."

"You're going to go out? In this?" She gestured to the back-yard that already had puddles obscuring the grass. "This is epic level rain, Mei. Everything out there will flood in a matter of minutes."

She was right, but I had no choice. It was now or never.

"I'll be careful. I promise."

We redressed at the front door, and I sent Akiko across the street with my nephews while I trudged off into the fields in the pouring rain. My boots stuck in the mud, but I pushed on, knowing it was now or never to investigate this. If I waited until after the storm was over, there might have been nothing left for me to investigate.

Rain ran in a river down my back under my raincoat, flying sideways at my umbrella as the wind picked up. The umbrella was doing a poor job of keeping me dry, but I didn't want to just abandon it in Akiko's fields.

I counted my steps as I got closer and closer to the spot Korota had pointed to.

What are you doing, Mei?

I should've at least called Goro for backup. He may have been dealing with the impending typhoon, but he would want to hear my suspicions and talk me down off the cliff I was ready to walk out onto. I glanced over my shoulder as I got closer, and no one was around.

Thank goodness for small miracles.

The mound of dirt in front of me was a muddy mess, and there was no way I was climbing over it. So I skirted the edge of the mound and peered down into the hole. It was filling with rainwater, and I squinted my eyes to see through all the muck.

"Of course. Nothing is going to be easy today," I yelled up at the sky. The rush of rain was deafening, but I was already wet to the bone and in the middle of a construction site. I might as well go all the way in.

The opposite side was lower and sloped into the depression, so I entered the hole from there. The edge towered over my head by almost half a meter, a wall of dirt between Akiko's house and me. This must have been a spot the heavy machinery had dug out for the administrative buildings. I dragged my booted feet along the bottom of the hole, hoping to find something, anything, that would justify this stupid excursion. My boots scraped against rocks, but that was about it.

I turned left and right, frustration building in my chest.

"What am I missing?" I asked aloud. I didn't expect anyone to answer, but just then, my eyes zoomed in on something flapping from the side of the hole.

Rain ricocheted off a piece of heavy-duty clear plastic exposed in the wall of the hole. I approached it slowly, wanting yet not wanting to see the real reason the plastic was there. Scratch marks around it led me to believe it had recently been dug at. By Kohei Watanabe?

Probably. We'd have to get the boys to describe him.

Since the umbrella wasn't doing me much good, I collapsed it and let the wind and rain have its way with me as I hacked away at the mud wall with the umbrella's handle. The whole process was slow, and my umbrella bent under the force with which I stabbed at the solid dirt.

Mud covered my hands, and my vision tunneled as I worked harder and harder. I forgot about Akiko, about Yasahiro waiting for me across the road, about Mom going blind, about my own baby growing in my belly, and I hacked away until I saw it.

I let my arms fall to my side and dropped the destroyed umbrella into the rising pool of rainwater.

There, beneath the clear, aging plastic, was a knot of long hair attached to the decayed head of a dead body.

I had finally found Ria.

CHAPTER
TWENTY-EIGHT

"Mei, you're a mess!" Mom cried as I stepped into the house and foyer. I dripped all over the stone floor, my muddy boots and hands creating a dark puddle around my feet.

My hands shook, and I couldn't stop them. Between the cool rain and what I'd just witnessed, I wondered if they'd ever stop again. Ria's face had been right there, her hair. I swallowed, trying to halt my thoughts from piecing the two together. Only a glimpse of skin had been visible, but in my head, my imagination had blown it up to her whole body.

Yasahiro emerged from the kitchen, wiping his hands on a dish towel, when his smile dropped, and he ran to me.

"Are you okay? What happened?" His hands skated over me, checking my shoulders, arms, and belly before peeling my raincoat off. Only about two square centimeters of my shirt was dry, if that. "Your face is so pale," he said, resting his hands on my cheeks.

"Your hands are warm," I chattered out. My jaw shook from trying to keep it steady. "I need my phone."

"You need to get undressed and in a hot bath immediately," Mom demanded. A hot bath sounded heavenly, but no.

"N-N-No time." I held out my shaking hand beckoning my phone to it. I had left it inside on the charger while out in the fields. I figured it should be at full strength before the typhoon hit.

Yasahiro retrieved my phone immediately. He must have known something big was happening because he didn't fight me. Mom scoffed, though. She hated when I went against her.

"I'll find you some dry clothes," she said, stalking off to the rear of the house.

I dialed up Goro, and he answered, shouting into the phone. "Mei! Where are you?"

"Out at Mom's. Look, I need —"

"Out at your mother's? Are you crazy? I asked for everyone out there to be evacuated!" His voice rose so high I had to pull the phone away from my ear.

"Evacuated?" Both Yasahiro and Yuna who'd been standing and listening stiffened. "No one came by or called." I raised my eyebrows at Yasahiro, and he shrugged.

Goro swore. "We sent Watanabe to your side of town to evacuate everyone. The Kino-Tsukoshi River is at its banks after thirty minutes of rain." He sighed. "We had so many rain storms this summer that it was already swollen before this. I expected you all to be at Yasahiro's place, not out at the farm!"

Kohei Watanabe was supposed to be out here evacuating us, not digging in the dirt looking for the girl he killed a decade ago. Why was I not surprised to hear he shirked his duties to cover his own butt?

The wind strengthened on Goro's end, and he swore again. "I'll try to send someone out there to retrieve you guys, but the road is flooded. So much rainwater is flowing into the sewers that the manholes are overflowing. If someone doesn't reach you in an hour, you need to prepare for the worst."

A new chill ran over my back. "Goro, listen to me. I think I found Ria."

"What?" he screamed into the phone, and I got the feeling he genuinely hadn't heard me because his end of the line sounded like complete chaos.

"I found Ria!" I yelled back. "She's buried in the fields behind Akiko's house!"

The whole house went silent around me. Even the wind seemed to gasp for a moment before it picked up its pace again. Mom stood in the hallway, her arms filled with clean and dry clothes, her eyes wide.

"And my nephews saw Kohei Watanabe right near her just before the rain started. You sent him out here to evacuate us, but instead, he was looking for Ria's last resting place." Silence stretched on the other end of the line. "Did you hear me?" My voice squeaked, and all the energy drained from my body.

"I heard you, Mei. I'll handle it. Whatever you do, don't try to drive out of there. The road is flooded, and your tiny cars will be swept away. Hold tight. I'll do what I can from here."

And he hung up. I stared at my phone for a moment before I used my shaky fingers to turn it off.

"We have to be ready to evacuate," I said, handing my phone back to Yasahiro. "The river is overflowing, and the roads are flooded. They're going to try to send someone out here to get us."

The wind picked up, and the lights flickered. My stomach sank, and finally, my body waved the white flag. I'd had just about my limit for the day, and it was far from over. My right side cramped, sending a shock of pain through me. I winced and placed my hand on my swollen belly.

"Mei." Yasahiro dived forward to put his arms around me. "What's wrong?" His eyes, usually so serene, were filled with worry.

I closed my eyes and concentrated on the spot. "Nothing. A stitch in my side. Not the baby." I was pretty sure. The pain reminded me of dealing with my pains from running, and considering I had just run across a muddy field in the beginnings of a typhoon, it was a likely story.

"You need to get changed into something dry. It can't be good for you to be like this."

I wanted to remind him that we were being evacuated, and I'd be wet again within the hour, but I was also seriously uncomfortable.

"Fine. Might as well."

In the tiny bathroom, my wonderful husband peeled the wet clothes from my body and wrapped me in a warm towel. I sat down on the closed toilet and stared up at him, the reality of the situation finally hitting me.

"I saw her." My lip quivered. "Her long hair and a glimpse of her decayed skin showed through the plastic she was buried in." A tear slipped down my cheek, and Yasahiro crouched down beside me, taking my cold, clammy hand in his. "Not even a proper funeral. It's such a shame."

Yasahiro wrapped my hand in both of his. "It is. No one should die alone like that. She was probably scared out of her mind too." He tugged on my hand. "But, Mei, you helped find her. Now they can figure out what happened. Akai can have her cremated and laid to rest with her parents."

I sniffed up and dragged my hand across my nose. "I didn't find her. The boys saw a man in a police uniform down in the hole digging at something. The man yelled at them to go away."

"Kohei Watanabe?" He nodded his head, and I was sure he had put the facts together like I had. Yasahiro had listened to every last piece of evidence I'd had over the last few days. He knew what I knew.

"And with Goro admitting that he sent Kohei out here to evacuate us, yet he never showed up, I'm pretty sure it was him. Who else would it be? He was missing from all the photos. He's obviously changed in appearance since he lived here last, probably to throw us off the scent. He was friends with Tama and ran with his crowd. And I don't trust anyone who would stick up for Tama."

The whole situation was as clear as day in my head. Like Ria's manga, she had been dating someone, maybe Itsuki, when she cheated on him with Kohei. Somewhere along the way, Kohei got angry with her, and he killed her.

I rested my head against the bathroom wall. This explanation still didn't make sense, though. Something was missing, like a good motive. Why did he kill her? I assumed Kohei had killed her because he knew exactly where to find her, and his actions for the past few months had been aggressive and suspicious.

But why?

A puzzle sat in front of me with a big piece absent from the center of it.

Where would I find the missing piece?

I got changed and opened the door, still chewing over this mystery, when I came back to the current situation. Yuna and the boys had packed their bags, and Mom stood at the front door peering across the street.

"Akiko went back home to be with Kirin. The wind almost blew her over. She was on her knees once. Look. The road is flooded up to Daichi Senahara's house." Mom's brow was creased with worry. "Help me get Mimoji into the cat carrier."

"Sure."

With a gust of wind, several roof tiles blew off and flew into the fields, then the power went out. Mom and I stared at each other for a long moment.

"They're not going to come for us," she whispered.

I knew she was right.

CHAPTER
TWENTY-NINE

The wind picked up into a howling, house-shaking and dangerous tempest within an hour. The gusts rattled the walls and plucked tiles off the roof like someone swatting ants off a picnic blanket. Thunder and lightning streaked the skies and scared my nephews. They huddled under blankets on the couch, playing their hand-held game consoles and giving no thought to when electricity might be restored.

No one had arrived to evacuate us, and the cell phone towers must've been without power too because I couldn't get a signal on my phone. We would have to wait it out now.

We, the adults, tried to remain calm. Mom's house had survived decades worth of typhoons, and we thought this time would be no different. But I was reminded of the several times the NHK weather forecasters said that this was the strongest typhoon to hit our area directly in over fifty years, and with all the rain we'd had this summer, we were already saturated. Also, Mom's roof was the oldest part of the house. With all the tiles flying off, we'd have leaks soon. Though we had renovated the inside once about twenty years ago, that was it. Getting a new roof had been way outside of the budget.

Mom and Yasahiro played Go at the dining room table while Yuna and I read books by candlelight. It was late afternoon, but the cloud cover was so thick that the house was as dark as night.

"We still have gas," Yasahiro said, breaking the silence. "So I was thinking about cooking up some soup. Better use up any fresh meat you may have in case it's a few days before power is restored."

"That's a good idea, Yasahiro." Mom bit her lip as she contemplated her next move on the Go board. "Would you mind handling the prep work? My eyesight is especially poor in low light."

I could tell how much it pained Mom to admit she needed help, but Yasahiro handled the situation easily.

"I'd be happy to. I have some ideas of what I could cook. Let's pause this game for now, and I'll come back to it in a bit." He turned to me, so I set my book down. "I bet you could use a snack. Come with me into the kitchen, and you can bring some snacks back for everyone."

"Sure," I said, not thinking much of the request. I *was* hungry, and if I didn't eat soon, my pregnancy hormones would surge, and I'd be a mess.

I followed him to the kitchen, trying to calm my nerves as the house shook around us. I was worried that the wind would pick us up and throw us into the next prefecture at this point. Creaks and cracks rang through the kitchen as a gust buffeted the house.

Yasahiro didn't stop at the stove and instead crossed the room to the shuttered windows on the side of the house facing the barn. He cranked open the glass window, and the fury of the wind filled the room. I hugged myself and stayed a meter back.

"What are you doing?" I asked, watching him slide the typhoon shutter to the side and look out at the fields.

"As I suspected." He shifted to the side and allowed me room to look out the window.

"Oh no," I breathed out.

The entire outside was an ocean, water as far as I could see.

And it was all the way up to the house.

"What are we going to do?" Panic seized my brain and caused it to race. I imagined us huddled on the collapsing roof, waiting for rescue to come. We had nothing we could use to escape either. We weren't a boating family. There had been no time or money for that kind of leisure, so floating out of here would be impossible.

Ugh. I couldn't help but feel I'd been completely irresponsible once again. I'd spent the last week flittering about trying to solve a decade-old mystery instead of paying attention to what was going on with my mom, the farm, the weather. Was digging up all of that information on Ria, Itsuki, and Kohei worth it?

Yasahiro, to his credit, looked unworried. He peered out the window again and shook his head.

"It's possible the water will rise up into the house before this is over. We haven't even seen the eye of the typhoon yet, so I think we have a lot more rain coming." He walked over to the island and pulled out a chair. "Sit. I'll cook, we'll eat, and then we'll plan for the worst."

I cringed every time the wind gusted, and the house creaked again. Yasahiro didn't talk while he chopped and cooked. I believed his mind to be elsewhere, planning for our eventual evacuation, and how we would get out. I knew him well enough now to understand his thought process. I was his wife, and I was carrying his child, something he had wanted for years. He wasn't going to jeopardize our safety if he could help it.

Still, a typhoon was out of our hands. Yasahiro couldn't reverse the wind or the water creeping up to the house. He didn't have the power of gods.

There was only so much that could be done.

The smell of food cooking roused everyone from their spots in the house. The boys came to grab everyone's chopsticks and pour water for drinks. Mom and Yuna cleaned up the kitchen and brought the rice to the table. Yasahiro had made a big hot pot of soup with chicken and any leftover vegetables in the fridge. We were able to set up the portable hot pot warmer on the dining room table to keep it warm while we ate.

Dinner was a quiet affair as if no one wanted to challenge the voice of the wind. I opened my mouth several times to tell Mom about the water encroaching on the house but stopped each time. I wanted the memory of this meal to be a pleasant one.

But there came a point when we couldn't hide the trouble we were in anymore.

The wind picked up, at least five times stronger than it had before. The boys were napping on the couch, and we were in the dining room, as usual, when the house shrieked in pain. Nails torn from wood screeched and echoed through the house, and everyone's eyes widened as we looked up at the ceiling.

"What was that?" Mom asked a moment before Yasahiro popped up and ran toward the back of the house. He swore loudly, something I hardly ever heard him do.

My body cooled and slowed down as I forced myself after him. I didn't want to see what had happened. Yasahiro was closing the door to my room as I rounded the corner of the hall-way. Water spit from under the door, and the door rattled in the wind.

"We need to get any valuables out of these rooms now!" Yasahiro stood at Hirata's old room, my nephews' current room, wind and rain buffeting him.

Yuna gasped behind me, her hand at her mouth.

"Trash bags! In the kitchen!" Mom hustled away, and Yuna went to grab Korota, the older of the two boys.

"Come help," she insisted. Korota drew himself up and got right in the mix. He was pretty brave for a nine-year-old.

Yasahiro tossed anything he found out into the hallway, and Korota ran it all to safety inside the house. Yuna opened her room, and the wind nearly knocked us over, slamming us into the other wall of the hallway. My heart skipped as I saw what used to be my room totally open to the sky. Wind and rain filled the room, but Yuna ran in. She grabbed a bag from the closet, swept everything still on top of the dresser into the bag, snatched a few more pieces of clothing from the drawers, and ran back out. We slid the door closed, but it rattled fiercely, and I wasn't sure if it would hold.

Out in the main room, we paused to take stock. My hair was curled around my head, and my heart beat at twice its normal pace, and Yuna looked to be in the same state. Mom threw everything Yasahiro and Korota had salvaged into trash bags and tied them up.

"How bad is it, Yasahiro?" she asked as he appeared out of the hallway. His face was pale, and he was wet from the top of his head to his waist.

"Bad. We should figure out some way to keep the rain from coming into the rest of the house through these two rooms."

"If only we had sandbags," I lamented.

Mom blinked a few times before perking up. "We have about forty kilos of rice. There's no way I'm evacuating it out of here, so we might as well use it for this."

"Right. Good idea," Yuna interrupted. "Let's fill some garbage bags with rice and put them on the floor in front of the door."

Yasahiro grimaced. "I don't know if it's necessary."

"What do you mean?" Mom asked.

We all paused as the wind picked up even more, and a low groaning moan echoed through the house followed by a smash and a car alarm going off outside.

"Uh oh." Yasahiro sighed as we turned to face the front of the house.

Those sounds combined only meant one thing.

I followed Yasahiro to the front door, and he looked out the side window facing the driveway. One of the many pine trees outside that framed the driveway was no longer standing and instead had flattened Yasahiro's car.

"Looks like we're going to need a new one of those." He grabbed his keys from the pocket of his raincoat hanging next to the door and silenced the alarm.

I looked out the window and panicked again at the sight of the cars in half a meter deep water. It's not like we could've driven them out of here anyway, and their engines were probably waterlogged.

"Mom, you have to come see this," I said, my voice monotone and grave. I stepped away from the door so she could look out. Her hand gripped the doorjamb, her knuckles turning white as she took in the view.

The flooding was up around the top step of the porch which meant that the entire underbelly of the house was in the water as well.

"I give it an hour before the house floods," I whispered to Yasahiro, Mom, and Yuna. "I think we're about to hit the eye of the storm, what with the wind picking up and the rain increasing. Then we still have the other side of the storm to consider if it doesn't weaken or turn."

I'd have given anything for internet access or a generator right then. Mom didn't even have a radio with batteries. Her last one died when it fell off the kitchen counter during a small earthquake. She never replaced it.

Yuna twisted her hands. "We need options."

"Let's try to save any valuables in garbage bags, plus any food or water in the plastic bins Mom uses throughout the house." I point to a few in the main room. "Unless they're already keeping something expensive, we empty them out and fill them up with the things we'll need in case it's a few days before we're rescued, or the water recedes so we can walk out of here. There's no way these cars are going to drive again."

We scuttled through the house, using the flashlights to light our way and gather up anything valuable. Mom emptied her plastic bins she kept bed linens in, and we used them for food, important documents, and the computer. The linens went into garbage bags, and anything else we thought to pack away, like clothing, got bagged up and piled on the beds.

Mimoji meowed from his cat carrier, both wanting to be out and curious about all our activity. Since I was sure everyone would evacuate to our apartment, I packed his wet and dry food plus a small bag of litter into a garbage bag as well. As soon as we were done packing, we let him use his litter box in the bathroom and then back into the cat carrier. The last thing we needed was a loose cat when we were in this situation.

Finally, it was only a matter of time before the bathroom stopped working, so we all washed up and used it, tiptoeing past the shaking bedroom doors.

Sitting around listening to the storm, my imagination ran at racing speed. I pictured the house, picked up and thrown into the sky Wizard of Oz style, twirling around and landing in the next town over. The walls shook enough for me to believe this was possible. Then my next daydream was more of a day nightmare as I envisioned all of us on the failing roof, scrambling to stay out of epic floodwaters with helicopters hovering overhead. I tried to banish these thoughts from my head, but then all I saw was Ria, dead and buried in Akiko's backfields. How did she die? I didn't want to know right then when it was possible this typhoon would kill us all.

As the sun began to set, water seeped up through the floors of the living room and the kitchen. We took the cushions from the couch and put them on the dining room table, draping dry linens over the table and cushions. The table was the most stable piece of furniture and the highest point in the house now since the dining room was raised up one step for the footwell.

Mom reached over and held my hand for a long moment. "You were right, and I was wrong. This is my punishment for trying to convince you to work on the farm when you didn't want to," she whispered.

I hushed her. "Mom, don't be dramatic. It's a typhoon. It's not some divine influence come to do you harm. Besides, I wanted to work on the farm. I just didn't want to give up the tea shop."

Yasahiro peeked over the top of Mom, and I popped a short smile to him.

"Don't worry about it. We'll stick together, and everything will be fine." Our roles were reversed. These were things Mom used to say to me, and now I was saying them to her.

Yuna curled up with the boys, and Mom, Yasahiro, and I drifted in and out of sleep, listening to the howling winds and hoping for rescue as soon as the storm ended.

We couldn't do anything else.

CHAPTER
THIRTY

"Mei! Tsukiko!"

My body ached liked someone had kicked me in every available soft spot, and I groaned as I came back to consciousness. I'd spent much of the night awake, the baby fluttering around inside of me, wanting attention... or snacks. It was hard to say. But no one was going anywhere as the water seeped up through the floor and covered most of the house.

"What?" I asked out loud, neither asleep nor awake. Who was calling for me?

A bright light cut through the slats of the typhoon shutters, and the low rumbling of an engine, the first man-made sound we'd heard in twelve hours, purred outside.

Yasahiro stirred beside me, and Yushin, the younger of my two nephews, was already awake.

"There's someone outside," he said, pointing at the window.

I rubbed my eyes as I took in the dining room around me. About twenty centimeters of water covered the floor. Bits of paper and other random objects floated along past the open door to the rest of the house. Weak light illuminated the living room and all the water in there.

What an absolute mess.

In all my years growing up in this house, this had never happened. We'd experienced earthquakes that knocked over bookcases and snows that once collapsed the roof over the kitchen. But this was an extraordinary amount of damage.

"Mei!"

I breathed a huge sigh of relief when I realized Goro was on the other side of the wall. Yasahiro sat up next to me and rubbed his eyes as well.

Grabbing the giant flashlight, I knocked the end against the dining room wall. It was a stretch for me to reach it, but the knocks were firm and loud.

"We're in the dining room! Take the shutters off the window!"

Goro swore on the other side, but it was a compassionate and relieved swear. "Thank Buddha you're still alive. My mom would've killed me if something happened to you. Hold on!"

"What's going on?" Yuna asked, sitting up with a yawn. "Is someone here?"

"I think we're being rescued," I said, a smile widening my face.

The house protested as Goro and whoever was with him pried the typhoon shutters off and let in the weak light of dawn. I gasped when I saw him because I wasn't prepared to see him in fly-fishing waders up to his chest and water not that far below him. The water level outside was higher than it was inside and the bottom portion of the window held back hundreds of liters of dirty, brown floodwaters. But Goro shimmied off the window anyway and let more water in. Might as well.

"Look at what we have here. Morning," he said, his wry smile making me laugh despite the situation. Next to him, other police officers, men I didn't know, worked to pry more of the typhoon shutters off. They must have called in reinforcements from other prefectures to help.

Beyond Goro, a small gray boat most people used for fishing puttered and waited for us with Akiko looking on. Kirin whined in her portable carrier next to her.

"Thank goodness," Akiko said, blowing out a big breath. "My house stayed dry, but that was about it," she called out. "I'm lucky that my house is on a hill. But my car is totaled, I have no electricity, and my plumbing stopped working about five hours ago." She looked disheveled and weary, and I assumed we were the same. "Kayo's going to take me in until the floods recede, and we get power back."

"And you all are expected back home. My mother is worried sick." Goro held out his hand to me, but I waved him off.

"Take Yuna and the boys first. We have valuables too, over on the couch."

"Mei, you're pregnant," he insisted.

"I'm well aware. Take Yuna and the boys first. I'm not leaving without Mom and my husband."

He sighed, and I felt sure that someone back at the station, probably Kayo, gave him strict instructions on "women and children first, plus pregnant ladies."

Yuna gathered up their belongings, and Goro and the men made a delivery chain outside to pass the bags to the boat. Then each of the boys and Yuna got a piggyback ride out. I waved goodbye to them all and Akiko as they puttered off toward town.

"It should take about twenty minutes round trip, so hold tight," Goro said, wading past us. "I'll retrieve your belongings."

As I watched Goro make his way into the flooded house, I gave Mom a giant hug.

"Mom, I'm so sorry about the house. I don't know what to say."

"Neither do I." She glanced around forlornly, her forehead pinched.

"Let's not say anything until we figure out how bad off we are," Yasahiro suggested.

It warmed my heart to hear how Yasahiro still considered this *our* situation. It wasn't Mom's hardship. It was ours.

Goro moved the belongings we were saving to the dining room table as we waited for the boat to return. Though the storm had passed, the air outside still held the late summer moisture hostage and the clouds raced by. The sun tried to climb out of its bed for the night, and I yawned in response.

"What time is it?" I asked Goro as he piled the last of the garbage bags on the table.

"Six-forty, or thereabouts. We mobilized around four once the majority of the storm passed." He whistled. "It was quite a doozy. Biggest typhoon this area has seen in almost a hundred years. It strengthened to a category two right before landfall, so it had a lot of wind and rain saved up to dump on us. Wait till you see the center of town." He shook his head, and I swallowed, wishing I had a hot cup of coffee and something to eat. I was feeling nauseous for the first time since my first trimester.

"Well, while we wait for the boat to come back, tell us about town," Mom politely demanded.

Goro's mouth twisted to the side. "The good news is that Sawayaka is fine. Water managed to get in the front, but the main dining area and kitchen are dry. Ana is there now with anyone who could come in. Oshabe-cha and your building are on a slight hill, so that whole neighborhood was spared, I'm happy to say. Our townhouse is also fine as is Kutsuro Matsu. But electricity is out town-wide, and many sewage systems are backed up by the sheer amount of water that came down." He wiped his face with a handkerchief he pulled out of his shirt pocket from beneath the waders. "Manholes all over town are gushing water. It's a mess. Train service has been suspended even."

"Wow. I don't remember the last time train service was suspended to this area." The damage must be particularly severe to have that happen.

I kept quiet for a few minutes while Mom asked after Goro's

mom, Chiyo, Kumi, and Taiga. They were all fine and worried about us, but otherwise unharmed. But in the back of my mind, Ria sat there tapping her foot. What about her?

Out the window, the boat was returning to take us to dry land.

"So..." I started slowly, drawing out the word. "Watanabe."

Goro turned around and raised his eyebrows at me. "You must have some sixth sense for these things, Mei. He ran."

"Ran?" I exchanged glances with Yasahiro.

"I don't know if he figured that this was the best time for an escape or what, but he took off, first with the police car and then on his own. We have police in from Tokyo tracking him down."

I looked out past the approaching boat to the drowned fields beyond Akiko's house. Ria was out there somewhere, now almost lost to the floods and mud of the typhoon.

"What did you tell the chief?" I asked him, eager for any news.

"Everything I could remember from you — that the kids saw him out there and you found a dead body where he had been. That's about it. If anything, they want to talk to him about deserting his post and leaving you all in danger. But I know in my gut" — Goro jabbed himself with his index finger — "that no one runs unless they're guilty of something. And he's always struck me as the guilty type. He was constantly asking about you, what you knew of Tama's case, and a bunch of other things. I always thought it was just morbid curiosity. Now I see it was much worse."

We worked in silence, loading the boat up with our valuables. Mom got a piggyback ride to the boat from one of the other officers, and I rode on Goro's back. It struck me that this was not the first time he had done this for me. He'd carried me when I was injured after going after Amanda's murderer.

Yasahiro refused to be carried. He got in the water and helped rearrange everything so we'd all fit.

"Wait a second," he said, raising his finger in the air. He waded back inside and reappeared a moment later with my painting, the one that had hung in the dining room for over ten years. My eyes watered as he handed it to me and climbed in.

"I always loved this one."

I thought I had been all cried out, but tears filled my eyes as we pulled away from the house.

"Oh, Mom," I groaned, doubled over. "I'm so sorry. Look what's happened to our home."

I reached over and took Mom's hand between my own. If we hadn't been in the boat, I would've hugged her.

"I know I've been an awful daughter, and I never told you how much this place has meant to me."

"Mei," Yasahiro whispered behind me, but I shook my head at him.

"Nothing in the world means more to me than this house and this land. This is where I grew up and where I wanted to grow old." I wiped the tears from my cheeks. "I have faint memories of Dad eating in the kitchen. I remember wearing my first party dress in the dining room with Akiko. And I wanted to have all those same memories with my kids there. I figured you didn't want to be separated from your family as you got older, and this would've been our chance to help make up for all the trouble I caused last winter. I'm sorry you felt like you had to go to Hirata for help." I squeezed her hand as she stared at me. "I'm absolutely devastated by what's happened this week and now."

Shamed by having Goro witness my breakdown in the boat, I bent over and pressed my forehead to our clasped hands. Mom smoothed out my hair and kissed the top of my head.

"Mei, I had no idea you felt so strongly about the house."

I sobbed a little louder and then sucked in a quick breath to stop it.

"I'm... I'm sorry things worked out this way," Mom said, leaning by my ear.

I waited for the excuse, the excuse that always followed an apology from Mom, but it didn't come.

"Sit up and look at me." Mom tugged on our joined hands, so I sat up. "Your husband here is a good man, and he stuck up for you when you needed it. I had no right to be so harsh with you. I thought about it all night, and" — she turned her head from me, ashamed — "I was wrong about the things I said. You haven't wanted a convenient life; you just wanted a fair one. Yuna reminded me of all the pain you've gone through, and still, you help people. That's something to be proud of."

Mom nodded as she patted my cheeks.

"I'm not sure what will happen with the house and the land now, but I promise to be kinder to you." She turned to look at Yasahiro. "I promise."

He smiled kindly. "We love you, Mom. We'll make it through this."

I glanced at Goro with embarrassed eyes, but he smiled back, his words from the other day echoing in my head. *"We love our families, but nothing is more important than being happy with your role in the universe... Your mother needs a push in the right direction."* Too bad that push had to be the size of a category two typhoon.

The boat ran aground about a hundred meters from the gas station on the edge of town where the land rose enough to keep the waters from the lower farm fields at bay. I was grateful to see friendly faces from the police station and other volunteers from in town helping load up vans with our belongings. Akiko waited for us, sitting on the open end of a van and drinking a hot cup of coffee. Kirin was asleep in the carrier next to her. As I waved to Akiko, she grabbed another cup for me.

I let the others unload the boat and went to sit beside her. She handed me the steaming cup of coffee, rich with cream and sugar, and I decided today was my day for a little indulgence. I deserved it after last night.

Akiko sighed as she looked out at the water leading away to our side of town.

"I just spoke with Senahara. They picked him up this morning before me." Senahara was our only other neighbor out in the farmlands beyond town, and he had saved Akiko and me from burning in the barn last year. "He's selling to Midori Sankaku. They offered to buy his house and land a month ago, and supposing they still want it in this state, he's going to sell it to them."

I pursed my lips and nodded. "That's probably the smart thing to do. He's getting old, and a smaller place would be better for him."

"He said he'll get an apartment in the assisted living place on the north side of town. He'll make enough from Midori Sankaku to pay for the place until he passes. His words, not mine," she said, holding her hands up. I was sure I was a shade paler than usual. I hated talking about death. There was too much of it between my elderly patients and the murder cases the last year.

"So, here's where I tell you, I'm going to sell my house and land too if I can get Midori Sankaku to buy it." Akiko winced and pulled back from me, freezing in place. Did she think I was going to attack her? Instead, I sighed and deflated.

"I think it's a good idea. You fought hard for the land and what you deserved, but..."

"But it's too full of bad memories and now" — she dropped her voice — "there may be a dead body out back."

"There *is* a dead body out back. I saw it for myself, and I'm pretty sure it's Ria."

Akiko's jawline tightened. "I just know I'm going to be called in for questioning on this."

"We'll see," I replied. The killer, as far as I was concerned, was on the run and guilty as the day was long. "Where will you move to?"

"The other side of town, if I can swing it. I'd like to buy a small house or a condo, and there are some being renovated for the new Midori Sankaku workers moving here. I'll have to ask about them."

This would mean Mom would be the only one left on this side of town. I didn't like the idea of her and Yuna and the kids out there all alone, and then I remembered the house. My heart ached knowing it was unsalvageable. What would Hirata say when we told him what had happened?

CHAPTER
THIRTY-ONE

The ride through town was disheartening. Overnight, Chikata had become a veritable dystopia of damage and decay. Several buildings were missing their roofs, the clay tiles smashed in the streets. Tree limbs and leaves cluttered the sidewalks, and people were cutting them to pieces with gardening shears. Looking down one side street, water gushed from a manhole and men hefted sandbags around it to direct the water away from the buildings. We even passed an NHK reporter, live on the scene, interviewing someone in front of her business that was soaked with floodwaters.

Sickness bubbled up inside of me, wondering how long it would take to recover, but then we turned the corner to our street and a TEPCO van, its bucket extended to the electricity pole, was repairing the power lines up and down the street. Someday they would have to bury them to prevent this from happening, but the town never had money for that sort of thing before. Maybe the power would be back on soon.

I sighed in relief when we pulled up to Oshabe-cha and the apartment. The streets and sidewalks were wet, but everything appeared to be okay. The whole block felt quiet without electricity, but people stood outside talking or sweeping. Once the power came back, everything would return to normal.

"See? All good here. But you'll want to check your roof," Goro said, as he parked the van and unlocked the doors. One of the other police officers popped out and opened the door for me, offering his hand to help me out. I accepted, grateful for the assistance. Sleeping on top of a dining room table, almost twenty weeks pregnant, hadn't been comfortable or restful. I was dead tired.

"This is where you live?" Yuna asked, and I realized she had never been to Yasahiro's place or ever visited the tea shop.

"Yeah, come inside. We'll get you and the boys a futon soon." I glanced past Yuna to Mom, and Mom nodded at me.

"I'll go to Chiyo's house with Mimoji," she said, which I saw coming a hundred kilometers away. She and Chiyo were inseparable.

Goro tried to hide a sigh. "The more, the merrier," he mumbled. Chiyo, Goro, Kumi, and Taiga all lived together in one townhouse. It was a decent size place (palatial compared to Tokyo) but not a house. They would be climbing the walls before long. "Everybody be sure to rest and bathe. I'll be back later to help out."

We said goodbye at the door as the vans drove off. Yuna watched them go with her arms crossed and a worried look on her face.

"I don't want us to be a bother to you, Yasahiro, Mei." Yuna picked up as many bags as she could carry.

"You won't be a bother." Yasahiro opened the door for us all. "We're happy to help."

"I..." Yuna's voice sputtered to a stop as she grasped my arm. "We should talk."

"Don't worry," I assured her. "It can wait." I figured she wanted to convince us she and the boys wouldn't stay long, that

Hirata would be back to help, etcetera, but she shook her head vehemently.

"No. We need to talk now."

———

THE SUN CRESTED THE TOPS OF THE BUILDINGS IN THE EAST as we opened up the apartment. Without the air conditioning on, the place was stuffy and warm, so we slid open a few windows and let the soft breezes leftover from the typhoon clear out the stale air.

"It's a beautiful apartment," Yuna said, bowing as she entered and ushered the boys inside. "Don't touch anything," she whispered to them, but I waved my hand in response.

"Boys, don't worry about anything. Claim a spot on the couch, and we'll cook up some breakfast before a very early nap time."

They both nodded and dragged themselves to the couch.

Yuna chewed on her lip as she set her bag on the table. "How long do you think we'll be here?"

Yasahiro and I eyed each other before he excused himself to what he did best, cooking.

"I'm not sure. We can house you here for as long as necessary, but I think you'll find the space cramped for all of us. We'll have to look for temporary housing until..." I thought about it for a moment. "Well, until we figure out what to do about the house."

"Right. The house."

We both sat across from each other at the table.

"Let's face it," I said, rubbing my forehead. "The house is a complete loss. Not only did we lose it, but we also lost a good deal of produce for the winter. I'm not sure how we'll come back now. I've lived through lean winters, and this would beat them all, especially without a house."

I was emotionally dried up and worn out. I couldn't even cry anymore. Confessing to Mom and having us patch things up had taken every last bit of strength I had.

Yuna ran her fingers through her hair. "I haven't spoken to Hirata yet, but..."

She stopped again, and irritation warred with sympathy in my head.

"What is it, Yuna?"

"The loan wasn't final yet. It still needed two more weeks and an inspection before it was finalized."

I groaned and rested my head on the table.

"There's no way the bank will approve the loan now. And our house hasn't sold yet either. We moved some items here, but the rest are back in Chiba."

I almost laughed, but I kept it in. The sheer unfairness of the situation and what we had already been through broke down any last bit of politeness I'd stored up in me.

"Aren't you lucky? You and Hirata just managed to dodge a catastrophe. Now you can go home and restart your life where you left off, and Mom and I will stay here to pick up the pieces, just like always." My voice tasted bitter, and I immediately regretted being so unsympathetic. I should've kept my mouth shut.

But this was what Hirata did. He moved away when we were poor and struggling. He succeeded when we failed. He had all the luck in life, and we had very little. He didn't do it maliciously, but he did it, all the same.

"Mei," Yasahiro admonished me, and Yuna broke into tears.

"I didn't want this!" she cried, tears coursing down her cheeks. "I didn't want Mom to lose her house or for all of our plans to go so badly. I feel terrible!"

I sighed and cursed myself. "I apologize, Yuna." I reached across the table and squeezed her hand. Sweet woman that she was, she squeezed back. "That was thoughtless and mean of me. I'm so sorry."

Even so, I imagined her packing up everything they had left and hightailing it back to Chiba where I wouldn't see them again until the next family holiday. I couldn't blame them for leaving, honestly, even though I felt that Yuna had started to like her new life in the few days she'd had as a farmer.

"It may have been mean, but it was the truth." She sniffed up. "There's no way Hirata will go through with this now. What will we do?"

She looked up at Yasahiro standing at my back. He rested his hand on my shoulder.

"I'm not sure," he said, "but we'll think of something."

———

THE GAS WAS WORKING IN THE APARTMENT WHICH MEANT Yasahiro could still cook, and the hot water heater was on so we could all bathe, which we did immediately. I slipped into the hot bath, savoring every moment of the quiet time while I had it. Yuna had washed up both kids and taken them outside to help with the neighborhood clean up. Last I saw them out the window, they were gathering fallen branches and pulling them into piles to be picked up and shredded.

"I've pulled the quiche out of the oven, and there's salad, too," Yasahiro said, peeking his head in the door to the bathroom. "I'm going to head over to Sawayaka now to assess the damage."

He looked as tired as I felt.

"Okay. Come back for a nap later, or you may die of sleep deprivation."

He rolled his eyes. "This is nothing. You should've seen me in culinary school. I barely slept an hour a night then, for months at a time." His face softened with the memories. "You take it easy. You're the one carrying a baby."

"Right, right." I waved to him. "I'll see you later."

"And we'll talk about what to do about your mom then, too,"

he called out from the other room. The door clicked closed not long after.

Yeah. What *would* we do about my mom? I sank down into the water, letting it come up to my chin. I had no idea. For once, I was at a loss. When I thought we'd help Mom, we had planned to knock the house down anyway and put up a new one. But that was before the Hirata mess and the typhoon, and now we'd lost all the crops as well in the flooding. I doubted many of them would survive, and I wasn't sure how long it would take for the flood waters to recede either.

After our heartfelt apologies, Mom had been quiet on the way back to town on the boat, squinting her eyes out at the water and not saying a word. If she had strong thoughts on what she wanted to do next, she wasn't telling anyone until she was ready.

When I entered the bedroom after my bath, Ria's red sketchbook on my bedside table caught my eye right away. I'd never finished the manga! I became so caught up with finding photos of Watanabe and then the typhoon that *After School* slipped out of my thoughts.

I dried off, dressed, and sat down on the bed to enjoy the rest of the manga. I felt I owed it to Ria. Even though I'd found Ria and knew she was dead, it would take days for the police to locate her in that watery landscape, and we had to catch Watanabe. There were still missing motives and unanswered questions. Maybe the manga could answer them?

Opening the sketchbook, I found my place again and raced through the drama. Shizuka was fretting over her affair with the boyfriend's best friend. She wanted to come out and tell the boyfriend, Hiromi. Kuro, the clandestine lover, cautioned that it was dangerous. Hiromi was way too jealous and controlling for that ever to work out.

Kuro hovered over Shizuka in the hallway after class was over.

"This is a bad idea. I think he'll go crazy. You've never seen him mad like I have," Kuro said.

"Yes, I have. He's always angry over his sister and father getting everything they want," Shizuka countered. "We should tell him now and get it over with."

Something about the way Ria had drawn Kuro niggled at me. He was tall and skinny, his shaggy hair always in his face.

Come to think of it, if Ria had put a cigarette in his fingers, this guy could've been Kohei Watanabe.

I stopped reading and flipped back through the manga. Now that I knew what Kohei had looked like as a teen, this Kuro was a dead ringer for him. And Kuro meant "black," a color Kohei wore all the time in his teens if Akai's photos were any indication.

I returned to my place, watching the drama play out. Shizuka went out on a date with Hiromi where she confessed to him that she didn't love him anymore. I thought the poor guy would be crushed. He *had* doted on her quite a bit during the length of the story.

But no. Ria had drawn him cold and distant. He withdrew so completely and easily that I actually got a chill.

"No one loses attention this quickly," he said, as Shizuka backed away from him. "You were fine the other day."

"I was pretending. I'm sorry. I didn't realize you'd be hurt."

"I'm not hurt."

And anyone who read the manga would know he wasn't hurt, he was angry. Vengeful. Ria had captured the emotion so perfectly, his state of mind jumped off the page at me.

I flipped the page, eager to see what happened next, but I was met with nothing. The rest of the sketchbook was empty despite my furious flipping of the pages.

Closing the sketchbook, I huffed a sigh and set it aside.

What was Ria's point? That the boyfriend, Hiromi, got mad enough to hurt or murder Shizuka? Did he confront Kuro?

I had too many questions, and my viewpoint of the whole situation flipped, changed in an instant.

What if Ria had been dating someone, someone other than Itsuki, but then she was having an affair with Kohei on the side? If the manga was the major clue, it wasn't Kohei who killed Ria. It was the boyfriend.

Panic surged through my aching chest again.

Oh no. It was the boyfriend, not the lover who killed Ria.

Who was the boyfriend?

I groaned as I laid down. Two steps forward and one step back.

But Kohei knew where Ria had been buried.

Either way, he had been involved, and when the police found him, I would confront him if it was the last thing I did.

CHAPTER
THIRTY-TWO

woke up in the fetal position on the bed, curled around the red sketchbook and my phone. It took me a few seconds to realize I was awake because the power had returned. Yay! Cool air wafted down on me from the air conditioning unit on the wall, and the boys in the other room cheered. I definitely couldn't be mad about them waking me because I was pretty happy about it myself.

Lying in bed, I took a minute to wake up, stretching and trying to reboot my brain. I turned on my phone, hoping the wifi and internet connection would be on. I was eager to see what had happened on the news, especially since NHK had been in town interviewing people.

But my phone rang in my hand. It was Goro.

"Good news! You have power again," he roared into the phone. I had to pull it away from my ear so I wouldn't go deaf.

"Yeah, we have power. I think it just came back. I was taking a nap." I yawned for good measure.

"Well, I hear there are only a few more streets to be taken care of. I just checked on Akai, and her place doesn't even look like it saw a typhoon. There are branches down in her yard, but she says all of her UPS's stayed up, and her generator kicked on right away. Plus she's on the side of town closer to the mountain so no flooding."

"What's a UPS?" I asked, still trying to wake up.

"They're like big batteries for computers. Anyway, the other good news I have is that Tokyo Metro Police nabbed Kohei Watanabe at Haneda about an hour ago."

I sat up in bed, and my stomach growled. "At Haneda? Was he trying to flee the country?"

"He had a plane ticket for Okinawa."

"Wow."

"Yeah. We'll have him back in the precinct in a few hours. Want to come by while we interrogate him? The chief said it's okay for you to be there."

"What kind of question is that? Of course, I do." I giggled, letting my imagination run wild with what he would say.

"Great. I'll send Kayo to get you around 15:00."

I hung up, finally feeling like things may work out for us. The power was back on, and the police found Kohei. What was next?

Lunch, apparently.

I exited the bedroom in time to see Yuna and Yasahiro bring rice to the table.

"Oh good! You're up," Yasahiro said, coming over to give me a kiss on the forehead. "I didn't want to wake you to eat, but I knew you had to eat. Catch-22," he appended in English.

"And the power's back on!" Korota smiled from his spot at the table. "We spent all morning helping outside. Everyone here is so nice."

"Well, that's good to hear." I sat in my usual place at the table and surveyed the lunch selection, soft-boiled eggs, broiled mackerel, steamed greens, rice, and pickles. My mouth watered. "How are all of my neighbors?" I asked him, wondering if he had run into anyone outside while I was sleeping.

His eyes lifted to the ceiling. "Hmmm, your next-door neighbor, the cobbler..."

"Hasé," I filled in.

"Yes. He says his shop is fine, and his home had no damage either. A branch went through one window of his parent's house, but they're fine too. He said you know them."

"I do," I replied, filling up my bowl with rice, greens, and fish. "I'll have to check up on them soon. They're the ones who gifted me the cups for the tea shop downstairs."

"And your other neighbor, Mrs. Murata, is fine, and her apartment is as well," Yuna said, helping the boys with their lunches. "She had one leak from the roof in the kitchen, but her landlord has come by to fix it."

The buzzer rang right then. Were we expecting someone?

"That's probably your mom." Yasahiro sprinted to the door to buzz her in. He left the door ajar, and Mom walked in a minute later.

She looked good, especially after everything that had happened the night before. She must have showered and had a nap just like I did because her hair was swept up in a twist and her skin was bright and shiny.

Everyone stood up to greet her, and the boys wrapped her in big hugs. I pulled out the seat at the opposite end of the head of the table for her and grabbed her a bowl and a set of chopsticks.

"Mom, you look well. I'm so pleased," I said, sitting to her left.

"It's amazing what a shower and a nap can do for you." She smiled at me, actually smiled with warmth and love. This was something I hadn't seen in a long time. I was almost knocked out of my chair by it.

"Before we eat, I'd like to take a moment to make some... announcements, though that's really not the proper word for it."

Korota and Yushin both sighed as they set their chopsticks down, their eyes on their bowls. Mom laughed.

"Okay, you boys can eat while the adults talk." Mom brought her hands to prayer position and chimed, *"Itadakimasu!"* and we all said it too. The boys dug into their bowls.

"What's going on, Mom?" Yasahiro asked. He pushed his glasses up his nose and gave her his full attention.

"I spoke with Hirata as soon as I could get through on the phone. I knew last night we were in major trouble, but this morning, seeing the floodwaters stretch out from the house, I came to a final decision. Hirata will withdraw his offer to buy the farm business. The loan wouldn't have gone through anyway now that there's significant damage to the property."

"I'm so sorry," Yuna said, bowing her head. "This was not what we wanted."

"I know," Mom assured her, handling this whole situation a lot more gracefully than I did earlier. "You can't predict the weather or the wrath of the *kami* anymore than you can predict who will win a race."

"So... What now?" I asked because there weren't many alternatives.

"Well..." Mom hesitated, and I held my breath. "The flood insurance will not pay for much. It'll only cover about five percent of the damage for the house, and then I don't think we'll get anything for the damage to the crops. There's some federal insurance, and then there's the private insurance." She sighed before taking a sip of water. "It'll be drawn out and complicated, and all the while, I'll be without a place to live. So, I called Midori Sankaku."

I realized I was still holding my breath, so I let it out slowly and looked down the table to Yasahiro. Oh no. He was frozen, waiting.

"They've been politely hounding me once a month, every month for the last year. They send someone by to talk, and I always told them no, I would not sell the land. Today I told them yes, and they accepted. They don't care about the flooding because they have big plans for the whole area, anyway. Rice and other crops I never wanted to do because they're too labor-intensive."

"You sold the house and land?" My eyes widened as her statements sank in. My home — our home — sold?

"I did. The house, the land, and all my assets there I promised to sell to Midori Sankaku." She nodded once. "I would never get such a good deal now that the land is damaged and the house as well. I figured this was my best way out of the whole mess, and I couldn't sell the property to you either, Mei. It would've set you and Yasahiro back way too far. Too much of a burden." She reached over and squeezed my hand. "I need to say this in front of everyone. I know I gave you grief about having your wedding at the house this summer, and I regret the things I said. I'm sorry."

I pulled back in surprise. My mom hardly ever apologized for anything, much less repeated those apologies in front of others. This was unprecedented. I held her hand in mine.

"I'm glad you were married there, and we'll have those fond memories and photos to look at when the house is gone."

My heart swelled with joy, though it ached. My wedding had been lovely, and I was doubly glad I'd had the ceremony and reception at the family home, that was for sure. I would still miss the house and the land though. A lot.

Yuna blinked a few times. "Where will you live? Would you like to move to Chiba with us? We have room for you, if we still have a house, that is." She blushed, perhaps realizing she needed to talk to her husband, soon.

"No, darling. Though thank you for the offer." Mom bobbed her head at Yuna. "I want to stay here in Chikata. This is my home. I couldn't live anywhere else."

Yasahiro stood up, gesturing for Mom's bowl. She handed it to him, and he filled it with hot rice. "Well, then, I have a new proposal."

Mom's face fell into a frown. "I feel bad we won't be able to implement your CSA idea at the farm. The proposal had been growing on me, and I know you worked hard on it."

Yasahiro shrugged. "It's nothing to worry about. I may use the idea again some other day. I have a new idea and an alternative idea as well. Mei and I are going to buy two adjacent vacant lots on the north side of town." He smiled down the table at me. "We're planning to combine them, build a new house and have a large garden there. We'd be honored if you'd come live with us."

"This is a great idea," Yuna said, brightening as she filled her bowl with food. "I love it, Mom."

"Well..." Mom drew out the one syllable into many. "I do think it's a great idea, but what will you do with this apartment?"

"Hmmm, we weren't sure yet. Maybe rent it out?"

Mom locked eyes with Yasahiro. He got the hint right away.

"Or, if you'd like to keep your independence for the foreseeable future, you could live here when we move. The stairs may become a problem eventually, but otherwise, everything is on one level." He glanced around the open space. "I'd hate to see this place with a stranger."

I laughed, tears forming in the corner of my eyes. "Oh good. I'd wondered how I would run the tea shop with someone I didn't know living above it. I like this idea much better."

"Then it's settled. This apartment is yours once we move." Yasahiro nodded once, the deal done.

"What will you do once the house is sold? For work?" Yuna asked as we all tucked into our meals.

"Oh, I'm not sure," Mom said, but there was a twinkle in her eye I hadn't seen in a long time. "I have to deal with my glaucoma and possibly surgery for that."

Right. The road ahead would be rocky, but at least we'd be together.

Mom smiled at us all. "But with my family surrounding me, I'm bound to come up with something."

CHAPTER
THIRTY-THREE

thought this would be easy — roll into the police station with Kayo, check in with Goro, and then watch the police interrogation from the other side of the one-way glass. I've heard police interrogations in Japan can be rough. Unlike the American TV shows I've watched where people can request a lawyer right away, that's not the way it is here, and Japanese police routinely get confessions from their suspects before the lawyers even show up.

"Hold up," Goro warned me as I entered the station and observed the hustling activity. People were still dealing with flooded roads, downed power lines, and older people who needed to evacuate their homes. In a way, we had been pretty lucky. We had places to go in town that had survived the storm. Many others did not have that choice.

"What's the matter?" I asked him. His face was pinched with worry.

"This is not going to be what you think, Mei. I haven't been able to bring the chief up to speed on everything regarding Ria yet, so we said we were pulling him back to the station to deal with administrative matters concerning leaving his post yesterday."

I narrowed my eyes at him.

"I haven't even been able to tell the chief that the body you found was possibly Ria's. It's been a mess here with the typhoon."

"What?" My blood pressure spiked, and the baby somersaulted. "If you give Watanabe any leeway, he'll find some angle to get out of this."

Goro sighed. "He's in the conference room right now with the chief. Care to come elaborate on the situation?"

"Hmph." I pulled my bag closer to my body, stepped around Goro, and proceeded to the conference room with Goro right behind me.

The conference room was brightly lit behind the wall of glass, and I remembered how I once sat at the same table and looked at pictures of Amanda Cheung, Yasahiro's old girlfriend, dead on the side of the road.

I pushed those memories aside.

Because Kohei Watanabe was a police officer already, they decided to give him the benefit of the doubt about deserting his post, obviously. He sat at the conference room table, a cup of coffee and a doughnut at his elbow, and he laughed with the chief.

Easy? I thought this would be easy? Try completely infuriating.

I approached the glass and stood on the other side watching them. They ignored me until anger sent me over the edge, and I rapped on the glass with my knuckle.

The chief smiled at me, but Kohei's face fell. Not happy to see me? I wouldn't be either if I were in his position. Upon being waved into the room, I opened the door and joined the chief on his side of the table. Goro sat at the end of the table nearest the door.

"It's good to see you, Miss Yama... Er, it's Mrs. Suga, now isn't it?" The chief rose from his seat, and we bowed to each other.

"It is. Thank you for allowing me to come down here today to talk to Kohei."

"Of course," he said, hesitating slightly. I wasn't sure if he had been briefed on everything I'd been doing regarding Ria, but he was about to find out.

"May I?" I gestured to the seat next to the chief, and he beckoned me to sit. I shifted into the chair, bent over and pulled Ria's red sketchbook from my bag, setting it on the table in front of me. Kohei's face paled by ten shades.

"Chief, I don't know if you know this, but I've been keen on solving a mystery that has plagued this town for over a decade."

He raised his eyebrows at me and sat back in his chair. "I heard from Goro that you were looking into the disappearance of Ria Fukuda. Is that what this is about?"

I nodded. "Ria's father died recently, and he left his house and all of his assets to a friend of mine who I believe you know, Akai." It occurred to me right then, I didn't know Akai's last name. But there were moments when I was sure Akai wasn't even her real name, anyway. When you were named after the color "red," it was quite possible the name was an alias.

"We work with Akai all the time. She inherited the house and his assets? Lucky woman."

I glanced across the table at Kohei. Sweat beaded on his forehead.

"She did, and she asked me to help her clean out the Fukuda house, just in case there were clues as to why Ria went missing all those years ago." I placed my hands on the sketchbook. "That's when I found this."

"What is it?" the chief asked. I pushed the book towards him, and Kohei jumped out of his seat. We both looked up at him.

Goro grunted. "You should sit back down. No one asked you to leave."

I was impressed by Goro's frosty attitude, and the chief picked up on the significance of Kohei being there right away. Kohei settled back into his chair.

"What's going on?" The chief opened the manga and flipped through it. What I always liked about this man was that he never said no to evidence that was right in front of him. Sure, it had led to me being interrogated in the past, but he was far from being corrupt. He often listened to reason and would put aside his own prejudices to solve a case.

His eyes skimmed the text as I plowed on.

"This is a manga that Ria was working on at the time of her death."

"Death?" This caught the chief's attention. "I thought she was just missing."

"No. She most certainly is dead. Let me lay out the story of the last few months of her life." I cleared my throat and turned so I could look Kohei straight in the eyes. "Ria Fukuda was in her last year of high school. She was bright and talented, one of the more popular yet quiet girls in the school. She had broken up with her long time boyfriend a few months before she went missing, and though the relationship had been good, she wasn't heartbroken. In fact, she went on to date two boys afterward. One boy, she dated somewhat openly. The other was an affair, someone she dated on the side. I'm going to guess that after a fairly boring life with a promising future in front of her and a family who loved her, she hungered for something devious and reckless. Two-timing a boyfriend was just risky enough to thrill her and not get her into too much trouble. She even wrote and drew a manga about the whole affair."

I waited while the chief continued to flip through the sketchbook. When he made it to the final scenes, he slowed down. This is what I should've done right from the beginning, but I'm one of those people who never reads the ending of the book before starting it. I want to be surprised at the end.

Looking across the table at Kohei, I knew I needed to surprise him. I needed to lure him out. He loved to be better than me even if that meant manufacturing lies to keep me down. He had an intense desire to be correct and for me to be wrong.

I could work that angle.

"I've done a lot of digging the last two weeks. I met Ria's previous boyfriend, Itsuki Kato, and I've spoken to many who knew her at the time. I've pieced together the last months of her life, and it's my belief she was dating Kohei at the time of her death."

The chief startled and looked up to take in the frosty stare between Kohei and me.

"Did you know he lived here briefly during his last year of high school?" I asked the chief.

"I did know that. His father is a big name in the police department, mostly administrative roles, and he had been stationed here for six months a little over ten years ago. It was before my time. They left as soon as his posting was complete. So Watanabe was dating Ria Fukuda while living here?" he asked me before turning to Kohei. "Is this true?"

Kohei didn't answer. He pressed his lips together and waited.

"Yes, he was dating her," I provided, "and considering I saw him in the backfields behind Akiko Kano's house looking at a dead body buried there, I'll hazard a guess that he killed her when he found out she was cheating on him."

Kohei's mouth twitched, and the chief became very still.

"A guess?" the chief asked. "We don't bring people in for murder charges on guesses."

"Yes. It was just a hunch that he killed her, and I needed more evidence. I had to link him directly to Ria. So I went to the high school and looked for photos of Kohei at the time he was dating Ria, and funnily enough, I couldn't find any!" I mocked surprise, and Kohei's lips twisted, but he kept his mouth shut. The chief still looked interested.

"So I went to the local library where all the school's year-books were kept, and the pages that should've had the photos of Kohei were ripped out."

"Ripped out?" The chief briefly fumed, and I was reminded of the librarian and how upset she was.

"Ripped out, I'm sorry to say."

Kohei remained silent on the other side of the table. This was the longest time we had ever been in the same room when he hadn't mouthed off or insulted me in some way. I was close to exposing him.

"It was hard to find photos of Kohei during that time. He often blocked the camera from capturing him or moved while the picture was being taken so he'd be nothing but a blur. I suppose he was camera shy. But I found one photo of him."

I pulled out my phone, ready to turn it on and show the photo Akai had given me, when Kohei huffed.

"There's no way you have a picture of me from back then. I never allowed photos to be taken of me. I hated the camera."

I opened the photo on my phone, flipped to the last two pages of the manga and set my phone next to the panel of Shizuka telling Hiromi she was breaking up with him. It was a close match, but not as close as how she had drawn the "other man" Kuro.

This was it. I had baited him as far as I could. I didn't know who the killer was for sure, but he did. What would Kohei say?

I expected bravado, a raging firestorm of anger and curse words.

Kohei leaned forward and moved my phone off the sketch-book, his eyes flitting over the last panel. His hand shook as he flipped back a few pages and halted at the panel where Shizuka declared her love for Kuro, how she was going to break up with Hiromi, and then they'd both go off to college together.

Kohei pressed his fist to his mouth and stared at the page for a long moment.

"I never saw these last panels," Kohei whispered. "We met the day before she went missing, and she was so scared. She was sure she was in a lot of trouble, and she told me to hold onto the sketchbook. Pleaded with me to take it. But I told her no. The sketchbook was hers, and I couldn't take it from her. Where did you find it?"

I was stunned speechless for a moment. This was not the same Kohei I knew. This was a soft-spoken man on the verge of tears.

"It was buried in her backyard."

"Under the cherry tree?"

I swallowed, my throat turned into sandpaper. "Yeah."

"This" — he laughed as he picked up my phone and looked at the photo — "was unexpected. I should never have gone to that hanami party. Always too many people with cameras."

He set my phone down on the panel where Shizuka looked up into the adoring face of Kuro. "*That's* me right there. You've had it backwards."

The room was dead silent for a few moments. Then Goro blew out a long breath, rubbed his face, and sat forward. He returned my phone to me and flipped to the last page, the one where Hiromi's vengeful face stared at Shizuka.

All Goro did was point to it, and Kohei laughed.

"You all are so short-sighted. I've been telling you for months that Mei is a complete idiot, and none of you listened to me."

I bristled, and the chief said, "Hey now," but Kohei laughed again, a tear rolling down his face.

"Did you honestly believe when Tama Kano tried to kill you a year ago that that had been his first time?"

All the blood in my head drained away, and I reached over to grasp Goro's arm.

"My life ended the night he strangled Ria in the fields behind his house. He led her back there and killed her to teach me a lesson." Kohei paused, his eyes unfocused. "Then he convinced me to help bury her and keep the whole thing a secret." He laughed bitterly. "He was such a good manipulator. He was sure he could pin the murder on me, and I believed him. So I helped him bury her, and I kept quiet."

He sat back in his chair, pushing out a relieved breath and wiping his face. "I actually became a police officer, so I could watch him. I knew he'd screw up somehow, and he did with his own father. What an idiot." He shook his head before pointing at me. "I got transferred here to watch you. I heard you were good at figuring out mysteries. Haruka told me so. And I just knew you'd poke around into Tama's past, eventually. Then I saw the Midori Sankaku deal go through a few months ago, and I was afraid they'd uncover the body before I could totally discredit you."

He shrugged his shoulders, and though I had a moment where I felt bad for him, that moment evaporated in a puff of air. He'd been willing to bring me down to save himself.

"It didn't work," I said, raising my chin. "And though you may not have killed Ria, you knew who had."

Tama Kano had killed Ria Fukuda. He'd killed his father, and he'd tried to kill Akiko and me. Tama was Hiromi in the manga, and Tama had not wanted to let go of Ria Fukuda when she tried to leave him for Kohei. It made perfect sense, but it also made me sick to my stomach. When I was younger, I'd loved Tama. What kind of person did that make me?

The chief stood up. "I think it's time to go to an interrogation room, Goro. I want this confession on camera."

"Yes, sir," Goro said, and we all stood up.

The chief led out Kohei, but Goro stayed back. "Are you okay?"

I shook my head. "I don't know."

He grasped my shoulder and squeezed. "It's over now, Mei. Time to go home to that husband of yours and put your feet up. You deserve it."

While I watched him walk off to the back of the station, I

tried to feel like I deserved all the rest in the world after pulling that off, but my brain was churning through this new information.

Why was I afraid this would not be the last I'd hear of Tama Kano?

CHAPTER
THIRTY-FOUR

The late morning sun beat down on our umbrellas as Akiko, and I stood in the new Midori Sankaku parking lot that abutted to the fields in back of Akiko's house. The yellow police caution tape fluttered in the wind in front of us as we sipped on our cold bottles of water.

"This place stinks now that all the water is gone," Akiko said, wrinkling her nose. She was right. The air had a certain decaying scent to it. But if I squinted my eyes, I could see rotting squash and other produce out in the trampled grass and mud. I was sure at least half of Mom's crops were either here or floating in the river on their way to Southern Japan.

It had taken two weeks for the fields to drain from the floodwaters. Midori Sankaku had wanted to get back on track, so they did everything they could to help the water abate, but some things had to be left up to Mother Nature. Now, the heavy machinery worked around us but gave us plenty of room to wait while the police forensics unit dug out Ria's body from the muck and dirt.

"Mei, I'm so glad I've sold this place. I can't live here much longer knowing Ria was buried in the backfields all this time." A tear sprinted down Akiko's face, and she wiped it with the back of her hand. "I know it's selfish, but I need to leave this behind me."

"I completely understand."

I took a few steps to my right to look out past Akiko's house to my mom's house beyond. A local arborist had cut up the pine tree two days after the typhoon, turned it into wood chips and logs, and Yasahiro's car had been towed away. Mom and Yuna were there, cleaning out the house and loading anything worth saving into a moving van. From there, everything would go into storage until our new house was built, and Mom moved into the apartment.

"Could it be any hotter out today? I thought the heat would lessen once we were in September." Akiko fanned herself as she gazed out across the fields. "I'm giving them ten more minutes before I get back in the car with the air conditioning."

I looked out at the fields again, and this time the situation at the site looked different. Many people stood around the hole in the ground, and they all had their hands on their hips. One man took off his hat and scratched his head. A photographer snapped away with his camera.

Goro turned and walked towards us, his face dark with determination. Worry grew in my chest as he approached. Something wasn't right about his demeanor.

"Come on," he said, lifting the yellow tape and urging us underneath it. "Your presence has been requested."

"By whom?" I asked, following him.

He didn't answer, so I just shrugged my shoulders at Akiko, and we continued behind him. Everyone parted to let us join them at the rim of the hole, whispering to each other as we stepped up to see what they saw.

I gasped, and my hand flew to my mouth. Akiko groaned and squatted down into a ball.

There were three bodies in the hole. Not one.

I opened my mouth to talk, and nothing came out. Three bodies? Three? Oh my god, Tama. Why would you do this?

I couldn't even guess who they were, their bodies were so decayed and unrecognizable, and the police had covered some of the most gruesome bits before we approached. But pieces of clothing remained even after all these years, thanks to synthetic fabrics, and I knew they were all women. He had buried them in their shoes.

"Mrs. Suga," the chief said, crossing behind others to come around to me. Bile rose in my throat.

"I-I-I didn't know," I stammered out, panic overwhelming me. "I swear."

The chief's face softened, and he rested his hands on my shoulders. "I didn't think you had. But we all owe you a huge debt of gratitude." He glanced over his shoulder at the hole and the dead bodies. "It looks like you've caught a serial killer."

Akiko let out a wail, but my brain had stopped functioning.

"A serial killer? Tama Kano was a serial killer?" My lips bumbled over the question.

"There's no other explanation for this. We must dig out farther from here, a wider radius of the field. But if one of these bodies is Ria Fukuda, which I believe the one on the far left is, then no one else besides Tama Kano or Kohei Watanabe would know to bury other bodies here." The chief squeezed my arms and then let go.

"And since we know Tama Kano stuck around town the last ten years, and he's the one with the arrogant ego who never believed he'd be caught, it has to be him," Goro said, wiping the sweat from his face. "Only someone with his personality would hide all the bodies in one place. He probably believed he'd own the land forever. Then Midori Sankaku arrived in town."

We turned to look at the greenhouse and the foundations for the new administrative buildings. When I first heard that Midori Sankaku had come to town to buy up land and start a new venture here, I thought *they* were the evil ones. I was suspicious of them and wanted to keep my town from being eaten up by a big corporation.

But that's not the way it turned out. Midori Sankaku ended up being the saviors of this town. They bought up land other people didn't want, they were saving Akiko and Mom from ruin, and just by being here, they'd helped us unearth a serial killer right in our midst.

"I think, with this new evidence, the prosecutor will ask for the death penalty," Goro said, and Akiko wailed again.

I dropped to the earth next to her. I didn't know what to say, so I extended my arm over her back and held her while she cried.

There were no words for this moment.

CHAPTER
THIRTY-FIVE

I held the letter in my hand for a long time before I even contemplated opening it. I sat and stared at the envelope as my palms grew sweaty, and my heart rate increased. No, not today!

Today was a special day for me. I'd asked Mom, Yasahiro's parents, Yuna and the boys, Kumi and Goro and Akiko and Kayo, everyone basically, to come over so we could announce the baby's gender. I didn't want to spread the news online or make phone calls. For once, I wanted something happy to celebrate, a way to put the last few weeks behind us.

Then I picked up the mail.

Bad idea, Mei.

Yasahiro entered the bedroom, took one look at me, and sighed.

"Are you going to read it? I don't think you should," he said, sitting next to me on the bed. I was dressed in one of my favorite pregnancy dresses, and my hair and makeup were perfect. I was ready for a party, not this.

"What should I do with it?" I flipped the envelope over,

examining both sides. His handwriting had always been so neat and precise.

"Burn it. Honestly, what does it matter what he has to say?"

I bit my lip and looked at it again. It didn't matter, but now that I had his words right here? No. I had to know.

I pushed the envelope at Yasahiro. "Here. You read it, and you tell me what it says."

He hesitated for a moment before ripping open the envelope and skimming the contents.

"Wow," he breathed out. He cleared his throat and began.

"*Dear Mei, I'll keep this letter short since all of my outgoing mail is read, anyway. I'm only allowed to write a letter every other week, so please tell Akiko that I did my part. It seems as though the police have found the bodies of the five girls I buried in the backfields. Originally, I denied it, but now I'm taking ownership of what I've done. They all deserved to die. Every last one of them.*

"*There's something so horrible about women who don't listen, and you were the first of them. I kept telling you to stop making fun of me, stop badgering me for being a skinny kid, and you and my sister just would not quit. I remember snapping and pushing you into the fire that day. I watched you burn, and I was happy about it. It gave me power I'd never had before, the power to get people to respect me, listen to me.*"

Yasahiro paused, and his voice broke. I was proud of myself for not crying.

"*But as time went on, more and more girls played with me. Ria, Ai, Yukie... other girls that I don't even remember their names. Then you came back, and you hadn't learned your lesson. It's a shame you never learned. I tried to teach you again, but I failed. But you need to never forget that you hurt me. You helped put me here. And I will die knowing it's your fault.*

"*I will go to death row now. I'm not appealing my case though I've been told by my attorneys that ninety percent of death row inmates*" *appeal their cases. Death by hanging. I won't know when until the day it happens, and Akiko will not be here. Your part in this death is clear, and you will have to live with that for the rest of your life. Tama Kano."*

I breathed a sigh of relief. I'm sure Tama thought his letter would chill me to the bone, and I would throw myself on the court asking for mercy for him.

"Good riddance," I said, and Yasahiro's sad eyes met mine. "Really. He kills women for 'not listening to him,' and it's my fault? No. Never. Not in a million years." I stood up, took the letter from Yasahiro's hand, and brought it out to the stove.

Lighting the paper on fire from one of the burners, I stared into the flames for a long moment before dropping it in the stainless steel sink. I remember when fire used to scare me to death. I couldn't even cook for fear of setting something alight. The fear controlled me for too long, and I wouldn't let that happen anymore. Tama Kano had no power over me anymore. He would go to his death with his own version of his life story in his head.

But we all knew the truth.

The door chimed. Our family and friends had arrived. Yasahiro took a deep breath and dried his eyes before he buzzed them in.

I raised my shoulders and greeted everyone at the door, a new woman ready to take on new challenges — a new house to build, children to raise, the tea shop to foster and grow, and so many more things beyond those. Everyone's smiles lifted my spirits and made me feel like I finally had my life under control. We talked and laughed and ate, and nothing was wrong or out of place.

Once all the guests but the kids had a glass of champagne in hand, Yasahiro cleared his throat to get their attention.

"Thank you all for coming today. It's great to see everyone again, especially since it's been a few weeks since the typhoon, and we haven't had anything to celebrate recently."

"Baseball season opened!" Korota called out, and everyone laughed.

"Yes, baseball season is super important," Yasahiro conceded. "And worthy of celebrating."

I reached over and pinched him before he could start musing about his favorite team and send us into a fit of boredom. He laughed and pulled away just in time.

"Anyway, so, we went to the doctor this past week for the big anatomy scan, and we have great news. All the tests have come back negative for any genetic abnormalities, and the baby is right on track weight wise. We also know the gender."

"It's a boy!" Goro called out, followed by, "It's a girl!" from Kumi.

"Hush," I said to them both, laughing. "It's a girl."

A round of cheers and applause rippled through the room. Mom and Yasahiro's parents came forward to give hugs and kisses. Kayo and Kumi both rubbed their fingers at Goro indicating he should pay up now because, of course, they all made bets on who would be right about the gender. I tried to make eye contact with Akiko, but she was politely listening to Yuna talk. I knew she was aching inside about her brother and the man he had become, but she needed time to figure it out for herself.

While everyone ate sandwiches and talked, Yasahiro and I slipped into the walk-in pantry to grab the cake we ordered. He closed the door behind us, and we stood over the cake with its pink sugar flowers and beautiful white icing and held hands.

"I'm so proud of you, Mei, and I don't think I've said recently how overjoyed I am that we're having a baby together. Boy or girl, I would've been happy either way. And I think we're going to have a wonderful life together, as a family."

"Me too."

He kissed me on my temple, and I wrapped my arms around him for a brief moment but long enough for the baby to squirm around inside of me. I imagined her giving us both a hug in return.

She approved, and so did I.

THANK YOU!

Thank you so much for reading *The Daydreamer Returns A Favor*. I was really excited to bring some of the story points from Book One to rest in this book. I hope you enjoyed that as well!

If you want the next book in the series... You can find *Matsuri and Murder* next!

Please leave a review of *The Daydreamer Detective Returns A Favor* wherever you purchased it. I welcome all reviews positive or negative. Reviews are so important to both authors and readers.

Want news of upcoming books, events, or free stuff? Subscribe to Steph's mailing list at https://www.stephgennaro. com/subscribe/

If you want more books like this one, you can check for more books on my website at http://www.stephgennaro.com/ books/

FROM STEPH

HELLO, READERS!

Well, I finally did it. The pieces of the story that I set up in the very first book have come to fruition in this fourth book of the series. It was always my intention to shed more light on Tama Kano and his murderous personality and answer the question of how Mei got her burn scars in the first place. So many readers asked me over and over for this! And I'm happy to finally give it to them. Did you suspect Tama was the killer? I stumped my two alpha readers! So I wonder how many readers caught on.

As for the typhoon sub-plot of the book, that one came to me while I was braving a typhoon in Japan in August of 2016. I watched the rain coming down sideways from my hotel room in Shinjuku, Tokyo, and I knit and drank Japanese beer while watching NHK report from Saitama prefecture. The typhoon (Typhoon Number 9, also known as Typhoon Lionrock) hit Saitama pretty near head-on and did some significant damage. It had been my intention to go to Saitama and sightsee the next day in Kawagoe, but the trains were out, and I couldn't visit. Everything that I described in the book was drawn from news footage I witnessed while waiting for the typhoon to pass. I just increased the drama a bit. Funnily enough, I did not anticipate Mei's mom selling her land, though, until it actually happened. This is the problem/wonderment of being a discovery writer. But I'm pleased with the outcome of this story because it sets up a few good plots for future books in the series!

Anyway, I'm happy that I was able to bring this main story-line to a close, and Mei is stronger than ever. She has quite a future in front of her now with plenty of room to learn and grow. I hope you'll continue on her journey with her. Thanks again for reading and giving this series a chance.

A NOTE ABOUT CHANGES TO THIS BOOK

In case you missed it in the Foreword...

In Japanese, the most common way of showing respect to another person's social standing is with the use of honorific suffixes that are appended on the end of either first or last names. The most common, -san, means either Mr., Ms., or Mrs.

In earlier versions of this book, and in the whole series, I did use these honorific suffixes. But for 2019 and onward, I have switched to the English way in order to make this series more accessible to English speakers. I hope you enjoy this version!

The town in this novel, Chikata, is completely fictional, though the area I put it in is not. Saitama prefecture is located to the west of Tokyo, and many of the eastern areas are considered to be suburbs of the city. Chikata is located farther out west, nearer to the prefectures of Nagano and Gunma.

ACKNOWLEDGMENTS

Big thanks goes out to all the people who helped or inspired me with this book including...

- Tracy Krimmer.
- Charity Vandehey.
- Germaine Fletcher.
- Cori Wilbur.
- Lola Verroen.
- Anne R. Tan.
- All those in my favorite FB author groups.
- My sibling, B.
- My mom, Claire.
- My husband, Keith.
- And my two girls, C and D.

ABOUT THE AUTHOR

Steph Gennaro is a long-time Japanophile, and she's been studying Japanese culture and language for over 20 years. She loves dreaming of far-off places, going for walks with her dog, Lulu Ninja Assassin, hanging out with her family, and reading outside in the summertime. There is no better season than summer. She's a Capricorn, mother, knitter, and web developer, and pasta is her favorite meal. Steph Gennaro is her pen name for cozy mysteries, but she also writes science fiction romance and many other genres.

Find her online at...
www.stephgennaro.com

f facebook.com/StephGennaroAuthor

BB bookbub.com/authors/steph-gennaro

www.ingramcontent.com/pod-product-compliance
Lightning Source LLC
Chambersburg PA
CBHW020318200626
46814CB00006BA/2306